Their HELL

A PENDLETON PREP NOVEL

H.L. PACKER

READER NOTE

Please note, The Sect, Her Devil, and His Angel should be read ahead of this story. The Sect is available for free here: https://dl.bookfunnel.com/t4aqupbw3, Her Devil is on all retailers: https://books2read.com/HerDevil as is His Angel: https://books2read.com/His-Angel

Editor – Vicki James at The Indie Hub

Cover Designer – LJDesigns

Formatter – LJDesigns

RECAP, TIME!

So, very briefly for those of you who read the first stories a little while ago and aren't bingeing the entire series in one fell swoop, let's recap.

Ivy had a fall out with her father when he demanded she put off her dreams of going away to university to become a psychologist in order to attend Pendleton Prep for a year. It wasn't up for negotiation, but she got to take her best friend Tamsin along for the ride.

Tamsin is a touch more free-spirited than Ivy and is determined to make the most of a year away from their parents overbearing supervision to enjoy her freedom. When they arrived, they found that instead of standard accommodation, they'd been upgraded, and are now in a pool house with four other girls and, despite a few challenges, they get on well.

They meet a bunch of guys at a mixer event and get invited to a party at their place—whispers of some secret fraternity being thrown around when dresses and an official invitation arrive for them.

It turns out the guys they met at the mixer live at the big stone house in front of theirs, and are, in fact, part of some secret society called The Sect. They're all introduced to a bunch of masked members before the party, and then the girls are raised up above everyone else through a fun evening of entertainment.

Things aren't quite as straight forward for the guys, though. They end up being dragged out of bed after the mixer event and are made to clean up the campus as part of their challenge criteria. They're put on a drink restriction and given a few other simple rules before being told how important the Angels are. Yep, they're the girls that live in the pool house.

A bunch of guys being trapped in a house with no way to burn off steam means that Nick and Jacob end up sparring. When that goes too far for other people, Nick storms off, only for Ivy to find him half beaten and bleeding on the driveway.

The adrenaline does a number on both their inhibitions when she realises he's okay, and they end up getting hot and heavy in the woods before going back to the pool house. The girls begin their peer training for a Big Sister project, and George is removed from the competition, and a few days later, they find out someone has targeted Stephanie.

Oliver rallies the Devils and makes an example of him, only for Nick and Wyatt to realise how exposed Ivy is, and they formulate a plan to keep her safe. Unfortunately, that plan doesn't go quite how they intended, and she ends up terrified but tied to Nick.

Tamsin decides to link herself with Taylor, and Leo and Jacob finally get together, before Nick demands time with Ivy after she gives him the silent treatment. They come to some kind of peace, and he helps formulate a plan to help win over her Little Sister.

The Angels host a pamper afternoon, and Ivy runs into Wyatt, who then turns up with some of the guys as 'shirtless butlers' for the afternoon. Not to be outdone, Nick and the rest of the guys (in their jealousy) crash the party, and the massages become a little less than professional.

The guys are pulled into another challenge—this one a series of escape rooms. Jacob almost gets hit with a dagger, Wyatt nearly ends up trapped with a killer, and Emmerson leaves the competition, and they're down to seven.

With everything getting so serious, they decide another party is in order. Tamsin and Taylor mirror themselves together, and Ivy finally starts to make progress with her Little Sister Ruby. They're all called in by The Sect to celebrate the new couple, only they're then removed from the competition because of broken rules.

Devastated, Ivy relies on the guys to hold her together through her grief, and the five of them find some kind of safety together, amongst other things. Leo and Wyatt try to tie themselves together, but they get interrupted, and it never gets finished when Nick begins to pull away.

As the girls begin to fight within themselves for position and power, Ivy decides a declaration needs to be made and gathers everyone together to make sure they know the Devils are off limits, and Leo puts in place a backup plan, just as Nick disappears.

ONE

Ivy

"Stop!" The word comes out in a panicked scream as I run across the car park, stamping up the ancient stone steps as the terror rushes through my veins. "Please, please, stop."

Yanking the handle of the door gets me nowhere as I yell, screech, and pound against the wood.

Someone's here; there are cars in the car park, lights on inside, but no security outside. I could let the concern of that sink in, but I daren't, instead continuing to attempt to push the fear that's so close to crashing over me deep, deep down inside.

This isn't the place to be weak, to let my feelings overcome what's got to be done, to be said. This is the moment to prove that I'm strong enough to stand as part of the elite, The Sect, beside the Devils, and not behind them.

This isn't the time to let myself be pulled under the waves. Instead, I need to become the wave, to crash through anything that stands in my way and retrieve the man that's mine. That's ours.

Eventually, Jacob catches up with me, twisting the

handle, and heaving the heavy door open with a creak as he shoves me through the gap. I'll appreciate how hard that must have been for him later—those precious seconds when he could have been in here, moving towards his own flesh and blood and whatever will meet him there, but he pushed me, sent me, his confidence in my ability bolstering the nerves filtering through me.

What if we're too late? What if it's done and nothing can be taken back? What if... What if... What if...

But there's no time for that—not now. Only time for strength and action.

"Stop," I repeat again, pressing forward, my heart pounding as two dozen men in masks turn in unison, their ominous presence like a heavy weight as blood tinges the air.

Leo, Jacob, and Wyatt stand behind me, their heat a safety I hadn't even considered in the blind panic that's consumed me since Jacob strode up those stairs with a swagger only known by one other man: Nick. But nobody moves. I sidestep, and still, the wall of men stand before me, an impenetrable force.

Jacob is nothing more than half a second away from barrelling through them, fists first, and I know his restraint is hanging by a thread, held back only by the knowledge that we don't need to be picking them both up from the cold concrete, but as the seconds tick by, I know that thread is fraying.

"Let them through," a man orders, the voice booming around the room as the slashes of silver, gold, and red move, once again, creating an aisle down the middle.

I almost wish they hadn't when my gaze falls onto the bloody mess at the other side, and my stomach lurches, but Jacob isn't waiting any longer. Already two steps ahead of me, he strides through the corridor, pushing past the parted bodies towards the crumpled and bleeding pile of a person ahead of us.

My vision tunnels as I follow, watching with bated breath for movement, for life.

Please don't let him be dead.

"There'd better be a good explanation for this interruption," that same man declares, and as I watch Nick's chest rise and fall, I finally manage to take that breath, sucking air into my lungs before daring to look up.

Sitting on the very same seat Nick and I sat on just a few weeks ago is a man in a black robe, with a black mask that has an ugly-looking, silver slash across it. He leans back casually, his legs parted as his dark brogues peek out below. He's clearly happy to watch the proceedings rather than take part, but he's definitely the one in control—the one with power.

"You can't do this," I declare with much more authority than I'm feeling. "Whatever he told you, whatever he offered, it's wrong."

My gaze leaves the black pits of Hell on the stage, catching Jacob's before lingering on Nick. He's barely conscious, with only a groan tumbling from him while Jacob seems to categorise the wounds.

"Is that so," the man says, dragging my attention back to him on the stage, the one who holds Nick's fate in his hands. While the mask and robes make his body language difficult to read, I can almost see the thoughts ticking behind his eyes: *irritation and intrigue.*

Leo presses in behind me, once again, with Wyatt going to help Jacob in my periphery, and as the gathered pack of masked men move inwards, the thought flickers through my mind that maybe we should have thought this through better.

Five of us, one already bloody and beaten, and more than four times as many of them… probably more.

"If you take him, you have to take me," I say, holding out my wrist defiantly.

They took Tamsin when they removed Taylor, so surely, if they're taking Nick, then they have to take me, too.

"Except, keeping you safe was part of his deal," he replies coolly.

The door behind us slams open, with everyone turning to see who on earth it could be. It's the second interruption in as many minutes.

"I suggest you listen to what they have to say," another voice booms.

I can't see through the throng of people between here and there, but somehow, this voice sounds familiar. Leo tenses beside me. Then the sound of shoes clicking against the concrete slabs echoes around us as the throng moves and parts like the Red Sea as a new man strides through them with nothing more than the power of his presence, and a glare I'd recognise anywhere.

The venom in that look would be enough to melt lesser men on the spot, but not here, not in The Sect. The suit fits him like a glove, the jacket falling open to expose the weapons I'm sure the men following him are also carrying—not that any of them would need them—and as he draws closer, I suddenly realise who is standing before us.

"This would be a good time to give them that explanation, son," he says, his icy gaze leaving mine and landing to my side on Leo.

Leo's fingers twist through mine, the tension rippling from him and filtering through me, simmering in my veins before he turns up his gaze back to the man on the chair—the man now leaning forward, with his elbows on his knees, fingers steepled, and his head cocked in interest.

I don't dare another look towards Nick, instead fixating on the one person who can make or break this situation, that can pull us from this hell, because I know that one look at the heartbreak on Jacob's face, or the fury on Wyatt's, I'll break, and breaking isn't an option. Not right now.

TWO

"**S**he's not the only one linked," I begin, pushing my sleeve back.

Wyatt does the same, as does Jacob.

"Windsor to Barrett, Chambers to Barrett, Barrett to Angel, and reverse," the man says, checking us off as he goes. "That's the play, is it? Tie the five of you together and hope for the best."

I nod. The silence echoing around the room is a weight I wasn't prepared for.

I knew that Nick had been pulling away, planning something, most likely. It's not a surprise he chose to sacrifice himself for her, for them, for us all. But it's too far, too much, so I stepped in, knowing he'd need us in the end.

Nick's bloodied hand reaches for the soft leather at Jacob's wrist.

No doubt he thought we'd completed the swap without him, the pompous arse. Luckily for him, we hadn't. So, with Nick already linked to Ivy, and Jacob to me, it was easy to link Wyatt with me, and Ivy to Wyatt. Chain reaction, baby. Take one, take us all.

"If you're taking Nick, you're taking us all. If you're willing to lose your entire intake in one move, we're here."

It's a bold statement, and one I'm praying to any god who will listen that they don't take us up on, but they'd be stupid to accept.

Harsh whispers come from the group of men surrounding us, and a pointed look comes from the man in charge.

My father adjusts his stance beside me, cracking his neck as he waits alongside us, impatient as ever. I have no idea how he got here so quickly, and I'm not sure I want to. If he's lingering this close, then we have a problem, but that's not something I can't consider right now.

No, right now, I'm either going down fighting, or we're about to save the fucking martyr of our group, and the weight of that hangs tensely in the balance.

My father's men take a step out, pushing The Sect back, seeming to buy us some breathing space. Not that it helps the strain running through me, or the rage as I steal a look towards Nick, Wyatt, and Jacob.

Categorising Nick's wounds takes time more time than I have, but quickly looking over him he's at least in one piece, his breathing is ragged, but most of the bleeding seems to have stopped. We may not have always seen eye to eye—in fact, most of the time we've been at odds—but he's important to Jacob, and to Ivy, and they're both important to me.

It takes more than a nice arse and a jawline handed down from the gods to buy my loyalty, but he has it. And not just because he's acted like a fool and gone off on his own to try and save a bunch of people who don't need it, but because, even though we've hit and hated each other, he'd still give himself for me.

I can't say there are very many people in this world I'd take a bullet for—the man beside me isn't even in that list most of the time—but Nick? Them? Any day.

The realisation hits me like a truck, with a well forming in the pit of my stomach. I get why he did this, as fucking stupid as it is.

"You don't think this has been done before? Linking one to another to another with the aim of keeping more than you should," the compare states from his seat, leaning back again. "Three Devils need to finish this, not four."

"Three Devils, and three Angels. That's six," Wyatt says defiantly, drawing all attention his way as I stretch my fingers out, already feeling the half-moons forming from where I've clenched my fists too tight. "There are only five of us here. We're not trying to keep more than we're owed."

"And how, exactly, will that work when three of you move on to your next roles?" the compare asks with finality.

Fuck.

"I'll step back," Jacob says. "Leo and I are linked, anyway. He can be the Devil, and I'll be his Angel."

My father scoffs beside me, the pitying look he sends Jacob's way not surprising. "If you're not strong enough to fight for your rightful place here, then you're not strong enough to be part of The Sect."

My father has never given a shit about women, proven by the fact that my mother would rather take her own life than deal with his shit any longer. He'd never see Jacob as my equal, as my partner, no more than he would Ivy. But he doesn't know either of them, and the steely determination that glowers at him from Wyatt's gaze is almost enough to convince me that could change.

"It takes more than being ruthless," Ivy says, the sound echoing against the cold, stone walls as all eyes divert to her. She squeezes my hand before caressing my cheek, her warmth fleeting before she steps away, her gaze dropping to where Nick's now sitting, partially propped up by Jacob. "More than dogged determination." She nears them, her hand going to the top of Nick's head as his eyes close, absorbing her strength as she stands up for him—for us all. "And more than wicked loyalty." Her other hand comes to Wyatt's sleeve.

Standing between Wyatt and Jacob, with Nick at their feet they look powerful, complete. She looks every bit the queen she should be treated as when she pulls her shoulders back and sets that determined gaze back on my father.

"Yes, loyalty, determination, and ruthlessness are all attributes for the Devils, for The Sect, but the Angels have to be all that and more. We have to be able to empathise, to manipulate a situation, to be able to calm the storm that rages around you with nothing more than a look or a touch." Her hands come to Jacob's shoulders before she looks my father straight in the face. "An Angel is everything your sacred Devils could wish to be and more."

And she's right.

She's so much more than any one part of us. Not that we don't have more than the one attribute, but The Sect is looking for particularly strong traits in each of their *candidates*. They're not looking at the big picture, but she is.

"They're a weak liability that can be twisted and bought. You're nothing more than a bargaining chip in a game you don't understand," my father counters, and movement to my side catches my eye as someone pushes through the throng to get closer, but not quite close enough. "Sit down, little girl," he sneers, drawing my attention back to the argument at hand. "Let the men come to an agreement about your fate."

He doesn't expect it and doesn't even see it coming before my fist lands squarely against his jaw, throwing his head to the side, but his feet stay planted as his furious gaze comes straight to me. He's demeaned and belittled women my entire life. He will not do it with the people I care about.

"Don't you ever disrespect them like that again," I say, managing to push the words out between gritted teeth.

I know more than anyone what it took for Ivy to place herself between us and the chopping block, to support what looks like the losing side, and then to throw that back in my father's face. Sure, she has no idea who he is, or the power he wields, but he's not the only one with power—not now.

Pressure ripples across the room, my father's men poised for attack, and whether that's with us or at us is yet to be decided as The Sect inch ever closer. Peering over his shoulder, I see men I've known my entire life. Men I've drunk with, laughed with, a man who knows me as well as I know myself, but whether they're with us or against us in this moment hangs precariously.

"Children, children. Let's keep this on task, shall we?" the compare says loudly before my father does anything stupid like returning the hit. No, he'll likely save that for later when the doors are closed, and the odds are stacked in his favour.

"Your roles were decided long ago, your paths matched," the compare continues. "It's just left to see which of you makes it to the end to begin their journeys. Now, Nicholas Barrett has offered himself up to allow his brother to take the place their bloodline is owed, and yet Jacob has an alternate offer. Interesting," he muses. "Still, none of you have completed the tasks set forth. There are still challenges ahead of you."

He nods twice, with The Sect barging their way through my father's security like they weren't even there. Within a second, their arms are wrapping around my chest, and my hands are being forced to my sides as I watch with horror at the same thing happening with Wyatt, Jacob, and Ivy.

So, this is it. We're all out.

There isn't time for the panic to set in before my father pulls a gun and points it at the forehead of the man behind me. I don't know these masks, they could be anyone, but he might. Would he kill a colleague? A friend? How far will he go for his sole blood heir?

His security follow suit as my panicked gaze flicks around. There's more than one face I recognise, and they're not only aiming to protect me, but also the rest of us. Nick is in no shape to help with anything, still barely conscious and breathing heavily, unaware of the chaos swirling around us like a storm brewing. And it's a storm emanating from the man on the stage.

He stands, the silver in his mask glinting in the sunlight

that streams through the glass window.

"Let's not do anything rash, Vincent," the compare says calmly, looking my father in the eye before dragging his mask off, dropping it on the seat, and pulling a knife from his sleeve as he steps down the two steps, closing the distance between us.

A lump forms in the back of my throat as I look towards Jacob, towards Ivy, and their panic and fear settles deep in my bones. I can't move or protect myself. If he takes me first, at least there's a chance they'll make it out alive; my father would murder everyone standing: friend, colleague or other.

I've taken more than one beating on the back of his whim and distaste, but what happens inside the house is one thing. Outside, I'm his to protect, and vice versa. It's the reason he's here, after all.

"Don't force my hand, then," my father replies, moving the gun to the compare.

The man in front of me toys with the knife, a smirk forming across his face.

They clearly know each other, but I don't recognise him, and I thought I'd met everyone in the business. I'm the one prepped to take over, after all. Pulling in close to me, his dark gaze meets mine, the coffee on his breath fanning across my face, with his nose just inches from mine as the blade teases against my throat, and he hovers.

It's not fear that rushes through my veins, but acceptance. Death has followed me for a long time, and if now is the time it's come to claim, then at least they'll all make it out alive. I promised her safety and vengeance, and if my death gives her and those she cares about the safety she holds dear, and the opportunity to take the blood they're owed, then so be it.

My jaw clenches as I narrow my eyes, peeking through the darkness within his—darkness that so closely matches my own.

I can practically feel Ivy's intake of breath, and a chill creeps through my blood the moment I hear the jostling going on behind the compare as one or more of them do their best to get to me. But it's not needed, because my father is here, and his gun and spine of steel should be more than enough warning to someone who knows him as well as this man seems to.

My father doesn't issue warnings, he gives out promises, but there's nothing I can do as the seconds tick by. Clearly getting impatient, my father clicks the safety off his gun and I swallow, the knife pressing against my throat as I do.

This is it. The moment that changes everything.

The compare chuckles, holding my gaze as he grins before dragging the knife along my throat, causing a sting to follow that would cause other people to hiss through their teeth, but it's not severed, and I'm not bleeding out in front of my father and most of the people I care about in this world. He continues pulling the knife down the length of my body, the blade doing nothing more than resting against the cloth, before it slices through the leather bracelet like butter.

THREE

Ivy

Ice slides down my spine as I watch the blood seep from his neck. It's nothing more than a trickle, but I've never felt anything like the combination of rage and terror that floods my body as the guys push beside me, both desperate to save him, to help. But as the knife droops lower, carving through the leather wristlet, it's clear it's not needed.

Leo holds the man's gaze, burning a hole through him even as he turns and faces Leo's father, and the very real threat of death held to his head.

Six months ago, my biggest issue was how to avoid my slimy ex-boyfriend at the next pretentious event my parents decided to drag me to. Now, I'm in an ancient building, seemingly held up by nothing but the egos of the men in this room, held hostage with guns, knives, and God knows what else.

How the hell did we find ourselves here?

"Next time," the man says, smiling at Leo's father before stepping away and coming straight to me.

The knife glints in the sun, double-edged, with crimson lacing one side as he waves it between us, and I still. Sure, he didn't hurt Leo in the end, but was that only because there was a gun pointed at his head? Will my fate be different without the same kind of support?

"That was a nice speech," the man says coolly, slicing through my wristlet before anyone else can argue, the leather falling to the floor gently. Leaning in so nobody else can hear, he whispers, "Open your mouth."

Whether the whisper is to avoid the complete hell that would break loose on the back of that statement, or just because he can, I don't really have time to consider. Acquiescing, he presses the tip to my tongue, pulling it away carefully as he watches my reaction with interest.

"How's he taste? The second man today willing to give his life for you."

Metallic, coppery, foreign.

He doesn't bother to wait for a reply, though, before he's dropping his hand down to Nick, while I tense, watching him run a finger along the cut by his eye and smearing the blood pooling there. Jacob practically vibrates with anger beside me as the man shoves Nick's pant leg up and slices through his band, and as I cast a glance across the small space, Leo looks ready to break lose and bring chaos too.

Coughing catches me off guard, and my gaze flicks back to the man in charge. He's closer than I remember, his smoky cologne wrapping around us now, and his dark eyes are focused and clear, with wrinkles appearing as he grins wickedly. It's a smile I'm sure has proceeded pain many times before. Instead, he offers his finger out to me with the tiny tilt of his head, his *suggestion* clear.

The last thing anyone needs right now is me being

held down while he forces that thing down my throat. So, wrapping my lips around the offending digit, I hold his gaze, swirling my tongue before sucking it clean. His pupils dilate when I release him with a pop before pulling back, despite the guy holding me in place.

"Such lucky boys," he comments with a smirk.

Bypassing Jacob, he nicks Wyatt's wrist when he cuts the wristlet off, offering me the blade to lick clean once again before turning to Jacob.

"Now, you're here for Mr Windsor and your brother, but are you here for them, too?" he asks him, cocking his head as he carves straight through Jacob's band. "Your brother's girlfriend and her other lover. That is complicated indeed."

Jacob doesn't need to think about it or consider his position before he nods. After all, just hours ago, he and I were the ones playing Leo's body together, even if it does feel like a lifetime ago.

Contrary to the almost functional collection of blood from everyone else, he hits Jacob so quickly that the movement barely registers, just the sound of bone smashing against bone that echoes around the room. The split lip must have been exactly what he was going for as he smirks, looking my way before gesturing to it with his head.

Only, it wasn't me he was gesturing to, it was the man behind me—the same one who now manhandles me until I'm facing Jacob, with his tongue dipping out to taste against the slit before he presses his lips together with a wince.

An hour ago, those lips were pressed against mine, his tongue tangling and tasting in my mouth, and not a second of it felt false or fake. We have a connection, even if it's not sexual in that way, and it took me a moment to realise it wasn't Nick, but that was different than this. So different. That was to show power, to save face in front of everyone, so we could come here and save Nick, just like this is.

Pressing my lips against his briefly, I drag his bottom lip through my teeth before turning to our master of puppets and raising my eyebrow in challenge.

We're pulled apart again with nothing more than a nod of his head—let's not forget who's in charge here—before his fingers push beneath my chin, his caustic gaze flittering over my every feature until he steps back, flipping the knife in his hand, and heading back to his perch.

"So, that's it, is it?" Wyatt clips "Nick offers himself up, Leo mouths off, and Jacob's questioned, but I'm, what, assumed? Great." He scoffs out an unimpressed noise and I can only imagine the way his arms would have been gesturing wildly had they not been restrained.

He hadn't been dragged into this ridiculous mess; hit, threatened or hurt, and now he's poking the bear. Why?

"Ah, Mr Chambers." The puppet master grins, his eyes sparking with amusement as he sits back in his seat, taking up position on his throne. "You're the man your Angel chose, the one she wrapped her colours around. Mr Unwavering Loyalty. That's what she said, isn't it? Do we really need to question that? Are you not here to save Mr Barrett for her?"

"I'm here because we're a unit, and because together, we work," he says calmly. "So, yes, I'm here to save Nick *from himself,* but not for Ivy—for us all."

Wasn't it Leo who suggested other people's sense of propriety wasn't his concern, and it certainly shouldn't be ours, but it was Wyatt that started the conversation about us all being together. Or, at the very least, he was the one who brought up the bubble and the safety and security of us all being together inside it. That wasn't just about him and me, or Jacob and Leo, but all of us.

I've never questioned the way he felt about me, it's just always been there, simmering away beneath everything. A constant. It was a friendship that turned flirtatious, and then those flirtations turned into something else that night at the masquerade party when he listened to Nick put restrictions on me, and then kissed me anyway.

As he watched Leo watch me, and Nick crave me, and me flounder in the middle of my feelings for them all. He was the one who gave us the space to be together. All of us.

"Beautifully put," the man declares, drawing me back to the here and now. To the blood on Jacob, Leo, and Nick. To the blood on my tongue. "Now, you still have challenges to undertake, so I suggest the five of you concentrate of getting through that."

Safeties click back on, and guns are holstered as our arms are released. Jacob pulls me into his embrace, with Nick at our feet as the four of us hover, not sure whether that means we're dismissed and safe, or what.

"And whatever he offered, whatever deal he bartered, that's off, right?" Wyatt confirms.

"Yes."

The single word is all we were waiting for before Leo comes rushing over, nodding to Jacob and pushing his shoulder beneath Nick's to haul him to his feet. Wyatt takes the other side as they half walk, half carry him to the door we walked through no more than thirty minutes ago, even if it does feel like an entire lifetime.

We follow, and I'm thankful the masked men leave a gap for us to get through.

"I'd like a word before you leave," Leo's father says as we pass.

"Yes, sir," Leo agrees without making eye contact—something I've not heard before from him laced through the tone: defeat.

"A doctor will meet you back at the house," our puppet master calls from behind, but none of us turn to address him. "And don't forget, The Sect sees and hears everything."

Fucking great.

Jacob lets me go, stepping around the others to throw open the door, while Leo and Wyatt somehow manage to get Nick safely down the stairs, though his feet stumble along until Leo gets him perched in the back seat and is able to take a closer look.

"There should be some wipes in the glove box," he says, tipping Nick's chin and running his hands down his side. "This is gonna sting."

He does his best to clean up Nick's face—there's one eye swollen shut, the opposite cheek and lip split—but it's his ribs that are black and blue as Leo shoves his shirt up, the bruises crossing one over the other as a myriad only broken up by the tattoos hidden beneath.

"You're a fucking idiot," Jacob complains, his hand twitching and ready to hit him, only holding back because he's clearly already in pain.

"Love you, too," Nick replies between ragged breaths.

The door opens behind us just as Wyatt's phone rings.

"Shit. I've got to take this," he says. "Are you guys okay here?"

We nod as I look over Leo's shoulder to see his father swaggering through the doorway just seconds behind us. It's like he already knows.

"Get him in the car," Leo whispers. "And lock the doors. You only let the two of us in, do you understand?" He turns, peering over his shoulder before looking at both Jacob and me earnestly.

"Of course," I agree with another nod, breaking Jacob from whatever silent conversation he's having with Nick. "We'll get him in."

Jacob manoeuvres Nick into the back and climbs in beside him. I follow, locking the doors as Leo walks away, but not before passing Jacob the wipes for his face, unable to ignore the sadness lingering as he watches the man he cares about walking towards possible further destruction.

FOUR

Leo

The unimpressed look on my father's face isn't a good sign, but at least the gun is holstered and we're in public as he strides down the steps towards me, Josiah not far behind. He's not likely to murder me, though. Not right now, anyway.

"So, this is the hill you're willing to die on, is it?"

I thought that was more than apparent, but I nod anyway, clenching my hands together behind my back. It would do none of us any good for me to continue pushing against him now.

"Your brothers will be hearing about this."

Fuck. "I understand, sir."

It's been nothing more than a handful of months at Pendleton Prep, but the words feel foreign on my tongue. Dex, Blaise, and I have been my father's go-to guys, following up deals and making a name for ourselves, uninterrupted and unhampered. Sent by the boss. Stone cold and deadly.

Nothing's changed, only the priority.

Sure, I can be soft with them, my blood brothers, and

share my vulnerabilities when it's needed, but that in no way takes from the fact that I'm next in line to a fortune amassed on blood—blood I've spilled.

"Parents aren't supposed to be involved in the induction process," my father says, looking past me to the car they're all sat in, or the call Wyatt's taking—probably his father intervening on our behalf, too.

I don't turn to check, though. It's not safe to take my eyes off my father right now. Just because murdering me in broad daylight in sight of The Sect would be a fuck up of major proportions doesn't mean he isn't waiting for any opportunity to do some damage.

"You did the right thing in calling me, but, son, where are their paths leading them, and how will that fit with yours? Make a decision. Pick one and get on with your life."

His words are like a punch to the gut. Not only because of the imminent threat to the two men who mean more to me than anything in this world, but the fact that he thinks loving these people is a choice, a decision to be made, or something I could walk away from.

I don't answer. I can't. There aren't the words to explain this to him. As if he'd hear them if there were.

"I'll be around," he says, before moving past me, with one of the guys throwing a smile and wink my way as they go.

Mostly, they're just bodies, whoever he had loitering around at the time the call came, but they've seen a lot more than I intended. A weakness I wasn't going to make public, not yet at least. And it's not like he's offered much reassurance in the grand scheme of things, but at this point it's all I've got, so I'll take it.

With a sigh, I head back to the car and climb in the front as Jacob passes over the keys. The cut on his lip isn't bad, it's already started to dry over, but watching him and Ivy be forced together is a trauma I'm not ready to relive yet.

Sure, if they wanted to get it on, that would be different, but Jacob's play at being Nick this morning was still fresh in my mind as their faces were shoved together, once again. Not fun. It took all I had in me not to rush over and save them.

Wyatt's gaze flicks our way when he kicks a stone into the shrubs at the side of the car park, looking back out at the graveyard as he talks. No doubt he's being read the riot act just like I was, the only difference being that my father does more than just talk big words. There are always big actions to follow it up.

I turn the engine over as Wyatt climbs in the passenger seat with a heavy sigh and an apology. The drive back is quiet, and I dread to think what classes we've missed today as we pass through the main campus, noticing the rest of the student body going about their day non-the-wiser to everything we've gone through.

Jasper doesn't say anything when we enter with Nick under my arms. He just gestures to the dining room and the man sat there waiting for us with a cup of tea. I step out to grab ice for Jacob's face, also grabbing a handful of breakfast bars at the same time before handing them out. No-one seems willing to leave Nick alone with this random unknown. Doctor or not.

After a thorough inspection, the doctor decides the eye

socket might be broken, but he'll be back to check on it in a couple of days. Nick's definitely broken one rib, badly bruised or fractured a couple of others, and his face needs stitching in more than one place. Luckily enough, the doctor has got everything with him.

Funny that. It's almost like someone gave him a heads up of what he might be walking into.

We stay while he does what needs to be done, listen to the instructions he gives us for the next few days, and write down the list of medications, and when to make sure Nick takes them. There's a list half as long as my arm of the emergency things to look out for, and a reminder that there's a contact number with the first aid kits, should we need it.

Wyatt thanks the doctor and sees him out whilst Jacob makes sure Nick takes the first batch of tablets. Ivy is frozen beside them, her fingers entwined with his the entire time. But all I can think about is the fact that he's just given them the perfect way to get rid of him. They could wipe him from the board whilst he's in surgery if it's needed. Or what if he's not quick enough off the mark, not fast enough in a challenge? Not thinking clearly because of the drugs or the face that is actually broken right now.

So, maybe The Sect gave him today, but tomorrow isn't promised, and Ivy's not even over losing her best friend. She won't recover if he goes out on the back of this because he tried to save us.

"Right, let's get you up two flights of fucking stairs and get some light bulbs changed," I say, clapping my hands twice.

Jacob looks at me in confusion.

"There's a box of blue bulbs on the bookshelf in the office in our room. I need them swapped out as close to as many windows as you can get them."

The time for discretion is almost gone. I need to warn them.

"Blue bulbs… but why?" Jacob asks, holding the door for me as I haul Nick up, supporting the majority of his weight.

"Because we aren't the only ones who are going to feel the fallout from today, and I need to warn them."

It's not like I can just call them up and be like, 'W*ell, I kind of lost my head today and punched my father in the face, so you'd better watch your backs.*' I mean, I could… but their phones are being watched, as is mine, alongside the camera we found in my room, and the ones around the rest of the house.

Fuck, this house is feeling more like a prison every damn day.

Eventually, we manage to get Nick upstairs and nestled in the corner of the sofa, propped up with a bunch of pillows, courtesy of Ivy. He sure as hell isn't going anywhere right now, and she's here to keep him in one place. Thank God.

When I head into the office, Jacob is already working on the bulbs, and I pluck Nick's schedule from the wall, flying off a few messages to get notes taken for the rest of the week. We've literally just stood in front of the student body and declared all the Angels and Devils are off limits in a show of strength and unity. The last thing we need is Nick crawling around campus like the weakest fucking link.

"Can I borrow your phone?" I ask Jacob awkwardly,

looking up from mine.

Mine's monitored, and anything I order going to their house is going to get flagged faster than you can say, '*Shit, that was a mistake.*'

"Sure," he says, dragging it from his pocket, unlocking it, and handing it over. "What's up?"

"Got to send a gift to a friend," I reply, catching his gaze.

The rest of the house has cameras, bugs, or whatever in it. This room is probably no different, and there's no way I can say the words I want to out loud. *I just need to send a coded warning to my brothers, because I fucked up, and my father is likely to be on the war path heading straight for them.*

"It needs to be a surprise," I explain.

"No worries. My cards are in the back."

I love him a little more right this very second. Not only because he doesn't question it, but because he knows we can't talk about it in here, and he trusts me enough to just hand everything over.

Your phone practically has your entire life in it. Add that in with your bank cards, and if I was a different kind of guy, I could make a whole mess of his life. Luckily, he's not a different kind of guy, and he gets it, going back to changing the bulb without a second thought.

I mouth, *"Thank you,"* before pulling up a florist and ordering a balloon gift congratulating them on the announcement of their new baby boy. It's probably not nearly as strange as it feels. People have babies all the fucking time, but not often intentionally in my circles.

"Thanks, babe" Jacob says with a smile, hopping down from the table and handing me over the white bulb. "One down, few more to go. How're you holding up?"

Because, obviously, his thoughts right now are on me and not the man in the other room.

"Me? What about you?"

Sure, I'm worried about what this will mean for Dex and Blaise, but this is shit we're used to. There's always been death hanging over our heads. Not so much for the rest of these guys.

"Keeping busy." He shrugs.

His hand comes to my chest, his vulnerability on display for only a few seconds before he blinks and it's gone, the shutters coming back down as he compartmentalises right before my eyes.

"I'm totally going to kick his arse once this is over," he says, looking over my shoulder towards the doorway.

Nick.

"I feel like there might be a bit of a queue for that," I reply, forcing a smile on my face.

It's a weird feeling, whatever *this* is.

Having something, someone, that I want to protect more than one person. People that I want to shield from all the dark and dangerous things that lurk around every corner. Jacob's made it more than clear that he's willing and able to stand up for himself, to face all that darkness with a strength not many find in themselves, but I don't want him to have to.

I want to be the one facing that gun, that knife.

I don't want Ivy anywhere near that life, or the rest

of them, and yet here we find ourselves, submerged in the mire, desperately attempting to pull ourselves free.

"Probably," Jacob says, puling me back into the moment, and my hand slides around his waist. "I'm not sure if Ivy's just terrified he's going to do something else stupid if she takes her eyes off him, or if she's really worried he's been beaten worse than we know."

"And it looks pretty bad."

I've seen men beaten and broken. I've made men that way and worse, but he looks bad, really bad. What would have happened if we hadn't arrived when we did, I don't know.

"Ain't that the truth." Jacob sighs, his breath fanning over my shoulder. "My brother is a fucking idiot."

"I've been telling you this for months."

"Helpful," he adds with the roll of his eyes, his lips pressing against mine briefly in nothing more than a tease. "Right, let's get this done and sorted, yeah?"

"Sure," I agree when he pulls back, knowing he's doing all this for me and nobody else.

Now all we have to do is to hope they see the warning before it's too late.

FIVE

Ivy

"I'm sure you're just trying to fatten me up," I say, sticking a fork in the fudge cake before dragging it closer. "If I'm not careful, these little treats are going to catch up with me."

I've never given one slightest thought about my weight, diet, or any other thing until I came here. Now I'm without the nutritionist and the personal trainer, and each time I think about the last time I hit the gym, took a class, or went for a run, I shudder. Too long, that's how long it's been.

Tamsin was always the one to pull me out of my comfort zone and get me moving, to keep me on the straight and narrow, as it were. Since we arrived at Pendleton Prep, we've both let ourselves enjoy the moment, not that it's served either of us well up to this point.

No, now I'm avoiding food and activity, and doing my best to stay rooted to Nick's side. Rightly or wrongly. Just being here has me itching all over to return to the safety of the house, and yet the familiarity of the place and the woman opposite is comforting. Kind of like the cake.

"I'm sure you'll be fine," Ruby replies with an eye roll,

pushing hers around her plate. It's what I should be doing rather than shovelling another amazingly tasting piece into my mouth. "You can run an extra mile or two with him." Her gaze flicks across the room to where I know Jacob loiters, anything but unobtrusively.

"Jacob doesn't jog. That's Nick, and he's not up to going out running right now."

"Oh." Her eyes narrow in Jacob's direction, her head cocking. "How do you tell them apart?"

"Not sure." I shrug. "I didn't at first, but once I knew, it was completely obvious. They're just different."

"Well, yeah, except they're kind of not."

I smile, getting it, although I'm not sure they would.

"So, you've swapped Tamsin's company for his today, huh?"

The question is innocent enough, but I can't help the stab of pain that slices through my chest. I think I manage to keep it off my face as I swallow the cake that tastes more like ash than food right now. "Something like that."

"I was hoping to ask her about the applique technique she used," Ruby continues, unaware of the way my stomach churns. "I guess you could tell me instead, though?"

"Erm, I can show you what she explained to me, but I don't have any of the technical knowledge to back it up, I'm afraid." I place my fork down and push the plate away.

Part of me wants to hold onto how easily this conversation is coming from her—finally some common ground. If only the topic in question wasn't my presumed dead best friend. Not that Ruby knows she's dead, clearly, but still, I don't hear any of the other words that come as she continues to talk, my mind anywhere but here.

"Sorry, can you excuse me for a minute?" I ask, cutting off whatever she was finally explaining before practically running to the bathroom and pressing my back against the cool tiles, my heart thundering in my chest.

It's always been Tamsin and me against the world. The two of us. Until now. My world tumbles and spins, the walls crumbling around me until someone knocks twice before entering. Instinctively, I know who it is before Jacob strides in the women's bathroom, no fucks given.

"Who do I need to kill?" he asks with a smirk, attempting to break the tension that crackles around the room. The meltdown I'm about to have.

"We probably shouldn't joke about that," I reply, watching his movements with interest.

I may have laughed it off a week ago, and I think Leo offered to do the very same thing at one point or another, but with so much death hanging over us, I don't know how he can make light of it.

"Fuck it," he replies, catching my gaze in the mirror when he runs his hands under the cold tap, shakes them off, and places them around the sides of my neck, the coolness acting as a balm I didn't realise I needed, making me sag against the wall.

"I'd better not mess up the makeup, though, huh?" he adds, swiping a wet finger across the tip of my nose before pressing it against the inside of my wrists.

I'm sure conversations continue out in the restaurant—the rest of them have no idea what I'm going through right now, and the world is still turning—but paused here in this moment, I take the opportunity to really look at him, with Ruby's words playing in the back of my mind: how alike really are the twins?

They both have that same cut jawline and dark hazel eyes, although the gentle way Jacob touches me right now is not the same. It's not that Nick doesn't care, just that the flame that flickers between us makes it different. There's no electricity zapping beneath my skin, for a start.

"If you're finished gawping, we should probably head back in," Jacob says, not taking his eyes off my hands.

"And here I was just thinking how you're nothing like your brother," I reply with a smile. It doesn't reach my eyes, but you've got to start somewhere, right?

"Oh, the sarcastic mouth definitely runs in the family. Just wait until you meet the rest of us," he says, stepping back and heading towards the door.

"I'm not sure the world could handle any more of you guys. I certainly can't," I say, handing him a paper towel as he holds the bathroom door for me.

He wipes his hands quickly before balling the towels up and throwing them across the room, his smirk growing when he lands it squarely in the rubbish bin. *Just like his brother.* Quickly, we make our way back to the main restaurant, with nobody else paying any attention as we slide back into the room.

Ruby has her face back in her phone when I look over. Jacob squeezes my shoulder before heading back to the counter and letting me make the move alone.

"Sorry about that. Where were we?" I ask, striding around Ruby and dropping into the seat opposite.

"Huh?" she asks, looking up. "Oh, I dunno. I'm sure it wasn't anything important."

We fall back into an awkward silence as she turns her phone over in her hands.

"Nice blouse," I comment, attempting to find something to talk about. "The colour really brings out your eyes."

"Washing day." She shrugs. "And my, erm, my friend likes it—said I should wear it because it suits me." Her gaze flicks to Jacob and then back to me.

"Well, your friend's right." I nod. "We should go shopping some time if you want?"

"I feel like we probably shop at different places. No offence."

"Hey, I like a bargain as much as the next girl," I argue, forcing a smile onto my face. "Next meet up, we're totally going shopping. My credit card hasn't had a stretch out in way too long, and if I'm not careful, my dad will think I'm sick or something."

"Are you guys close?"

"Me and my dad?"

She nods.

It's a loaded question.

"We used to be," I reply, thinking back to the whiskey spilling down the wall of his office.

He was everything. The standard set. The one all men had to live up to. And the second that mask broke, and I saw what was underneath, my entire world collapsed.

The man who was strong and loving. The doting father. The one who bought me the pony and helped me with my politics homework. The man who showed up to every dance competition and riding show. But it was all just a lie. A facade. A ruse.

I don't even know who that man is anymore.

"Don't tell me it's complicated." She laughs depreciatingly. "I know all about that."

"So, you're not close with yours, either?"

"Absolutely not. He went out for milk when I was a baby… you know how it goes."

"Sorry." I go to reach out for her hand but stop part way, leaving it hovering in the middle of the table as her eyes widen, and she pulls it back protectively.

I should have remembered how she felt about physical touch and personal space. Not that Tamsin gave a shit about that at the end of the party when wrapping her arms around her and squeezing tightly.

No, she allowed that one, almost as if she knew it would be the last opportunity for her to do it… but that's absurd, isn't it?

"It's fine," she brushes me off, and a lump forms in my throat as my eyes water from nothing more than thinking about the best friend I'll never see again. Her death and the conversation about my father has caused me to see lies, deceit, and connections in places where they don't exist. "I guess our time's up, anyway."

"Right." I nod, pressing my lips together and praying to everything that's holy that I can manage to keep my shit together for five more fucking minutes. "Well, let me know where you want to go shopping, and we'll do it. Seriously, my card needs a workout, and Tamsin usually has a big bill, so the sky's the limit."

"She won't be joining us?" she asks with her hand on the back of the chair, her step not quite taken as her head turns my way and her eyes narrow.

"Ladies," Liselle calls, giving me a moment to gather my shit together, and when I look her way I see the baby pink mask she's wearing matches her dress perfectly.

Looking back to Ruby, I shake my head. "No, Tamsin won't be with us."

Confusion crosses her face before she walks away silently and joins the rest of the Little Sisters as they walk out. When Jacob comes to my side, my composure is nothing more than a fragile shell.

"Shall we?" he asks, gesturing to the door.

"Absolutely."

To say Liselle was unimpressed at Jacob deciding to tag along this afternoon is the biggest of understatements ever— she was fuming. Apparently, she said this is important, and not the kind of thing to bring your boyfriend to, clearly not realising this isn't Nick. In the end, she conceded to Jacob driving me, so long as he stayed out of the way. Whether that's because she was there when everything went down with Tamsin, or because she noticed the lack of leather on my wrist, I'm not sure, but either way, she conceded the point eventually.

Jacob helps me into the passenger seat before climbing in himself, and the engine rumbles as he revs it up.

"Such a child."

"Made you smile, though." He winks before setting off, heading back to campus.

"Have you heard from Wyatt?" I ask, pulling out my

phone and checking the messages.

"Yes. Nick's fine." He answers the question I didn't even ask with a smile, knowing that was going to be the exact thing to come next.

It's not that I haven't been busy or had other things to do, it's just that sitting there with Nick calms me. For whatever reason, he went and did what he did alone, without us, and I'm not willing to give him the opportunity to do it again. Oh, and he's a complete mess who would forget his own head if he didn't have someone to remind him, never mind the tablets he's supposed to be taking.

"You know that splitting time to babysit us both is not sustainable, right?" I ask Jacob.

"He's going to get his shit together," he replies, gripping the steering wheel tighter. "And you can't sit there keeping an eye on him all the time, either."

"Means only one of you has to sit guard, though." I shrug, trying to play it off.

It's not just that he fucked off and tried to hand himself into The Sect as some kind of sacrifice for the rest of us, but the fact that he did it while we all sat there with him, around him, that even us being there together wasn't enough. Or maybe it was too much. Maybe he really doesn't want it all.

We all said we were in it together, and we confirmed as much to The Sect with knives pointed at us. Fuck, I really thought for a second we were all dead. But not Nick. He was too beaten to even breathe properly for the first thirty-two hours… not that I was counting.

But then if he wasn't here for us all, he wouldn't have done what he did… and I'm back to going around in circles with these men, only now I have no one to talk it through with.

Tamsin.

"How're you holding up?" Jacob asks, clearly picking up on the sombre look on my face.

"I'll admit, I've had better days. Ruby mentioning Tamsin didn't really help, either, not that she knows, but still."

"Yep, get that." He nods. "But it looked like you two were getting on better if that helps at all? You're making progress with her, despite everything else going on."

"Yeah," I muse. "Man, do you remember how damn terrified I was about failing?" I scoff out a laugh. "That first day when Wyatt dropped me back off at the house after the cemetery trip, and the explanation about that damn unmarked grave. Hell, did that turn out to be realer than I imagined. All I could think about was fucking up with Ruby and not moving her forward like The Sect was expecting. I guess I wasn't looking close enough to home, huh?"

And it's not an exaggeration. I was so wrapped up in failing them, I never stopped to consider what that would look like. That the people closest to me were the ones who would be taken from me.

"You say these things like we have all the answers," he replies, his hand dropping down to squeeze around mine reassuringly. "We're all just figuring this shit out as we go."

I nod, and we fall silent, the music occupying the cabin as we pass through what are quickly becoming familiar roads.

"So, do you think we should find them some treats in

the kitchen when we get back, or not?" I ask, lightening the conversation. Sure, I got to sit and eat cake for the first time in what feels like weeks, but we've been on Nick rotation for days and days, with nobody really looking after themselves like they should be.

"For sitting on their arses all morning? I don't think so. I'll help you take up some coffee or something if we must."

"Will Leo be back from class?"

"He already is." He smiles, the dreamy look of someone absolutely smitten smeared across his face.

"And you're still okay with me and him… with us…" I stumble, unable to put the words together in the right order, so they don't sound as smutty as I think they do.

With me wrapping my lips around his dick and using him as a lollipop? Or any of the myriad of disgusting thoughts that have been tangling around my head over the last week or more. I couldn't even admit half of them if I wanted to.

"If it makes him happy." He shrugs with a smile. "And you're not so bad." He winks. "If I was ever going to entertain a partner in crime, it would definitely be someone that pisses my brother off as much as you do. Oh, and who brings this much heat to the equation."

"Now, are you talking about me or Wyatt?" I ask with a smile, grateful for the easy distraction.

"Do I have to pick?" He smirks, pulling into the garage.

"Guess not."

He turns the engine off and hops out while I look around, noticing their cars lined up safely in a car-lover's dream.

"Do you reckon there would be space for Debbie in

here?" I ask absentmindedly as Jacob opens my door, then holds his hand out for mine.

"Who?"

"Debbie the Discovery. Seems a shame to leave her unloved out by the pool house when she could be tucked in here with all the big boys."

"Debbie the… Jeez, you fit in here better than I ever imagined. Next you'll be sitting up and talking horsepower with them, getting all hot and bothered."

"Not quite." I chuckle. "And I didn't realise that kind of conversation got Leo hot under the collar."

"Not quite," he echoes back to me with a wink as we walk through the boot room, then head through to the entranceway.

Aimee and Charlotte come striding through the moment we make our way to the kitchen, with their arms full of stuff. They both smile our way before heading up the stairs without breaking their conversation.

"I guess that means they went ahead and did it," I say quietly. "Oliver and Stephanie."

"Ah, so we've got new floormates. Although, I guess now we're not a mirrored set or whatever, we should probably head back to our own rooms."

"Not happening," I clip out, banging the coffee powder harder than necessary before pouring the water into the machine. "If you think, after everything that's happened over the last few weeks, and after everything your brother did, that I'm letting him or any of you out of my sight, you must be out of your damn mind."

"Okay," he replies quietly.

It's taken a few days to get used to my bare wrist, and it's annoyed me more than I care to admit that I'd become so reliant on the safety that band represented. Not that any of it is real, but still, it was something I was unknowingly clinging to and, as with plenty things I thought were mine before we came here, they continue to be stripped away and I can only feel their loss for a moment.

I moved away from my home, from my family, from the safety that place represented. Despite all her flaws and the way she stood beside my father, even though it was adamantly not what I wanted, my mother is my mother, and her mask isn't fake. It's just who she is, and she's far away, with no idea what's going on.

The friend I brought with me is now gone, too—another support I didn't realise I needed so badly until I no longer had it. Never in a million years would I have told you that I'd be leaving this place without her. She's been my friend since we were six years old. She's an extension of me, myself, and I, and now she's gone, and I'm alone.

Except, I'm not alone.

I was linked to one man and picked up by three others.

I thought I had Nick beside me, and I do, except not in a way that's going to be recognised by the biggest current threat: The Sect. He's beside me so much, he was willing to leave to keep me and the guys safe, but that's not the kind of thing that's going to keep us safe in this game.

Division is the key, and they almost got it.

Not on my watch. Not on Jacob's.

Wyatt keeps telling me that diamonds are forged under pressure, and if how I reacted the other day is anything to go by, I could be the strongest one here, though it doesn't always feel that way.

Jacob makes small talk about our sociology class while we make the drinks before grabbing all the travel mugs out and loading them up to make our way upstairs, passing the giggling coming from the other bedroom as we do.

I'm all poised to call out, *'Honey, we're home!'* when Jacob pushes open the door with his elbow, holding it there with his back, and the words die on my tongue as I take in the state of the room.

Bedsheets are strewn everywhere, with pillows abandoned haphazardly across the floor as Wyatt and Leo sit opposite each other on the sofas. They're glowering wordlessly, with their arms crossed, and fury huffing from each one of them like caged bulls, but Nick is nowhere to be seen.

"What the fuck?" Jacob says, stealing the words right out of my mouth. "Is that blood?"

"Someone better start talking right fucking now," I demand, slamming the mugs on the coffee table between them, making the liquid slosh everywhere. "And where the hell is Nick?"

"Shower," they reply in unison.

We left them for an hour.

Well, slightly more than an hour once you take into consideration the coffee, but they said it was okay. Wyatt said everything was fine. Panic grips me while Jacob calmly crosses the room and places the mugs on the table beside me before looking from Wyatt to Leo and back expectantly. When neither of them start talking, I wait, and Jacob sighs, shaking his head before marching to the bed.

I don't even want to think where the blood came from. Probably one of these two if the split brow is anything to go by.

"What the hell happened?" Jacob seethes, ripping the sheet back. "I swear to God, if I have to bang your heads together to get an answer, I'll do it."

And yet, silence.

"If you think we're going to come in here with coffee and clean up your mess like the damn maids, you'd better think again," I say, crossing my arms.

But Jacob doesn't stop as he throws the sheet in a heap on the floor before snatching up a pillow and dragging the cover from it, then throwing it at the back of Leo's head with a thump.

"Someone decided Nick needed some tough love," Leo finally spills. "I didn't agree."

"And the blood?" Jacob asks, pointing at the sheets, even though both Leo and Wyatt are still glowering at each other and not taking us in for a second.

"I don't think he's popped the stitch properly, but it's definitely a close call," Wyatt admits, though there's no sign of remorse on his face. "At least he's up and getting cleaned up. That's better than he was before."

"Cleaned up, as in, he's in the shower, alone and unstable? Jesus Christ." I sigh, leaving Jacob to deal with the petulant children while I storm into the bathroom.

But Nick's not in the first one, so I move on, finally seeing the steam billowing as I close the door behind me. Even black and blue, he's a sight to behold. I'm supposed to be in here checking he's okay—he's clearly fine—and yet, I can't help but stand and stare at the sight before me: thick muscles, a tight arse, and thighs I can't wait to straddle again one day when he's feeling better.

He tips his head back, his hands braced against the wall as a groan tumbles from him.

"I can feel you staring, you know," he rumbles, the sound hitting me deep in my core, making my stomach twist. "The least you could do is give me a hand."

Caught out, and not for the first time today.

"Do you want me to wash your back?" I ask with a smile, stepping closer and reaching for the body wash whilst attempting to keep out of the spray.

He's standing, that's something, and the casual indifference tumbling from his lips means he's okay, of sorts. So, I attempt to keep it light to shove down the fact that I can't wait to ride him into oblivion.

"Or a little lower," he replies as I smooth the silky cream along his shoulders, that familiar sizzle building in the air.

"Well, it's good to know you've not lost your sense of humour."

He quiets as I work along his back and down his sides, attempting to be as gentle as possible while pushing the suds along his skin. I'm doing a rubbish job of avoiding the spray bouncing from his skin, and my arms and chest are already soaked when he shuffles his weight from one foot to another. A grumble of pain echoes around the room, just as one of the sprays hits me right in the stomach.

Turning, Nick turns one of the nozzles off before resting his back against the tiles, but the damage is already done.

I'm soaked.

"Well, I guess you may as well take it off now."

With the raise of an eyebrow, I peel the soggy material from my skin and drop it behind me as the temperature in the room skyrockets. It's been nearly a week since his hands touched my skin, since he looked at anything or anyone with more than pity and sadness, and for the most part it's been a feeling reciprocated.

The five of us have huddled and moped, hoping and praying we would come back together somehow. That the jagged pieces that were left behind on that church floor would somehow meld back together properly. But they aren't, and they haven't—not without action. And I'm done waiting.

They've taken and taken, and I'm over being pushed around.

I know Wyatt meant well by pushing Nick, and maybe it worked—it got him out of the bed and into the bathroom, I suppose—but if we're going to make it through this, then it has to be together, and that starts right back at the beginning… with us.

Him and me.

A push. A pull.

A claim I never wanted to accept but couldn't deny.

While holding Nick's gaze, I flick the button on my trousers and let the material pool at my feet. He doesn't falter or look down, and the air becomes thick and heavy between us as I unclip my bra, letting it join the rest of my clothes on the floor. The silk French knickers will probably never be the same as they land in the suds, but who fucking cares? None of us will be the same when we leave here.

I watch his Adam's apple bob as he swallows thickly, his gaze a scorching heat that descends over my skin taking in every delicate inch.

"You gonna get washed up, or what?" he asks, his voice as strained as his dick.

"Are you going to wash my back?" I ask, throwing the proverbial ball back in his court.

He smiles, nodding as I step under the water I've been doing one hell of a shit job avoiding this far. I completely understand the moan of appreciation when his hands run over my skin, building something I know neither of us are going to be able to sate the moment he brushes against my nipples.

"You're so beautiful," he whispers, the words almost lost under the sound of the water rushing around us, but they hang in the air as his body hits my back, and my head falls against his chest.

"You're not bad yourself," I reply with a smile, turning in his grip to look up into those deep eyes. A million words seem to cascade from him: pain, regret, an apology? Or perhaps that's pushing it too far. "Let's get you dry; you're shaking."

It's probably the strain rather than the cold, but neither of us move. His dick bobs against my stomach, and my arms are wrapped around his waist. It could be some ridiculous attempt at holding him up, but it's not.

I want to wrap my legs around that waist, and my arms around his neck when I plunge my tongue into his mouth and sink onto his cock. I want to connect us so deeply that he never considers walking away from us again. That even the thought brings him physical pain. But I can't... not yet.

And still, my body moves of its own accord, my hands sliding up and over the water that falls, and my nails pushing against his beaten back as I tip my head in invitation—one he finally acquiesces after the longest seconds of my life.

My lips press against his while the waterfall shower tumbles over us both as we tilt and turn. His hands grip my arse, pulling me against him, and then his tongue rages war against mine, no longer meek, no longer pitiful. But we both know this can't go any further, and quicker than either of us are ready for, we pull back, our breaths ragged, and our disappointment swirling between us.

"Soon," I promise.

"Soon," he repeats, kissing the spot where my shoulder meets my neck, making goosebumps break out across my skin.

"Are they still arguing out there?" he asks, turning the water off, allowing me to step out and grab a couple of towels from the side.

"I don't think so," I reply, wrapping the towel around my chest and taking a step away, looking him over now the steam is beginning to dissipate. "You should probably get that checked out again," I comment, noting the fresh blood at his brow.

"Nah, it's clean, and it's healing."

"It'll scar."

"Are you worried about my pretty face, sugar?" he asks with a smirk, the movement opening it up farther.

Rolling my eyes, I throw him a face cloth. "I'm good.

Jacob will still be pretty."

"Oh, ouch." He chuckles, feigning pain this time instead of feeling it as he presses the cloth against his face.

"Let's get you some clothes. You'll be pleased to know they're in the walk-in with mine."

"Yeah, thanks for that," he replies, embarrassment creeping across his features as he adjusts the towel low on his hips before linking our fingers together.

The room goes quiet when we step out of the bathroom, three sets of eyes coming our way before we slip into the walk-in wardrobe to get changed.

"You know they're talking about us," Nick says, distractingly dropping the towel the second the door closes behind us.

"Yes." I turn and pull out a pair of yoga pants and an oversized tee. "What do you think we've been talking about for the best part of a week if it wasn't you?"

"I dunno." He shrugs, sliding the jeans up his legs. "The weather. Sports. Classes. You know, normal, boring, life shit."

"Because we're living with normal, boring, life shit right now, huh?" I pin him with a look and hold my top against my chest.

He concedes the point with a tip of his head and a shrug of his shoulders. The water is dripping off the ends of his hair, making a pattern down his shirt. Even battered and bruised, he's still beautiful, but how long do we have until he tries to protect us again? And what will the cost for that be?

SIX

Nick

She turns, with a combination of disappointment and concern flickering over her features, but it's the fear and pain that worries me. I know I fucked up, and hell, if I haven't been paying the toll for that since.

Stepping towards the door, I wait until she's ready before pulling it back, noticing a pregnant pause being put on whatever conversation the guys were having.

Jacob is already on his feet and closing the distance between us before anyone can say anything to him. Not that there's far to go as his hands comes to my face, tipping it up to check it out before pressing his lips together and shaking his head. I can't work out who he's most disappointed in: me for needing the stitches in the first place, Leo and Wyatt for picking a fight over it, or himself for leaving me.

His hand slides around the back of my head, then he's pulling my forehead against his while I close my eyes and take the deepest breath I've managed since four guys broke my ribs. Peace washes over me, creating a calmness I've not felt in far too fucking long.

Ivy helps to dissipate the tension and electricity that zaps beneath my skin on a regular basis, but there's something about my brother that just absolves it—always has.

"Well, at least you'll smell better now," Leo quips.

Pulling away, Jacob hits Leo around the back of the head before stepping away and dropping onto the sofa beside him, clearly finished playing referee as Wyatt looks at me expectantly.

Ivy picks up on the tension immediately and pulls me around and down into the corner between everyone before asking, "What's really going on?"

"Sitting here isn't going to get him ready for the next challenge," Wyatt states, repeating the start of the conversation he and Leo have already had over the top of me.

"And killing himself in that gym won't, either," Leo replies, their argument playing on repeat.

They bicker for another minute or two like I'm not even here while I attempt to drown out the noise. Jacob joins in, and it continues to escalate… again, until Ivy intervenes, physically putting herself between the three of them.

"I'm just surprised it's not Leo trying to get me back in the ring," I say, cutting through the distortion, causing all heads to turn to me. "What? It's no lie there's been no love lost between us."

Yeah, there's been a truce, of sorts, but like everything else in this place, it's held together by hopes and dreams. Hopes and dreams that are being so casually smashed to pieces, it's not even funny.

"Yeah, well, shit happens," he grumbles by way of a reply. "And for the record, he's right. Sitting here isn't going to get you ready for the next challenge, whenever and whatever that turns out to be. But your body is still healing, and that takes time."

"You think I've been running him aromatherapy baths because I like it?" Wyatt clips out, his irritation lacing every word. "Made up and dished out arnica salve because it smells nice, really? Healing, bruising, recovery." He marks them off on his fingers as he says them, his agitation growing again. "They should halve his recovery time, but the longer you sit there, sinking mentally, emotionally, and physically, the more off your game you're going to be, and we don't need a repeat of that."

"Uh—" Leo starts before Wyatt cuts him off again.

"Yeah, you didn't know what I've been doing. Whatever. It's fine. I'm just the toff plucked from the ivory tower… or beachfront, which is probably closer to the truth, and I don't know shit about anything or care about anyone else. I'm just trying to get him to run before he can walk again, right?"

"Thank you," I say before Leo has the chance to retort. I'm sick of listening to the two of them. "Thank you for helping quietly in the background. For doing what you can. It's appreciated."

He nods, sitting down again.

"I know I'm not ready for the gym. Hell, I've not even made it downstairs yet. Maybe we should start there and build up to it, yeah?" I ask, looking from Wyatt to Leo and then Jacob. "I'm not out of this, I'm in."

It's the reason I went to The Sect in the first place. Not because I was out, but because I'm so far in this with these people, just the thought of Ivy and Jacob getting deeper with Leo and Wyatt and then them losing them hurt. If I could stop any of them going through what Ivy has with Tamsin, I would.

"Say it again," Ivy whispers, her fingers clutching mine, and hope glistening in the deep green of her eyes. "Please."

"Huh?"

"Say it again."

"I'm not out of this, I'm in."

She pushes a breath out through pursed lips, and her eyes close as she nods. Then she's opening them before jumping up and disappearing back to the wardrobe. My confusion is mirrored on everyone else's faces until she returns with something black in her hands.

"Right, I don't know how you're supposed to do this in real life. I'm sure smutty romance books make it out to be sexier than it is, but…" She unravels the strap, pulling out a short but sharp looking knife."

"Where the hell did you get that" Wyatt asks, horrified.

"It was a gift." She shrugs, not taking her eyes of the glittering knife in her hands. It's not the first one she's received from us, the chastity belt I gave her a much hotter thought than the knife. "I get them from time to time."

"Is that a leather thigh strap?" I ask, attempting to work out exactly what she has in her hands.

"Yep," Leo replies smugly. "Just be careful, it's sharp." And we watch her slice her palm open.

Wonderful. Now she's bleeding, too.

Taking a painful breath in, I push up to move and get her a cloth or something, but she holds her hand out for me to wait before passing the knife to Wyatt.

Warily, he takes it, slicing his palm before then passing the knife on. It's not like we haven't all done the same and more for The Sect. They've got our blood safely stored somewhere for whatever reasons they might come up with in the future, so how is this any different?

"Fuck, I can't remember how you're supposed to do this. They always have the right words in the books," Ivy says as Jacob hands the knife to me, allowing me to slice my hand before giving it back to Ivy.

It wouldn't be my gift of choice but whatever.

"Okay, so we're all in this, yeah?" she asks, looking at each of us and waiting for confirmation. "To love," she says, pressing her palm against Wyatt's, causing a pang of jealousy to wash over me.

Sure, we haven't said the words, but I thought it was pretty obvious that my feelings for her are more than platonic.

"To care for," she continues, turning and pressing it against Leo's.

Because it was his father that turned up to back us up. He's the one rocking up with the muscle here.

"To protect," she says, locking her gaze and hand with Jacob before turning to me.

But it isn't Jacob they've had to protect. It's me.

A lump forms in my throat as our palms press together and our fingers twine as she pins with me with the same determined look she gave each of them.

"Until death," she whispers.

"Until death," I repeat.

Emotion is heavy in the room as she repeats it all.

"We're together to love, to care for, to protect, until death."

Wyatt goes first, pressing his palm from one to another, with Leo following, then Jacob. My hand stings by the time it's my turn, and whilst looking each of them in the eye and declaring us a team feels like it should be awkward as hell, it isn't. It's like a weight is lifted from my shoulders. A confirmation I didn't realise I needed.

It's the five of us against the world now, and nobody and nothing is going to stop us, not even each other.

"Now, that means no more going off on your own, no making decisions for other people, no second guessing, and no holding on to shit," Ivy says from beside me. "You'll talk it out like fucking adults."

Both Leo and I attempt to smother the laughter bubbling up inside us as the tension and emotion crackles around the room, sizzling to boiling point, but when my gaze connects with his, there's no damn chance, and as much as it burns like hell, I can't help the laugh that tumbles from me.

"I guess we could try that," Jacob says. "But all this testosterone is going to end up somewhere, chick. It's fuck or fight."

His words only make it worse as both Leo and I clutch our sides, the laughter so painful, yet completely unstoppable.

"Fucking children," Wyatt says, probably rolling his eyes.

Eventually, we manage to get ourselves together. Wyatt hands everyone a cloth to clean up with, but as I look at the throbbing smear on my hand, I'm only hit again with the lengths I'd go to in order to keep them all safe. But it's not just about them anymore… it's about all of us.

Finally, I realise I'm going to have to face what's happened. Eventually, I'm going to have to face the rest of the world, and that moment is getting closer and closer.

"So, what do they know?" I ask, acknowledging a weight in the pit of my stomach.

I never considered what would happen afterwards…

I planned and prepped what I'd say to The Sect, how I'd convince them to take me, and leave everyone else in the race. If they fucked up, then that's on them, but I only wanted to give them the best chance I could.

It never occurred to me that there would be fallout I'd have to face, or that the rest of these guys would come to rescue me, and bring back-up, too. But her battle cry is what I held on to, and what pulled me back from the brink as they pummelled my body—a body I'd gladly give to save them. It was a siren song, drawing me closer and closer to them, the start of the end, and the moment they saved us.

Then we came home, and I was broken in a different way.

Physically, The Sect did plenty of damage, and I'm more than sure Olly and Jasper saw that when the guys dragged my arse in. But mentally, I was broken, too, because I'd failed.

I failed to save them. I failed to stop my brother from offering himself up, too. Now, we have no bands, and no way to get them. We have to go through whatever challenges they throw at us and face the fallout from my failed martyrdom.

I know these guys understand why I did what I did, but what about everyone else? What do they know? How far has my failure spread?

"Nobody outside the Devils and Angels knows anything at all. They've been told you're ill and to take your notes because I asked them to," Leo says. "Inside these walls…. Well, they know you've had a run in with The Sect, and that it didn't end well for you, but they don't know anything else. And the fact that nobody's been at that door chasing down answers tells me they'd only be interested in the gossip, anyway, not wanting to make sure you're safe."

"And what are we going to tell them?" I ask, knowing more than well there'll be questions once they see the state of me. The damage is hard to miss.

"Whatever you want," Wyatt says, adjusting the cushions beside him.

"Or nothing at all," Ivy suggests. "Oliver and Stephanie have swapped bands now, and I imagine Jasper and Aimee aren't far behind them." She ponders, her thoughts ticking behind her eyes. "That means Charlotte and Penelope don't have partners."

"Right, but how is that relevant?" Jacob asks.

"We can't request any more bands, and we can't even cobble together enough from other people now either, so telling them you were willing to back out of the race to ensure everyone in here finishes only draws the divide between you, Oliver, and Jasper wider. There's half a chance we can keep the Angels that aren't yet linked up completely out of it, and safe."

"Okay, so we don't tell them anything, and don't make this any more of a competition than it already is. We keep things going as normal, but move forward knowing we're working against them, whilst trying to keep as many people safe as we can," Leo says. "Am I following that right?"

"Yes," she agrees with a nod.

"How and when do you want to talk to the girls?" Wyatt asks. "Is this something you want us to pitch in with, or do you just want leaving to it?"

I'm not sure how the hell me attempting to convince three girls to go it alone against The Sect would go down, especially considering the state of my face right now, and the rest of me, but I can give it a go if needed.

"Leave it with me," Ivy replies from my side. "I'll shout up if I need some help, but I've got something in mind."

"Cool," Wyatt says with a nod before turning his gaze to me. "So, are you ready to pull your head out of your arse, apologise, and get on with the stairs?"

Tension ripples around the room as my jaw clenches. "I'm not apologising for anything."

"Your reckless idea almost got us all killed. You might not have been able to see the knife against Leo's throat, but the rest of damn well could," he clips out.

"Look, that wasn't my fault or intention. I went there to keep you guys safe, and then you all came running straight into the line of fire." Someone attempts to say something, but I cut them off, the words rolling as it all finally spills out. "And it's not that I'm not grateful you did, that it isn't appreciated. I am, and it is. It's just that I was doing what I thought was right, and I'm not going to apologise for that, or for trying to keep you all safe and in one piece."

"Because you thought we wouldn't notice you were gone?" he asks. "That we would magically realise it was for the best that you left us as we were literally telling the rest of the world that together we were united. Obviously." He scoffs out an unimpressed laugh, holding his hands across his chest and turning away.

"I left a letter…"

"What?" everyone says in unison, their confusion evident.

"I left you a letter explaining everything." Yep. Sad, and cliché as fuck, but they had to understand and had to know how I felt. *Fuck, so pathetic.* "If you didn't find it, then how did you find me? How did you know?"

"You'd been pulling away for days," Leo says, his dark gaze catching mine as he drags Jacob into his side. "That's why we tied everyone together. Incidentally, that was the night before you did what you did. Talk about timing."

"Then, when we were supposed to meet outside the administration buildings, you were nowhere to be seen. Luckily for you, I managed to fill your shoes," Jacob adds with a roll of his eyes, while Leo's hand finds his thigh. "But I knew you'd done something stupid. I could feel it."

"Great," I grumble.

"It's a twin thing." He shrugs.

Of course it fucking is.

"It didn't take a genius to work out what you'd be doing if it wasn't something with one of us or the rest of the Devils, and it was lucky for all of us that Leo's father was nearby," Wyatt says. "I can only imagine how that would have gone down without his backup."

Wonderful. Now I'm in debt to Leo, too.

"Okay, so Nick did a thing, and we did a thing, and

now we're all on the same page, together, 'til death, right?"
Ivy asks, squeezing my knee. "Can we just move past this,
because arguing over context isn't going to get any of you
through the next challenges, and that's where we need be
directing our focus: outward, not inward. We've got the
rules from The Sect, and the challenges to keep on top of,
as well as all the damn work and navigating living with the
competition, because that's how we need to view this now."

"Cold."

"I like Stephanie a lot, but if it comes down to her or
you, then you know where I stand." She rises to her feet,
then turns to me and holds her hands out. "Now, it's time
to get your arse up and get moving, buddy." As if she could
support my weight if I used her to get up.

But she's right.

It's time to stop sulking, to stop worrying, and to start
working together, because we're not making it out of here
alone. We're going as a unit, 'til death.

With a nod, I plant my hands in hers, using her for
nothing more than balance as I haul myself up, my lungs
screaming in protest.

"Your next painkillers are in half an hour," Leo says.
"Do you fancy grabbing them from the kitchen?"

Hell no. But what choice do I have?

The Sect isn't going to let me skip out of anything
because of a decision I made, because of a punishment they
handed out. They've already proven that with George. So,
unless I'm planning on ending up in the same place he is, I
need to get a fucking grip on myself and prove I'm worthy
of the place I've found myself in, as well as the people I find

myself besides.

"Let's do this."

Time to let the real work begin.

SEVEN

Ivy

"An audience isn't required," Nick states, looking over my shoulder sternly.

"And when you fall down the stairs and take her with you?" Jacob asks with just as much indignation.

Nick's eyes narrow before he whispers, "Wait here," in my ear, pulling me into his chest and wrapping his arms around my waist. "This will be embarrassing enough without any more of an audience." He places a kiss on the top of my head before stepping away, with Jacob and Leo following. "You're not needed," he growls, glowering as Leo pushes past him to grab the door and hold it out for him.

"Tough shit," he replies, his smile saccharine sweet.

Any retort dies on his tongue as Jacob comes to Nick's side. The two of them walk through with Leo following, and the three of them bicker on the other side, their voices getting quieter as they move slowly down the corridor.

"Well, the coffee was much appreciated," Wyatt says, handing me my untouched drink before gathering up the bloody cloths and throwing them in the bin.

"Anytime," I reply with a weary smile, plopping back on the edge of the sofa.

He returns with his tablet, flicking the TV onto one of my favourite programmes, and pulling me in against his side before dragging a blanket from the back of the sofa and over my legs.

"How did it go with Ruby?" he asks, evidently wanting to move away from the deep and dark as I rest my head against his shoulder.

"Ugh," I groan, not really wanting to go over it again. It was embarrassing enough the first time. "Running away from her wasn't really part of the plan, but it's what happened," I admit. "We're going to go shopping at some point, and hopefully she'll stop asking about Tamsin."

"Her not being there is a reasonably big variation from the norm," he says, opening up his workbook. "And this first meeting was always going to be tricky, but balancing our life and the outside world is going to be something we have to manage for a long time."

I hope.

"Yeah, sounds like it." I sigh. "Did you know this was a forever thing before we came here?"

He adjusts beside me, tucking me under his arm better as he moves the tablet on his lap, probably buying time while he thinks about his answer.

"I didn't know for certain, but looking at my parents and the life they live, with the information I have now, I can see it. It makes sense, you know?"

"What are they like?" I ask, conscious that family isn't something we've talked about a lot, and that's partly because Nick and Jacob have only recently lost their father, and that's a pain they're still processing. But also because I now know Leo's father is scary as fuck.

"Busy," Wyatt replies absentmindedly. "I've often wondered why they're together. Don't get me wrong, it's not like they hate each other. There are no screaming matches at 3:00 a.m. where they throw glasses at each other, but it's weird, and I didn't realise it until I came here. It's like they're just roommates that happen to have a child together."

"Huh, that's an interesting observation."

"It's not that they don't care about me or any of that. Whilst business has always been important, there are very few occasions it's taken precedence over any of my things. But at the same time, I know they don't have that same commitment for each other."

"It's like they're living alongside each other rather than together," I add, thinking of my own parents.

"Exactly."

Not that my mother has or would ever go against my father, but knowing this world like we both now know it, I can see why. Their lives haven't been in their control for a long time, and it's clear to see that's had an effect on how they relate, if they even chose each other.

I suppose they must have at some point, or maybe our mothers were just the ones left after everyone else had picked or disappeared, but that's not a conversation I want to have with either of them. My relationship with my parents isn't good at the moment, I did not leave under favourable circumstances. I think *hanging on by a thread* is closer to the phrase I'd use.

"We won't end up like them," he promises, squeezing me.

"Until death, baby," I reply, as dread curdles in my stomach.

There's nothing to say that the Angels are sent here by design, similar to the blood lines like the Devils, but what if they are?

What if, once upon a time, my mother was here, dropped off unknowingly into a game with all the cards held by someone else? What if she was forced into a position to choose or die, but somehow, she made it out, only to find herself tied with the kind of man who would choose power and status over anything?

Yet, that's not the kind of men I find myself with now. Sure, those things are important to all of them, but Nick gave himself up for the others, and Jacob offered the same. Leo stood with a knife to his throat for us, and Wyatt's here silently holding us all together, pushing when needed.

But they're not the only men here, and I can see it of the others.

There's something manic about Oliver—the same man that beat someone half to death for threatening his girlfriend—something not quite right, and whilst Jasper doesn't have that same kind of energy, there's something hidden behind his playful acquiescence that I can't quite put my finger on. This is the same man who dragged me out of a broken car window by my hair, after all. Whatever it is, it's not good.

"Are you really worried about him?" I ask when I hear

a door slamming somewhere down the hall, dragging me back into the conversation at hand.

"Who?" he replies, stilling.

"Nick."

"Not now," he replies on an exhale. "He was sinking, and I don't mean physically. He was shutting down, switching off. He was—"

"Giving up," I finish.

"Pretty much. I know Leo wasn't happy about it, but sometimes you've got to push Nick forwards. The timing is important, obviously, but if I hadn't pushed in the past, then Leo wouldn't have Jacob right now, and the whole lot of us would still be floundering around. My father said to be sure, and to be strategic, and whilst I'm reasonably sure *this* wasn't what he had in mind, that's just unfortunate."

"So, we're your best bet, huh?" I ask with a smile, trying to lighten the mood since we've found ourselves back in the thick of it. I place my cup on the table and turn my head to look at him.

"Something like that," he replies, looking down at me from the corner of his eye, the edge of his lip turning up in a smirk. "It does help that you're hot as fuck, too."

"Is that so…"

Pushing the blanket off, I climb onto his lap, straddling his legs as he lifts the tablet in one hand, moving it out of my way as surprise crosses his face. Sometimes, it's felt a little one-sided between us. Not that there isn't that sizzle of attraction, but the undercurrent is different, and with him being more laid back than both Leo and Nick, it's often felt like he's being dragged along by my infatuation. But it's nice to know and believe he's also here by choice, and that he wants us, too.

Not that he hasn't made that clear plenty of times recently, but it's different admitting that in the quiet of our safe space than it is when it feels like lives are on the line.

"You say that like those guys don't whisper dirty things in your ear a dozen times a day," he says quietly.

"Oh, they do." I nod. "But it hits differently when you say it."

"Yeah?"

The tablet finds its place on the sofa as his hands slide under the edge of my top, one holding my hip while the other brushes up my spine, and my anticipation coils deep in my stomach.

"So, this isn't just because things got steamy in that shower with Nick earlier on?" he asks, his head tipping back against the sofa, and one eyebrow rising.

Oh, he knows us so well.

"Absolutely not."

Sure, it got hot, but that's got nothing to do with the declarations we've just made, or the way need rushes through my body right now.

I settle in against him, finding a more comfortable spot as he traces patterns against my skin. My nipples tighten, thinking of the time he did that against my thigh with his tongue somewhere else entirely, and my cheeks redden.

"What Nick wouldn't give for that blush," he comments idly, and as the seconds drag out, I know it's intentional, both the way my body responds to his innocuous touches, and the time they take.

He's patient, he'll wait, but I'm not sure I am.

The TV plays behind me. I drop my forearms either side of his head, and his grip leaves my hip and squeezes my arse—the other hand soon following as he grinds me against his thickening length, causing a shiver to ripple over my body. Gently, his lips come to the column of my neck, placing soft kisses along the delicate skin while our clothed bodies rock together.

"Do we have time before they get back?" I ask.

"Who cares if we don't?" he counters, pulling my top up and off before doing the same with his.

The frenzy building under my skin only intensifies when the cooler air in the room kisses against it, and his sizzling gaze holds mine in a challenge. *Who's going to break first?*

I forewent the bra, only wanting to get dressed quickly and get whatever the hell was going on between the guys resolved. Now, sitting here with my nipples hard, and my chest bounding, I could almost long for a scrap of the delicate lace to give me some semblance of control. Control I don't own.

Instead, we both wait, my gaze as desperate as his to drop to the glorious muscles I know are on show.

His hips push up, his jeans doing nothing to hide the hard bulge, but it's my turn to tease and taste. After dropping my hands, I steady myself against the back of the sofa before trailing my fingers against his abs. My tongue twirls over his nipple before my teeth graze against it, and he moans, the guttural sound being ripped from him as his hands slide in my hair and pull me against his lips.

And, oh, God, his kiss is everything.

It's not frantic like Nick's—an overpowering need that has to be sated that second lest we die—but it's hardly lackadaisical. It's intoxicating in a way I've never encountered before, as if he's consuming and devouring, drawing out parts of my soul to entangle with his.

It's a joining, but not like I expected, and by the time he's ready to release me, the only thing I can think about is getting the rest of these clothes off and getting him so deep inside of me that I don't have to think any more.

My leggings and thong are gone before he's even fully out of the jeans. He's still kicking them off his ankles as I clamber back over him.

"Protection?" he asks, sliding down the sofa, his wet fingers gliding over my pussy before teasing against my entrance.

"Until death."

I'm not sure it's the answer I should give him, but right now, I couldn't care less. This isn't what we were talking about when we made those promises, but if we're in this together to the end, then we're in this together until the end. And if that means I leave this place with a part of them, then so be it.

It's reckless, and stupid, and the sober, straight-thinking part of me knows that, but as he teases his dick against my entrance, I can't find it in me to care. Especially when his hands thread through my hair, swallowing my gasp as his lips press against mine.

Right now, there's only us, this feeling, and this connection that grows stronger by the day. As I sink down onto him, and he pushes up into me, it's never felt so real.

We move together so in sync, it's strange to think we've not been together forever.

He squeezes my arse, and I tighten my grip in his hair. He bucks up harder, and my head tips back as sweat slips down my spine. My entire body is on fire as oblivion teeters just seconds away.

"Go on, take it," he says, the words strained, but I shake my head, not ready to fall. Not ready for it to be over.

"Do you need me to hold you down and fuck you?" *Like Nick.* "Or to whisper filthy words of encouragement in your ear?" *Like Leo.* He doesn't say their names, but I can hear the comparisons on the tip of his tongue. "Or will you take what you want, what you need?" He pants the words out as I grind against him, chasing but still holding back. And I don't know why.

He feels so fucking good. Amazing.

His fingers wrap around my throat, the momentum of his body pushing me upright making him hit me deeper, slower. It's a torturous pace I love and loathe at the same time.

"I'm not going to push you, Ivy," he says, way too calmly for the frenzy we're currently in the midst of. My skin is on fire as every nerve ending screams for blissful release.

Taking a breath, I steady myself against his chest, and lean into his grip.

"That's it," he praises while I push harder against him, my body taking over as instinct kicks in, the primal need all I can think about. "You're strong, you're beautiful, and you have ownership here, too."

"Fuck," I rasp, pulling back slightly and dragging more air into my lungs as need curls through my every extremity. My legs shake from the orgasm I can't quite reach teetering on the edge.

"We've got you, Ivy. Now, let go."

His quiet, confident command echoes through my mind, while the TV becomes nothing more than white noise, and I tumble off that cliff, bucking and bouncing against him… but he holds me firmly. With one hand at my hip, and one at my shoulder, he finally gives in to his needs and chases his own pleasure before coming deep inside me with a groan I feel right down to my toes.

"Wow." I sigh, collapsing against his chest, with nothing more than our panted breaths attempting to overcome the sound of the TV.

"Here," he says, grabbing his shirt whilst I manoeuvre my way off him.

Accepting it with a smile, I slide it on before standing on wobbly legs.

"Uh, it was for cleaning up, but that works, too." He looks at me with a whole new level of appreciation, a sense of ownership finally showing through.

"I need a wee, anyway," I say, excusing myself as I hurry across the room and slide into the bathroom.

Gravity, however, has got the best of me, and our sticky come makes itself known before I can manage to get washed up.

"Are you okay in there?" Wyatt asks, knocking on the door.

"Fine," I reply, shutting the water off quickly.

My mind is a million miles away, still stuck somewhere between climbing into his lap and his hand around my throat. While he held my body and worshipped me, he also let me lead.

A shiver ripples over my skin before I snap back into reality and fold the towel before throwing it in the wash basket.

"Sorry, it's all yours," I apologise while opening the bathroom door, not in the slightest bit prepared for him to be half-naked on the other side, even though I should be.

Logically, it makes sense. His shirt is on my back, after all, but the top button of his jeans is still undone, and I know exactly where that tiny trail of hair leads: to Heaven. His abs contract as he reaches for the door, and his hair is already tied back when he winks at me. *Caught out again.*

Quickly, I grab my things, and slide them back on before attempting to fold his shirt, with my mind wandering again.

What would have happened if Nick, Jacob, and Leo had come back? Would they have been mad? Jealous? Would it all have been over? Or would they have joined us, too?

I'm still glowing after what Wyatt and I just did, and I can't stop thinking about the what-if situations with other men.

Leo fucking Jacob beside me. Nick's hands on my skin. His harsh touch the very balm for the fire inside me. Or Jacob fucking Leo, and his lips finally touching mine—the only one of our weird and wonderful group I haven't yet kissed.

"Uh, Ivy. I think it's folded," Wyatt says from behind me, taking the shirt from my very distracted hands. "Not that it needed it."

He slides it straight on with a grin. Like some mind of mind reader, he knew exactly what I was thinking about as I stared at the spot we just had sex in. The same place we're all going to sit around later on today.

"Shall we go see what's taking them so long?" he asks. "I'd have expected them to be back by now."

Shit, yeah. Nick's body is still broken, and here I am working that out with someone else.

"Yeah, that sounds good."

A tiny bit of unease crawls through my insides.

This is the first time we've done something, anything, one-on-one and not as a group since I moved in here after running away from the memories of the woman I've lost. And it was amazing, unbelievable, and empowering in the weirdest kind of way. But do we only do this together now, or was this okay?

What on earth are the rules here?

EIGHT

Nick

"**A**nd I'll expect the rest of chapter eleven to be finished before I see you all next," the professor says as we all pack away. "There may or may not be questions on that section coming your way imminently."

Because it's not been hard enough work keeping up with everything from the house, now there's half a chance I'm going to fall behind. I've still got an assignment to finish as it is. I guess it's a good job nobody said this year was going to be easy.

They also didn't explain that I'd have a gruelling academic workload, extra-curriculars that I'm really not interested in, and a secret society breathing down my neck. Okay, so I kicked the hornets' nest with the last one, but still, it's a lot, and with Christmas looming, too.

After slinging my bag on my shoulder, I step out, completely oblivious to the guy heading straight past me until I end up colliding with his shoulder. Pain ricochets through me, my entire body ready to collapse in on itself.

Oomph.

"Don't mind me," I grumble, but he doesn't even

acknowledge my comment, striding on, non-the-wiser. "Oi, dickhead. An apology wouldn't go amiss."

"What, me?" he asks, turning around.

There are only two other students left, and both of them scuttle out of the room as quickly as they can manage.

"You might want to consider watching where you're going."

"Uh, you walked right into me," he argues, looking around for someone to back him up.

"Nobody here is going to help you." I grin, pushing past the pain as I close the distance between us. I can't let any weakness show. Not now. Not here. "Don't you know who I am?"

It's pompous, and I can hear the condescension dripping from my own words, but I can't help it. We're the Devils of Pendleton Prep, and we have a reputation to uphold, bruised and broken or not.

"Oh, you're…"

"Yep," I reply, popping the p as I square my shoulders just inches from him, our chests practically brushing.

This ridiculous superiority complex used to feel forced, but after everything we've been through and all the things we've done, as well as the friends we've lost along the way, it's not forced anymore. We've been hand-selected, chosen. We're going to do amazing things if only we can get through these next few weeks and months, and if this dickhead doesn't realise and acknowledge that, I'll be more than happy to educate him.

"Shit, man, I'm sorry. I didn't realise," he says, stumbling over his words as he steps back, his fear finally showing in his eyes.

He takes another step back, while I take one forward, hearing the door closing somewhere over the other side of the room—probably the professor making his escape—until I hear the cough.

"If you're ready, brother," Jacob says calmly.

There's a tense moment where I consider my options. Yeah, I'm still really feeling the after-effects of my run in with The Sect, and I'm grumpy because of it. God knows Leo's been giving me enough shit to really hammer home the point. But I'm also more than ready to remind everyone who the fuck I am.

I'm not done yet, and if some jumped up little shit thinks he can shoulder check me without any come back, he's got another thing coming.

The guy shuffles awkwardly from one foot to the other as he waits with bated breath for my answer. There's a slight tremble in the arm that holds his books, and it's all I need to see really.

"Sure," I reply, turning away from the idiot who wasn't watching where he was going, and stomping straight out. I don't have the fucking energy for it, anyway.

At least that's what I'm telling myself.

"I don't even know why I've got to do this shit," I grouch once Jacob catches up to me. He was probably apologising to the guy or something. Always the peacekeeper.

"You picked the course," he replies cheerily.

"What's the point of having a twin if you won't help me out every now and again?"

"It's time you got on with your own classes again, and

you know it.”

“Yeah, well… I don’t have to like it.”

“At least Ivy’s makeup tricks hide the bruising pretty well.”

“Let’s not say that quite so loudly, huh?” I hush him and look around self-consciously.

“I still don’t know why anyone in their right mind would want to study maths.”

“Because some of us want to make something of ourselves, not just enjoy slacking off in sociology.” I roll my eyes. *Such a waste of time.*

“Ivy and I are thoroughly enjoying that class I’ll have you know.” He gently bumps my shoulder with his. “History and law aren’t exactly a walk in the park, either.”

“If you say so.” I brush him off but hold the door open for him. I’m more than aware his workload isn’t light, but he didn’t opt for the additional subject that I did. Clearly, he had more foresight.

“You might want to be nicer to me. I have the car keys,” he reminds me.

I’m off the worst of the pain meds now, so I’m reasonably sure there’s no real reason for them to not let me drive. They just enjoy the power trip their little gang allows them. *Dicks.* It won’t last, and they all know it. I guess that’s why they’re making the most of the opportunities that present themselves.

“Hey, I can walk.” *Though it might cripple me.* “Maybe even jog.” *Hell no.* “I’m totally good.”

Lies. Lies. All the fucking lies.

“Oh, Ivy will be excited to hear that. She was talking

about going for a run later this afternoon."

And… kill me now.

"I think that's probably a bit more than I'm up to just at the minute," I say, backtracking as quickly as I can. "But soon!"

"Sure thing," he says with a knowing smirk, flicking the lock on the car.

We both clamber in, glad we don't have to wait for anyone else as the doors close and the music turns on.

"So, all good in your classes, then?" I ask.

"Yeah, just about."

"Cool."

"Everything is starting to settle back down to its usual whatever," he says, reversing out of the spot. "Not that anyone has really questioned much after our declaration the other week, but you know how it is. There's always someone with a big mouth waiting for their moment."

"Isn't there just."

It takes less than a minute for us to make our way down the driveway, the garage doors opening automatically once we arrive.

"It's weird, isn't it? All these cars parked here, but no owners to drive half of them."

"That's a creepy thought; a vehicular mausoleum," he replies.

"Let's not call it that."

"Yeah, I heard it the second the words came out of my mouth," he says with a shudder before climbing out.

"That wasn't here before, though, was it?" I ask, looking at the Range Rover on the far side.

"No, I don't think so."

With a shrug, he pulls open the door and walks through the boot room to the entranceway, pulling up short when I see the card.

"So, who's got the new car?" I ask, gesturing to the sideboard.

"Me," Leo declares, appearing through the changing room doorway.

"You went car shopping without me?" Jacob asks with the raise of his eyebrows. "That's just rude."

"That new Discovery?" I ask.

"No, not my style, but this is good news. News we've been waiting for."

"What is?" I ask, looking between them.

"*Ohh*," Jacob replies, his eyes widening. "Oh, you've got a *new car, and it's blue.*"

"Whatever," I say, dismissing the two of them. This is either code for something else, or I'm completely missing the point. Either way, I'm not interested. "It's quiet in here. Where the hell is everyone?"

"The girls have taken over the movie room for some film bonanza or something, but Wyatt and I are downstairs."

"Are you on your way to get cleaned up?" Jacob asks, gesturing to the towel around Leo's neck.

"Not at all. Are you up for some sparring?" he asks, looking my way.

Hell no.

"Sure."

What an idiot.

"Really?" Jacob pins me with a look that says *what on*

earth are you doing, before rolling his eyes and looking back at Leo. "Just take it easy on him, please." His palm finds Leo's chest.

Gross.

The last thing I need or want is someone pleading my case.

"I brought your gear down," Leo says as I brush past the pair of them, heading for the stairs. "It's in the changing room."

"Great," I grumble, heading to the changing room, both glad that I don't have to make it up two flights of stairs and back, but also anxious knowing the pain is only going to come that much quicker.

The bruising on my face may be nothing more than shadow now, but those on my ribs are still a combination of black and yellow. They look just as bad as they feel, but broken ribs were never going to heal overnight. And whilst I absolutely don't need anyone hitting or kicking them, I do need to keep on top of my fitness, and there's something about a mat beneath your feet, and an opponent standing opposite you that hits differently.

In the same way that there's something special about hitting a trail on a crisp afternoon compared to the treadmill, or working the boat with your friend instead of the rowing machine. They work the same muscles in the same way, it just hits your soul in another.

"Is it just us?" I ask as we head down the stairs, my eyes taking a minute to adjust to the lighting, the concrete floor cold underfoot.

"For now," Wyatt replies from the depths of the gym.

"I imagine Oliver will be down here with bells on when he gets back from class. He's been waiting for the opportunity to get you back in the ring."

"Yay," I reply, throwing as much sarcasm into my tone as I can. "Are you guys really working out down here with no music on? What the hell?"

"Good point," Jacob says, following me down and heading straight for the sound system, no doubt picking out his favourite playlist.

My groan of irritation is echoed by Wyatt and Leo as the theme song to Rocky blasts through the room.

"What?" Jacob asks with mock surprise written all over his face. "I honestly didn't know this would be the first one. It's on random."

"Of course it is," Leo says with a roll of his eyes, climbing through the ropes.

"Why the hell it's even in there is a mystery to me," I add.

"Gloves and pads," Wyatt says, throwing them in the ring behind me. "As much as I know we all want you fighting fit, now is not the time to overdo it."

"Fine," I agree, secretly more than happy for the reprieve. "Can you at least turn this shit down, though?"

Jacob wanders off, muttering, but the volume eventually drops, and by the time we've warmed up and done fifteen minutes of pad work, my insides are already screaming.

"Jacob, you're up," I say, stepping back.

"One more set," he replies from the side, taping the mat twice.

"Fuck off," I argue through panted breaths, resting my

forearms against my thighs as I bend over, unable to ignore the sweat slicking down my spine.

"Can't hack it?" Leo goads from the other side of the ring.

I know he's only trying to push me, just like Jacob and Wyatt are, but hell if he doesn't have the most irritating way of going about it. I suppose that's the idea.

"And you can shove it, too."

"Come on, just one more set," Leo continues undeterred as he bounces on the balls of his feet. "Then we'll have to get someone in here who's capable of giving me a proper workout."

"Gross," I reply, shaking my arms out, but I make it through one last set… just.

"Well, if that isn't perfect timing, I don't know what is," Oliver says, strutting down the stairs. "You keep hold of those pads, Leo. Nick's gonna show me how it's done."

I'm not sure when Oliver's obsession with proving me wrong began. Maybe it was the night I asked him for help with Ivy and the wristband. There's a good chance it was when I told him that he'd gone too far with the guy who threatened Stephanie, or one of the many occasions he's run his mouth and been told to shut the fuck up.

Now he can smell blood in the water, and like the shark he is, he's here to capitalise on it.

"Next time," I say, straightening up and rolling my shoulders. "I'm just stretching out for now."

"Really?" he says sceptically. "Because it looks like you're fucked, mate."

Jacob bristles from the side of the ring as Leo throws

down the pads, glowering at Oliver before unwrapping my gloves. Tension ripples across the room when Oliver swaggers towards us, clearly ready to prove some point to himself.

"Why don't I jump in with you?" Wyatt offers, and my stomach sinks.

I saw the state Oliver left the guy who overstepped with his girl, and whilst we've all worked out together for a while now, I don't recall a single moment when Wyatt climbed in the ring. My concern is mirrored in the look Leo sends my way.

"Nah, you're good," Leo says, intervening. "I need the workout, anyway. Nick was just helping me to get warmed up."

And under normal circumstances, he'd be right, but I'm not sure I could even hold the pads for him right now.

"Next time, I suppose," Oliver says, winking as he passes Wyatt to push through the ropes and join us.

I offer him the boxing gloves, but he shakes his head.

"Aren't you up for sparring?" he asks Leo as he kicks the pads to the side.

"Sure, let me grab the tape."

"The kid's scared of a little blood." Oliver laughs, slapping his hand down on my shoulder as if we're suddenly best mates. Like he doesn't know exactly who the people are that I share a bed with at night. Strange as that should be.

"I think that was more for your protection than his." I shrug, despite the pain jolting down my arm and across my chest as the contact vibrates through me. "But, whatever."

Oliver shrugs, and Wyatt throws him a roll of tape to

wrap his hands, but he makes a shitty job of it, so I grab the roll and do it for him. To be fair, it's not the easiest job to do on your own, but it's like he doesn't care and can't be arsed to do it right. *Thank fuck it's Leo he's in with.*

I don't know why, and it's entirely possible I'm wrong, but there's just something a little more delicate about Wyatt than the rest of us. Sure, he works out, he lifts, he climbs, and his muscles are leaner, tighter, but there's a raw animalism to Oliver that I've seen first-hand, and that's not something I want Wyatt on the receiving end of.

Leo, however, can take it.

"Thanks, man," Oliver says, testing out the flex, and rotating his wrists.

"Good luck," I reply, picking up the gloves and scooting out of the ring, with Leo already making his way back across.

"It's funny, you sticking up for Wyatt," Oliver says to Leo with a smirk, the two of them sizing each other up. "After all the noise coming from your room the other afternoon."

"What's that got to do with anything"?" Leo asks, jabbing.

"Stephanie said you three were on the way to the kitchen when she came up, but Ivy sounded like she was having a real good time."

I don't have the time to reply before Leo clocks Oliver in the jaw, throwing his head, and the rest of him, to the side.

"She's a big girl," Leo says. "She can do what she wants."

But I can't help the jealousy that swarms through my veins, the pain that still echoes through me from the workout now drowned out by the green-eyed monster. Not an hour after we all shared a moment were the two of them at it without me? Without us?

And that's not to say that Ivy and I haven't been together without them, but I thought it was different now.

But then, I guess everything has been back to normal pretty much. We hadn't known anything had happened between them until Oliver decided to open his big fucking mouth just now. Ivy's been her usual self with me, and I think with everyone else, too. I haven't noticed Ivy and Wyatt cosying up more than usual, but maybe I haven't been paying attention.

Fuck.

The temptation to storm out of this room and up those stairs to interrupt their movie and remind her exactly who I am is consuming, and I know the guys notice.

"Are you good?" Wyatt asks, moving to my side.

"Not as good as you are, it would seem."

"Fair enough." He shrugs, unphased as he watches Oliver attempt to get the upper hand and fail. "There are no rules here. Ivy, you, me. We're able to do what feels right in the moment, you know?"

"Do you really think this is the best place or time for that conversation?" I clip, refusing to turn and acknowledge him.

"I think you need to hear something right now."

"Maybe what I need is upstairs. Maybe I should just leave you guys to it and go find her."

The thought of his hands on her… Her hands on him.

But I've seen both those things before. I've watched her wrap those luscious lips around his cock while her pussy squeezed the fuck out of mine. I know more than well how hot she gets for him—for all of us. Leo included, as much as that still grates.

God, I knew she was something special the second I laid my eyes on her in that elevator. With an attitude and a mouth like hers, how could I not have?

Most of the women here are self-important, bitchy, and it oozes from their plastic smiles and fake faces, but Ivy's not the same. Sure, she's gorgeous, confident, and not in the slightest bit interested in standing for anyone's shit. I guess that's why she's struggling so much with The Sect. Cloaks and daggers are not her thing.

She also has a heart of gold, and when we agreed to care for and protect each other, that meant all of us. Together. Individually. However it was needed.

So, who am I to argue with them being together, too?

NINE

Ivy

"**W**ell, it looks like you've got me today," Leo says, popping his head around the doorway and making me jump and grab onto the top hanging in front of me. "Is that okay?"

"You know that I'm quite capable of going shopping all by myself, don't you?" I smooth down the fabric before flicking through the hangers in search of the red top I want.

His silence has me turning to see his eyes darkening, and suddenly I'm very aware that I'm wearing nothing more than trousers and a bra, and it's been way too long since I felt that sizzling heat on my skin.

At least the silence is positive this time.

He smiles, breaking the spell much easier than I ever could have. "Of course, but you don't have to." He peeks over his shoulder, grimacing when he turns back to me. "But if you want to make it out of here unravaged, I suggest you get finished up quickly."

Yeah, because leaving here unravaged is exactly where my head, and other things, are right now. Holding out while Nick's body heals is proving to be trickier than I anticipated, and every time we're all in the same room, there's this undercurrent of sexual tension wrapping itself tighter and tighter around us.

"Thanks for the heads up," I say, wishing we could just give in and do all the damn ravaging.

Finally, I find the top I'm looking for, slide it on, and fasten the neck, just as Nick and Jacob walk in, both of them looking hot and sweaty. *Damn.*

"Sorry, we'll be out of your hair in just one minute," Jacob apologises, grabbing the clothes he set out earlier on and thrusting them in his brother's hands before shoving him out of the door, calling, "Have a great time shopping!" over his shoulder.

Clearly, I'm not the only one aware of the heat simmering away.

"Thank you," I call, and pick up my bracelet.

Unfortunately, getting the damn thing clipped together is tricky, and for a second, a wave of sadness sweeps through me. Tamsin would have had this done straight away. But she's not here, and I have to keep forging a path forward. For her. For her life to not have been wasted in vain.

Eventually, I get the stupid thing done, as well as my mules on, feeling ready to push the sexual tension and sadness to one side for a fun afternoon with Ruby. Hopefully, it will be a good distraction from everything else that's going on.

Leo is sprawled on the sofa when I step into the main room, watching some ridiculous video on YouTube, but he turns it off and grabs the keys as the two of us head out, no ceremony required. We're just two people going for a drive and a shop, with probably some coffee and cake here or there.

There's no need for any masked men to arrive and ruin the day, one way or another. There's enough of a shadow over this because I'm doing it without Tamsin without anything else going wrong.

"I thought Wyatt would have been back by now," I comment while we walk through the entranceway, passing Oliver and Stephanie as they head for the stairs with a smile and a wave.

"Yeah, I bet you did," is spoken quietly by one of them, and I'm just about to turn around and question who when Leo hauls open the door, shaking his head as he holds it for me while glaring at their backs.

Somehow shoving down the desire to march after them and demand answers, I walk through, waiting until we're safely tucked in the car before asking, "What was that all about?"

He turns the music down, and the engine roars to life as he presses his lips together, clearly working out the best way to say whatever it is he has to say. "They heard you and Wyatt the other day, uh, in the room, while we were all downstairs with Nick. Oliver felt the need to try and rub it in our faces when we were in the gym."

Oh, shit.

"And that explains his black eye."

"Pretty much." He shrugs, clearly not wanting to go any further into it.

Anxiety swarms through my belly like I've swallowed a fistful of bees while we wait for the garage doors to open, the radio being the only sound. Like it wasn't awkward enough knowing what we'd done behind everyone's back, but to have it out there is a whole different thing, and not something I can leave be.

"So, you're all pissed off about it?" I question.

I'm still unsure whether we should have done it at all. Not that it wasn't amazing and exactly what we'd both needed at the time. But tiptoeing around four other people's feelings is tricky, and we're still just figuring it all out.

"I can't speak for Nick and Jacob—they're their own people—but I'm only pissed off that Oliver threw it down solely to wind Nick up. And that's not only because Nick's still recovering, and I don't think we've given him enough credit for that, but because Oliver is an absolute dick. He's going to do everything he can to get ahead in this competition, including pissing Nick off enough to set him back."

"Great, so now we need to worry about what Jasper and him have got up their sleeves, too." I sigh.

"Competition is competition, angel. I'm not sure we've considered that much so far, but things are getting tense, and it's time we noticed and did something about it."

I've been so worried about keeping my head above water, attempting to deal with the overwhelming grief that tumbles through me every time I think about my best friend and everything we're going to have to do without her, that I never stopped to think about everything else that's going on.

This is a game, a competition, and there are other players that want to get ahead, too.

The two of us fall quiet as we reverse out before heading

down the driveway and across the campus.

"So, you're not angry with me?" I ask, circling back to our conversation.

"Why would I be?" He pulls out onto the main road, not giving me his eyes as he concentrates on driving.

"Because Wyatt and I were alone, not part of the group."

It's been itching under my skin for days, and as much as I've tried to cover it up, it's seriously worried me that we did something that would hurt everyone else, when I'm sure that was neither of our intentions.

"So, you don't think that I'm jacking Jacob off every time we jump in the shower together?" He scoffs out a laugh at the sheer ridiculousness of it. "Come on, angel. This is about doing what feels good, when it feels good, with people you trust and care about. If that extends to one, some, or all of us, then that's awesome. But if you think for one second I'm calling you all in every time I want to see that blissed out look on his face, you're out of your fucking mind."

The relief is immediate and immense. I can't believe how much that was stressing me out all this time when I could have just asked, and they already knew.

"And Nick?" I ask, screwing my nose up. I'm not going to like this answer, I can already tell.

"Is jealous as fuck, but his body is also broken as hell. He'll get over it."

I nod, knowing he would be, but I guess this is new territory for all of us, and we'll just have to figure it out as we go.

"Don't go out of your way for him about this. He's

known about this since yesterday and he managed to get over himself enough to crawl into bed last night. That's saying something."

"I suppose."

"You didn't do anything wrong—neither of you did." His hand comes to mine over the centre console to stop my fidgeting. "Let him sit with it for a bit, then let Nick and Wyatt work it out. Nobody is going it let it get out of hand."

"Promise?" I ask, with way too much hope laced through my words.

"I promise. Now, what are we looking for today?" he asks as we weave our way through the grim winter weather towards the address Ruby text me.

"A connection with the girl I'm supposed to be mentoring…" I offer.

"And does that come in red, blue, or black?"

"I think it comes in heartbreak, death, and destruction, but not necessarily in that order."

"Well, it's good to know you're looking on the brighter side of life," he replies with a smile. "Let's see how we get on, shall we?"

"Sure."

"Did you get an opportunity to speak with the girls about the bands?"

"I did, but it's not good news." I grimace, thinking back to the awkward conversation we had. "Aimee is determined that she's going to link up with Jasper. They've had a thing going for quite some time from what I can gather but they were worried about bringing it into the light of day after everything else we've all been going through."

"I figured as much. He asked me to witness."

I nod, thinking back to the awkward conversation we had between films the other day. None of them were convinced that being alone was the way to go. After all, Liselle has been pushing pairing up since day one, but I know that forcing someone to be with you for the wrong reasons isn't the way to go. Especially if there's a chance this is for more than the year.

Leo squeezes my hand and turns the music up as we drive ever closer to our destination. The collection of stores is nearer than I anticipated, and the nerves really kick in when we pull into the open-air carpark.

"Do you know where we're supposed to find her in here?" he asks, looking for a space.

"Apparently, there are maps at the entrances, and she'll be in *Jess's Juices,*" I say reading from my phone.

"What an unfortunate name."

"Yep!"

"And who the hell wants juice when it's freezing outside?"

"Got me." I shrug.

After finding a space to park, we climb out of the car, grabbing the coats he stashed in the boot earlier on our way, and wrestling them on. Finding the map and juice bar is straight forward, just like she said it would be, and we make our way there, my anticipation mixing with anxiety as the moment draws closer.

Mistletoe hangs off the lampposts next to the stalls, and fairy lights trail from one to the next, with the stalls scattered through the pathway that I'm sure manages to look festive and inviting even in the worst of the British rain and snow.

Once we turn the corner, we find Ruby perched on one of the stools at the bar, chatting happily to the redheaded barista-bartender—what even do you call someone who works at a juice bar?—something I'm not sure I've ever quite managed.

"You've got this," Leo whispers, pulling me into his side before straightening my scarf.

"Nice of you to finally get here," Ruby says as she turns. "I can honestly say I expected you to turn tail and run when you saw the word '*outlet*' on the sign."

"I'm sure you did."

"And an entourage, too. What a surprise." She takes a sip from her steaming cup, eyeing Leo suspiciously.

"Hot juice?" I ask, ignoring her sarcastic comment. I'm finally learning that dodging the barbs is just a part of communicating with Ruby.

"It's mulled wine, but they do a good hot chocolate, too."

"Ooh, mulled wine. My favourite."

I close the distance between us and order two as I pull out the stool beside her. The redhead smiles and disappears, too busy making the drinks to continue whatever they were talking about before.

Ruby fidgets with her phone while we wait, checking and rechecking it, while Leo simply hovers, making the moment even more awkward.

"Is everything okay?" I ask, accepting the drinks silently and handing one to Leo.

He winks, taking the hint and stepping away a touch

while I attempt to get to the bottom of the deal with this phone and the man she's no doubt waiting to hear from. We've been making slow progress on this particular topic, but it's a sticking point, and if I could only get to the root of it, I'm sure we'd be able to connect better.

"Are you waiting to hear from someone?" I ask when she doesn't reply, instead, shoving the phone in her pocket. "Your friend, maybe?"

With that, she stands, turning her back to me before clipping out, "Yes, but it's fine. Let's just get this over with."

Shopping is not something I've ever felt the need to *get done*. It's been a day out with friends, or an afternoon spent browsing and sipping coffee. It's been something to enjoy, and time to savour, but this doesn't seem like that and, once again, I feel the sting of loss shoot through me.

Tamsin would have known how to navigate this—how to break this wall that keeps building between the two of us. I don't think it's intentional, but it's there, and it's a problem. We were given these Little Sisters for a reason, and I can't fail this task.

"Was there something particular you were looking for, or are we just seeing what feels good?" I ask, changing the subject just as Leo starts coughing and spluttering behind me.

Panicked, I abandon my cup on the table, going straight to him with no clue what to actually do. *What if someone has poisoned them? How do I get it out of him?* Slapping him on the back barely registers anything on his face as he coughs again.

"What the hell is this shit?" he asks, dragging breath

back in his lungs before placing the cup on the bench and pining me with a look. "*That* is absolutely vile."

Fucking hell.

"Are you kidding me right now?"

Realising he's not actually being poisoned has relief coursing through my body, and after a second, Ruby and I both burst into laughter, calming down only to start again when he orders a hot chocolate, shoving the mulled wine in our direction.

"Honestly, your taste buds must be fucked. How the hell can you even drink that?" he asks, glowering at the offending cup before accepting his new drink with a warning of, "It's hot."

"It tastes good," I reply, with a shrug of my shoulders and a tilt of my head, before turning back to Ruby and grabbing both cups. "Now, where are we starting?"

With a groan, she jerks her head at one of the smaller stores, the dark exterior looking more like a warning to stay out than an invitation for customers to come in. Following her, we eventually meander in, the dimmed lighting and array of black definitely more her style than mine.

I watch her fingers trail over this jumper, and that top, over and over. She pulls out a pair of jeans only to return them seconds later with a crinkle of her nose.

"Nothing you like?" I ask, taking another sip of the now-warm mulled wine.

"It's fine." She shrugs, peeking in a glass cabinet before stepping away.

"So, were we looking for something specific?"

"You were the one who wanted to come shopping."

"I was?"

"Yeah. Do you think I do this for fun?" she says dismissively while Leo hovers in the doorway.

"Clearly not." Moving around the room, I throw one of the empty cups in the bin, spotting something that Tamsin would have loved out of the corner of my eye.

"I can honestly say, of all the things in here, *this* is not what I expected you to find," she comments, joining me.

The black lace of the corset is delicate, with red ribbons running through it. It's strong but delicate.

"Tamsin would have loved this," I say quietly.

"Why not get it for her? Just because she couldn't come shopping today doesn't mean you can't take something home for her."

If only she knew.

"What have you been told?" I ask, stepping closer. Just because we're out of the house doesn't mean we're safe. "What was Mercedes told?"

"Just that Tamsin won't be taking part in the Big Sister programme anymore." She shrugs, flicking through the rail to find the right size before pulling it out and hanging it on the front. "I don't get why she'd back out, but then it's none of my business anyway, is it?"

The hurt in her voice catches me off guard. I've been so wrapped up in how losing Tamsin has affected me, I never took the time to consider how anyone else is taking the news. Especially not the ones who don't even have the full story.

"That's not quite the whole truth," I hedge, seeing Leo moving in closer.

Sure, I can't tell her exactly what's going on, but I can give her more than the lies she's already been fed. My overreaction at the coffee shop and my refusal to pick her anything up today aren't going to go unnoticed by Ruby. She keeps her mouth closed about her own things, but she's more than observant as to what's going on around her.

"She's not at Pendleton Prep anymore."

"So, you'll give it to her at Christmas?"

"I won't be able to see her at Christmas, either."

"Oh."

I can't exactly spell this out for her. The Little Sisters don't know that they're just more pawns in this stupid competition.

"Yeah. She's not at Pendleton Prep, and I won't be seeing her at Christmas, as much as I'd like to."

"You haven't had a fall out, then?"

I shake my head, not daring to look her in the eye. "As much as I'd love to buy this for her, to see her wear it, I can't."

Quietly, Ruby picks it up, turning it in the light before putting it back with a resigned sigh. Maybe she does know this is a game. Maybe she does know what happens to those who don't make it. Maybe she's more clued in than I've given her credit for this whole time.

"So, if Tamsin isn't about, then maybe we need to find something for ourselves," she says astutely.

"Yeah," I agree sadly, stepping away from the corset.

"We'd better give that credit card a workout and make sure your father knows that you're here and you're doing okay."

Because appearances are everything, and as long as money is going out then I must be okay.

I nod.

"There's going to be nothing in here for you. Let's go find something expensive and useless."

After scoffing out a laugh, I smile. Of course, she picks up on more than I give her credit for. Why would I have expected anything less? The mulled wine is now cold, and I abandon it in the bin before the three of us walk out of the store.

"Have you got all your Christmas gifts?" she asks conversationally, my shock evident when I turn to look at her.

"Yeah, I think so. You?"

"Absolutely not, and I won't be either, so don't even suggest it."

"Fine," I say, holding my hands up in surrender as we walk past some small boutique store, the name of which I've never even heard of. But we both stop dead in our tracks when we see the most gorgeous, black jumper dress. It's flowing longline tunic would end somewhere mid-thigh, and as we both gravitate towards it, we see the crocheted wrap around scarf is separate.

"Okay, now, *that* I could get behind," I say. "I wonder if they have it in something other than black."

"Who cares? This is perfect," Ruby dismisses, looking at price tag before dropping it like a hot cake and mouthing, "Wow." She looks around. "I don't think this is my kind of shop."

"Ah, because it doesn't say outlet above the door." I

nod. "If you're not happy with the price, then my credit card won't care, and it needs working out, anyway, you just said."

The cashmere is soft to the touch, and despite not being able to find the jumper in another colour, I spot something else whilst Ruby hovers near it, not ready to leave the beautiful piece behind.

"Hold that thought," I say, heading right for Leo.

"I don't care what you say, you can't make me wear a dress," he warns, holding one finger up with a smile.

"As if I'd even try." I smirk, plucking the bluebell, ombre-coloured blouse from the rail and taking it back to Ruby. "Isn't this gorgeous?"

"Wow."

"And it's the same colour as the top your friend said you looked nice in."

"Yeah…" Her gaze flicks over my shoulder to Leo, and I turn, attempting to figure out what's going on right now.

"You slide that on with some black jeans, and probably a silver belt, and you'll have him eating him from the palm of your hand," I tell her.

The top's not overtly sexy. The round neckline is broken up with a slit from the collar to the right breast, with silver buttons holding the fabric in place. It covers everything it's supposed to, but the soft silk and the colour would be absolutely perfect on her.

"A blue top," Leo says, catching my attention as he narrows his eyes and walks over to join us. "When was this?"

"When we were at the coffee shop the other week," I

reply while Ruby eyes him warily before taking the top and the jumper and turning away. "Why?"

"No reason," he says, watching her carefully.

I know better than to take those words at face value. Something's got his back up, I just don't know what.

"Right, you try those on," I say, turning back to Ruby, knowing Leo's not goingto talk about it here. "We can grab those black jeans you liked but pretended you didn't from the other place, and then you've got a Christmas outfit to wow your man."

"Oh, he's not my man," she argues without looking our way. "He's just a friend, that's all."

Sure he is. Isn't that what I used to say about Wyatt and Nick?

Still, she takes the blouse, as well as the jumper, and heads to the changing room without any more arguing. Maybe I need to get Leo closer on a more regular basis. It seems to have her finally doing what I've asked her without any argument, but then the thing that allowed her to open up the most was being honest with her about what's going on.

Not the whole truth, but closer than what she's been led to believe so far.

An olive branch I didn't realise I was offering.

Of course, the blouse fits perfectly, and the jumper is gorgeous, but then comes the argument about the price tag and who's paying for it.

"Look, I told you, my father will be worrying that my credit card has pretty much been sat unused for the last three weeks. I need to get some money spent today," I argue.

"Yeah, well, your daddy problems aren't my issue,

and as much as these are lovely, they're too much," Ruby counters while the store assistant watches our tete-a-tete with amusement, hangers in hand.

"Seriously, are you two done yet?" Leo asks, stepping around the corner.

He snatches the hangers from the assistant and storms his way to the counter while the two of us stand in the changing room entrance, gobsmacked. Slamming his card on the desk, he demands, "Bag it, box it, throw smelly shit in it. Whatever. I don't fucking care."

Pressing my lips together, I attempt to smother a smile, and fail if Ruby's indignant snort is anything to go by.

"Guess that leaves your daddy issues wide open," she snips, heading for the counter.

"Guess that means we'll have to do some more shopping, then, huh?"

Her steps falter for half a second as my words penetrate before she shrugs it off like it's no big deal. And an afternoon shopping is no big deal for most people, but for some reason, she's determined to make this a war. Well, if she doesn't want to let me pay for anything, and really isn't interested in anything for herself, she's just here because I suggested it, so I may as well make this a little fun.

"Here," Leo says, pushing the bag in Ruby's direction "Merry fucking Christmas."

"Thanks," she mumbles, and the three of us head for the door.

There are less arguments when we return to the previous store. Ruby finds the jeans and pays for them without so much as a hint of antagonism, even if she does pay for it herself.

"I guess now we just need something decadent and useless."

"Why?" she asks, confusion wrinkling her nose.

"Because you two won't let me pay for anything."

We meander through the stalls outside, with Ruby stopping to look at some handmade bags whilst Leo peruses a selection of leather belts, and that's when I see it. The perfect thing.

Excitedly, I wander over to the pen that has huge rows lined up all ready for the choosing. I've never picked one of these before, but it's where the festive spirit starts, isn't it? The wonder of the lights, the decorations, the boose whilst you do the decorating.

"Christmas trees?" Ruby asks from behind me. "You want to buy a Christmas tree."

"At least one." I nod as the winter chill bites at the tips of my ears.

"For our room?" Leo asks.

"Our? Because obviously you share a room with *him,*" Ruby says.

"Actually—" Leo starts, but I stop him with a shake of my head. She's not going to get that. She probably still thinks I'm leading them all on.

"Whatever," she says with a roll of her eyes. "Can't you just grab a plastic one like everyone else? You've got to be extra and get a real one. So much work."

"Well, you'd think that," one of the assistants says, pulling his cap down over his head, his plaid shirt covered with a black Christmas jumper. "But most people find they're much easier than they anticipate, and the self-watering system only needs topping up once a week."

"That isn't going to fit in the car, angel," Leo warns.

"We offer delivery and set up if it's needed. Why don't you come through and take a look?" he offers, pushing open the little wooden gate. "What size are you looking for?"

Excitement trickles through my fingertips, and I rub my hands together, attempting to breathe warmth into them as I step through, with Ruby and Leo following without anything near as much interest.

"I think... one for the entranceway, one for our room, and then one for the den. Ooh, and do you have little ones we can use as a centrepiece for the dining table or in the kitchen?"

"The store opposite has all the decorations you'll need. I just deal with the trees." He grins. "So, sizes?"

Cringing, I turn and look at Leo, hoping for some assistance. I'm not sure a bedroom size, a normal room size, and a huge entrance size are really going to help us here...

"Two six foots and an eight foot," Leo says, the pine scent thick in the air as we move farther into the rows of trees.

"And are there any styles you particularly like the look of?"

"Erm... Christmas tree style?" I offer.

With a bemused smile, the salesman walks down the line, pointing out different things about the different trees, but they all look the same to me. Eventually, I pick out the ones I like, and he bags and tags them, making a note of what goes where while he books delivery for within a few days. With a swipe of my credit card, and half an hour of our lives, the first items are purchased.

"Yes, now we get to do the fun bit," I say.

"That wasn't the fun bit?" Ruby asks dryly.

"Nope. Now we can pick the lights and decorations. Come on."

Excitedly, I look at the Christmas grotto-looking building opposite, more than ready to jump into the throws of the festive spirit.

Standing in front of the rows and rows of lights, though, I realise I'm completely lost. Luckily, one of the store assistants takes mercy on my overwhelmed brain and helps us to get the right length and colour of lights for the boxes upon boxes of baubles, ribbons, bows, beads, and just about everything else you can picture I've already gathered together.

"It's entirely possible I went a little overboard," I admit, looking at the amount of bags we're going to have to attempt to shove into Leo's car.

"You think?" Ruby asks, amusement crossing her face.

"Well, at least it got a smile on your face. Here, there's one of these for you, too." Pulling one of the Christmas headband boppers out, I hand it over, not daring to attempt to put it on her head, but wanting her to have it all the same.

"Ooh, yay," she says, but she puts it on anyway, and it matches my own.

"Do you need a lift home?" I ask. "Assuming there isn't anything else you want whilst we're here?"

"No, thanks. Someone is coming for me. If you're done, I'll let them know we're ready."

"I just need to pick up some chocolates, but that will only take ten minutes, then I'm done. You don't have to hang on for us, though. If you're ready to go, then feel free to escape my Christmassy clutches."

I'm not sure why, but it feels like the ice has finally broken between us. Sure, she's still prickly to talk to, but I think that's just part of who she is. There's also this other side to her—one that's fun and a little bit quirky.

"Cool." She nods, pulling out her phone and texting whoever it is that's picking her up.

"Let's get this lot in the car and then we can go find your chocolates," Leo suggests.

And so, the three of us meander that way, with Ruby loitering by the huge entrance gates as we make our way across the car park to Leo's car. She's still waiting there when we get back, and as much as I'd like to give her a hug and wish her a merry Christmas, I'm not sure we're ever going to be quite there.

"Well, have a good Christmas, and we'll see you in the New Year," I say.

"Yeah, have a nice Christmas," she replies. "Car's almost here, so I guess I'll see you in the New Year."

"See ya soon," Leo throws out before we turn to walk away, and he draws me in against his side.

"Not if I see you first," she replies over her shoulder.

Leo stiffens just for a second before he tilts his head. "Can we nip back to the car? I just need to check something," he whispers.

Nodding, we turn and head back, and Leo explains how he's forgotten something, then we disappear through the throng of vehicles. But instead of pulling something out or looking for something, he drops down, moving away from his sporty little Lexus and waiting farther down, looking like he's trying to find his keys.

"Leo, that's not your car," I comment quietly, stepping up beside him.

"I know. I want to see what car picks her up."

"We could have just waited with her…"

"He wouldn't have come then," he comments, looking over his shoulder to where Ruby still waits.

"Who wouldn't?" I ask, my confusion evident.

"Will you just let me know when she's climbing into a car?"

Nodding, we continue to wait, with him looking like he's lost his keys in his pocket forever as the seconds tick by, one after another. Sure enough, though, a black car pulls up, and Ruby goes to get in it.

"It's here," I say, not sure how he's going to see anything in this darkness.

Quickly, Leo glances over his shoulder and narrows his eyes as he takes a step to the side, peeking through the cars to get a better look, but it's too far away for him to be able to tell anything other than the fact that some kind of black car picked her up, surely.

The car pulls away, with Ruby safely tucked inside. Leo's silent as we head back across the car park, picking out chocolate before getting in his car and heading back to the house.

"What was that all about?" I ask, unable to take the tension anymore.

"I'm not sure yet, but I'll find out," he replies ominously.

TEN

Nick

"**I** mean, honestly, how long does it take to go and buy a few things? It's pitch-black outside."

"It's been dark since four o'clock," Jacob replies, then throws a stress ball at my head before peeking through the curtains, clearly as concerned as I am.

"Not the point."

"They've gone shopping with one of the Little Sisters. It's hardly a nefarious trip gone wrong, is it?" he asks, turning back to face me.

"You say that, but the *let's celebrate the newly paired couple* trip hardly went to plan either, did it?" I clip out.

Part of me knows Jacob's right while the other part is still pissed as hell that Leo decided I wasn't up to the task and went in my place. I'm done being babied and mollycoddled, and I've sure as shit had enough of being told what I can and can't do when it comes to the woman in my life.

Fuck that.

"Where's Wyatt?" he asks, changing the subject.

"He's upstairs finishing a project," I reply as one of the chefs comes in and prepares the table. He doesn't pay us any attention as he pulls out the plates, somehow knowing who's here and who isn't without even asking. A useful skill, I'm sure. "How's that sociology thing coming along?"

"Slowly," he replies, rolling his eyes. "Ivy and I really need to nail some time down to get it finished."

A door bangs closed, and a girly giggle follows before the two of us rush across the room and into the entranceway like two excited children when their favourite aunties turn up. Ivy's eyes light up when she tumbles through the doorway and takes in the two of us. Leo follows holding an arm full of bags out to her, and she rifles through them, searching for something.

"I know we aren't doing gifts or whatever, but I couldn't resist these." She grins, holding something behind her back as she closes the distance between us. Jacob's gaze flicks around her to Leo, I assume, only mine is stuck on the flush that covers her cheeks, and the myriad of reasons it might be there.

"Had a good time, did you?" I ask, struggling to hold in the jealousy. Maybe Leo's getting some one-on-one time with her, too.

"Absolutely."

She pulls out two bands with green and red ribbon wrapped around them and Santa hats on the end of coiled, springy stalks. She shoves one on Jacob's head and then mine.

"What the fuck is this?" I ask, looking at my brother as he looks at me.

He bursts out laughing when I yank the thing off my head, glowering at it before looking up too see Ivy's pouty face. Leo is sliding a matching band over her head, too. *Fuck, how can I say no to that?* He laughs even harder the moment I slide it back on, the little shit.

"We got one for Wyatt, too. Is he upstairs?" Leo asks, looking around for the rest of the welcome party.

He's wearing one too because, of course he is, and it almost suits him, obviously. If I could dislike him for one singular reason, this would be it: Christmas head boppers.

"Cheer up, babe. You look cute," Ivy says, pressing her finger against my nose before snatching it away quicker than I can grab hold of it.

"That's exactly what I was going for," I reply, pulling her in and pressing my lips against hers.

She tastes like peppermint candy canes, sweet but naughty. The kind of thing you know you should leave in its perfect position on the tree yet can't help snatching off, anyway. And one is never enough. She melts against my chest, her hand coming to my waist. I slide my fingers through the length of her hair, brushing against her scalp as I deepen the kiss, until our stupid Santa hats bang together, tangling up.

We pull apart, my headband staying attached to hers as it swings precariously, almost hitting her in the face.

"Uh, sorry about that," I apologise, pulling them apart before awkwardly sliding it back on my head, while Jacob pats me on the back with a smile.

"Let's get this lot upstairs," he says. "Looks like dinner isn't far off."

"Perfect, I'm starving," Leo adds, grabbing a handful of bags and heading for the stairs.

"Worked up an appetite, did you?" I ask sarcastically.

I've no right to be jealous even if they did *work up an appetite,* but still.

Ivy straightens my band with a smile. "Behave," she whispers, taking my hand and following the two of them upstairs.

"I thought this was supposed to be a trip for Ruby?" I ask, gesturing to all the bags.

"So did I," Leo grumbles in reply.

"You have to shop when you go shopping," Jacob argues, dragging his gaze from Leo's arse when we get to the first-floor hallway, the silence of all these empty rooms finally feeling a little lighter as a TV plays in one.

"Well, I know that, but all this?"

"This is nothing," Ivy dismisses as we head up the secret stairs to the second floor. "Just a couple of bits to top up what I forgot from home."

"A couple? If you say so."

"You should see what we left in the car."

The disbelief on my face must be apparent because Jacob shakes his head as Leo opens the door to our room. It still feels strange sharing a space with these guys, but somehow, pulling Ivy into my arms every night makes everything else feel worth it.

Ivy grabs another band from Leo's outstretched hand. Wyatt's quizzical gaze follows her movements as she hides it behind her back and makes her way to the corner of the sofa he's currently lounged in with a laptop on his knee. I can picture the cheeky grin on her face as she drops it on his head, then wraps her arms over his shoulders and kisses his cheek.

It's what she did with me only ten minutes ago, after all, and despite the tiny amount of unease tingling in my fingertips, nothing happens.

There's no swarm of jealousy, no green-eyed monster going smash, threatening to rip him limb from limb. Don't get me wrong, I'd rather those lips were on mine than his, but at the same time, I'm surprisingly unaffected.

I know Leo has a thing for Ivy, and that Jacob and her got very up close and personal with him, but for some reason, he still feels like Jacob's rather than someone interested in Ivy. And I know he is interested in her, as well as her in him, but I don't know how to explain it… it's just different.

"Proud of ya, man," Jacob whispers at my side.

And that's when I realise Leo's hovering halfway between Wyatt and me, that unwarranted, overprotective look on his face.

"Fuck you," I grumble, shoulder checking his as I move towards the sofas. "And fuck you, too," I say, pointing at Leo with a glower as I pass him.

"You only have to ask," he replies with an amused chuckle.

"Hungry?" I ask Wyatt as I drop on the sofa, far away from his myriad of papers while I do my best to ignore Leo's stupid remark.

Wyatt's hand strokes Ivy's forearm, his gaze swinging to mine, like he's only just noticed the rest of us are here before replying, "Absolutely."

"Best get this lot packed up then. Dinner's almost ready."

"Shit, is it that time already? I thought I'd set an alarm."

Ivy raises an eyebrow as she stands, and Wyatt quickly gathers his things together and disappears into the office. When I turn, I notice Leo and Jacob have disappeared, leaving just the two of us and the tension that's been building for weeks.

There have been glances, touches, and kisses even, but barely anything more on account of my 'broken' status, but I'm done waiting. It's time we got back to being us again. All of us.

"Have you had a good time?"

"Yeah, it was… dare I say it? Nice," she replies, a small smile playing out across her features.

"That sounds like good news."

Pink still kisses the tip of her nose and her ears, the wind chill having clearly caught them, but it doesn't seem to bother her as she looks up. "Yeah, I think we've finally made some progress."

"That's awesome. Do you need to change or anything before dinner? They were setting up just before you got back, but I'm sure there's time." *I could help you take that blouse off, peel the jeans from your legs, and then bury myself between them, too, if you don't mind.*

"I'll go wash up. Thank you for the heads up." She nods and disappears into the bathroom, just as Jacob appears from the walk-in wardrobe.

"Right, are you three ready?" Jacob asks, with Leo quickly following him out. *I don't want to know.*

"Sorry about that," Wyatt apologises when he comes back in.

"I'm good," Ivy declares, throwing the towel on the counter before the five of us meet at the doorway and head down. Jacob slides Ivy's arm through his, demanding she tell him all about her shopping trip.

"About that," Leo says, falling into step with Wyatt and looking over his shoulder to check he's got my attention. "We need to talk."

I nod, and Wyatt agrees, both of us aware we can't talk freely in here, and if it's important enough for him to mention now, it's probably not good news. *Great.*

Charlotte and Penelope join us once we get to the first floor, the girls all but abandoning the pool house and moving in here. Nobody said anything about it, and the chefs are just getting on with catering, enjoying having Aimee's input and help, as far as I can gather.

It's nice.

Their laughter breaks up the empty space as we pass the rooms where Emmerson, George, and Taylor used to be, ours no better, but it makes it easier in some ways to know not everything is gone just yet.

Stephanie, Oliver, Jasper, and Aimee are already seated when we make it to the dining room, the seven of us joining them with perfect timing as the first plates arrive. More bloody witchery, I'm sure.

"Dinner is served," the chef says, placing the last plate down with a head nod and leaving us to it.

Conversation continues, and we fall into what feels like another easy meal, the girls discussing the latest episode of some celebrity, real-life drama thing, like *our* real life doesn't hold enough of that as it is. That is until the sound of the door banging open silences everything, with our forks hanging mid-air as all eyes go to the doorway.

"What was that?" Stephanie asks, looking at Oliver, but he doesn't even have time to answer before a masked man strides in, shoving the door out of his way, and resting his arms over the back of the nearest chair, security flanking him on either side.

"Good evening, ladies and gentlemen. Doesn't this all look very civilised?"

If the voice is anything to go by, this is the same man who told us he wears his mask to protect us and not himself, and whilst the take-no-shit attitude is the same as Leo's father, the voice isn't. Our father was never going to turn up here—not even The Sect can raise a man from the dead— but ever since I realised that four of us are legacies, or birth right members of this old-man's club, the thought has been ticking away in the back of my mind.

What if their fathers are coming in and giving them a hand? A secret warning or a head's-up, maybe.

It's pathetic, and the thought sours my stomach every time it crosses my mind. We're a team, after all, but something tells me The Sect will expect three winners, not four, from The Devils, and will Jacob saying he'll step back be enough?

"Masks on, then, boys. It's time for us to make tracks. Wouldn't want to be late," he continues, despite the lack of reply, and the anxious tension rippling through the room as his caustic gaze judges each of us, weighing us for merit.

It's not just a social call, then.

"Late for what?" Charlotte asks with a far too innocent

tilt of her head.

"The next challenge, of course," he replies, adjusting a large ring on his right hand before focusing his attention on Stephanie. "It looks like you get to ride along for this one too, sweetheart."

Fuck. They're bringing the Angels.

Aimee and Penelope place their napkins on the table as we all stand, until he cuts them off. "Just her and The Devils. Nobody else is tied."

My heart sinks to my stomach, and I swallow thickly, catching Jacob's eye. Kissing the top of Ivy's head, I attempt to quash the panic before it grips me. We all file out, refusing to look back as we silently head to the hallway, ready to retrieve our masks, with Stephanie chirping on as we go.

"Terrible timing, Aims. If this had only been tomorrow, you could have come, too," she says condescendingly.

The smug look on her face as she flicks her hair over her shoulder gets even my back up, and I barely know the girl. Jasper looks ready to murder her in her sleep. Unsurprisingly, I didn't realise they were quite at that point yet.

I know Ivy was trying to get the girls to back off, to keep them safe, but I guess Aimee wanted him, or the security she thinks he provides despite that. Either way, there's no need for the spiteful words. I don't know whether she just doesn't grasp the seriousness of the situation, or if she's completely oblivious, but it's not helpful.

"Five minutes, boys!" he calls from the doorway. "We've got a long drive ahead of us."

Great.

"Ladies, you can either make yourselves comfortable in the movie room or the pool house for the evening, but security will be here shortly. I suggest you locate your masks and make a plan."

Which means, without a shadow of a doubt, one of us isn't coming back.

Stephanie continues to blabber on about what an amazing opportunity it is to come with us and *support her man*—insert vomit here—as we make our way upstairs before escaping into our room in silence, the door closing behind us.

"She'll be fine. We'll be fine. We've got this," Wyatt says, reaching for the box we stashed the masks in above the clothes rails.

"Are you trying to convince yourself or me?" I ask as Jacob and Leo are hang back in the main room.

"Either… both?" he offers, handing my mask over.

"You're failing," I reply, sneaking a peek through the doorway. "Is Ivy's on there too?" I ask, buying my brother two minutes alone with Leo. "We'd better take that down as we go."

He nods, adding her delicate face covering to the pile of black while the two of us hover in the wardrobe doorway.

"We giving them a sec?" Wyatt asks.

"Yeah."

"We didn't get that with her," he comments, jealousy laced through his tone.

"Neither did they."

It's not just about the two of us and Ivy, or Jacob and Leo. We're in this together. The five of us are entangled.

Until death.

Wyatt elbows the door before pushing me through it with a sigh, catching Leo and Jacob in a frantic kiss.

"We're all coming back," I say as Wyatt hands them their masks and we abandon our Christmas boppers on the sofa, not phased for the second it takes for them to pull apart, that half a lifetime when your twin brother's tongue is tangled with someone else's is barely awkward these days.

"Exactly." Wyatt nods, shoving the three of us towards the door. "We've got this."

"You feeling okay?" Leo asks as we leave, passing Oliver and Stephanie's room.

I wonder if that's going to be the one that's quiet tonight. Silent. Empty.

"As good as I'm going to in the next hour," I reply, flexing my shoulders before pulling my sleeves back into place.

The gym hasn't been going quite to plan, but I don't regret the steps we've been taking to get me back into better health. Whether or not that is going to be needed is yet to be seen, but I guess we won't have too long until we find out.

There's no time for goodbyes or good lucks. The girls have already been sequestered away when we get to the entranceway, with the masked man's security waiting to guide us straight to the waiting cars, forcing a sense of dread to creep through my veins.

Wyatt disappears into the movie room to give Ivy her mask, and the three of us are ushered into one car, not waiting for him before setting off. I guess that means he's with Oliver, Stephanie, and Jasper.

Us leaving the house knowing someone isn't coming back, someone we know, someone we've built a friendship with doesn't get easier. The drive is tense, quiet, and much longer than I'd hoped before we pull into the warehouse where we faced the escape rooms, only it's different this time.

Instead of two sets of rooms in the middle, they line either side of the building, and there's a winner's circle set out at the end. Oliver marches Stephanie down there while we loiter in the entrance, getting her as comfortable as he can in a security-lined warehouse.

It's feeling less like a victory every time we make it through a round, that's for sure.

Wyatt ambles over, Jasper following, as a new master of ceremonies appears, sliding out of one of the rooms and flicking a switch. The main lights dim, a different colour lighting up each room as he garners everyone's attention.

"The rooms have your surnames on. Jacob, Nicholas, you can decide which of you takes each door. If you require your Angel at any point, please ask, and she'll be delivered to your room," he says, looking at Oliver.

Short. Sweet. To the point.

I guess the rest of us will have to figure it out on our own, though. Fine. It's totally fine.

"There's no time limit on this event," he continues. "You're only competing against yourself and each other." He gestures to the doors, and we all step forward, searching out the right ones. "Phones are to be left outside, please."

Nervously, we step forward, Jacob and I having the first doors—him taking the left, me taking the right—with

Leo and Wyatt on the other end while Jasper and Oliver are sandwiched between us. The rooms are smaller than before, though. They don't look big enough for a decent workout, and we're not being put against each other, so at least this one isn't likely to be physical.

I sigh a breath of relief, my ribs thanking me before we even begin.

Turning, Leo winks, and Jacob and I nod at Wyatt. We've got this. Until death. No matter how soon that may be.

The doors unlock, a timer clock starting above each door as I carefully place my phone inside the provided box and push open the door. The gold-coloured light gives the room an eerie glow as it reflects off the white table, the black paper a stark contrast when I pick it up first, eying up the rest of the items with trepidation.

Your team (aka me) *is presented with twenty-seven cubes and six riddles.*

Using the twenty-seven cubes, you must create one large cube with a completed image on each face, which must answer one of the riddles.

Your challenge is complete when the cube is correct and you read the riddles with their correct answers.

There's no need to add anything as asinine as *you'd better do it quickly or your dead.* The implication is more than enough.

After dropping the paper on the table, I pick up one of the cubes, all six faces having some part of a picture on them. *Fucking great.* This is going to take forever. Picking up a few of them, I turn them over but get nowhere. They're all different parts of different pictures, or maybe the same picture. They're blurring into one.

Is one part of an eye… or a door? Who the fuck even knows?

Abandoning them on the table, I turn and look at the walls, hoping for better luck with the riddles.

"What breaks but never falls, what falls but never breaks?" Fuck knows. "What is cut on a table but never eaten?" Okay, that one I know. It's a deck of cards.

Turning, I realise there are a couple more on the left wall. "What can run but never walks, has a mouth but never talks, has a head but never weeps, and a bed but never sleeps?" Shit, I have no clue. "What goes up but never comes down?" My blood pressure in this damn challenge?

The other wall has the final two, and I pray to God there's something on this one that's going to help me. "The person who makes it has no need for it, the person who buys it has no use for it, and the person who uses it can neither see nor feel it… what is it?" Hell if I know. "What has many keys but can't open a single lock?" A piano.

Finally, one that makes sense.

It's two, but it's a start. Hopefully, once I find the pieces for those, the rest will be easier.

While spreading out the cubes, I realise this is going to be a bigger job than I anticipated. Twenty-seven cubes, six sides each, that's one hundred and sixty-two options. *Fuck.* Even if I know what I'm looking for, this is going to be a mission, on the clock, whilst the guys are also doing the same.

Grabbing one cube, I turn it around, attempting to find

something that looks like a deck of cards or a piano before giving up, moving it to one side, and starting with another one. Process of elimination it is.

The bass notes for some MGK song come on. Acoustic. Piano. I pay attention for the first three beats before blocking it out and concentrating on the task at hand, working out where the hell these pieces are, making everything else disappear into the background.

Which, I suppose, is what's meant to happen.

With no idea when Oliver requests Stephanie's help— and he will request it because this kind of stuff is really *not* his forte—or when the other guys finish, the pressure is really on to get this done, and done quickly.

There's no room for error here, and no room for messing about.

Head down.

Find the pieces.

Until eventually, the stress and my frustrations build and finally tumble over the edge of irritation, one of the blocks soon hurtling across the room before smashing into a wall. With a sigh, I slide down the opposite one, pulling my knees up to rest my elbows on, with my head in my hands. Then I close my eyes, letting the lilting acoustics lull my senses so I can finally breathe.

Don't worry about Ivy; she's safe at home.

Don't worry about Jacob; he's only on the other side of the building.

Don't worry about Leo or Wyatt; they've got this.

Just focus on the task at hand. One simple task.

And to be fair, I manage to get the cubes together with

the image of the cards on. So, one side down, but the rest is still evading me. Taking one final, deep breath, I open my eyes, the gold light catching off the edge the of the cube resting on the floor, illuminating a thick line.

A line. Is it a line?

An edge, maybe?

Crawling across the floor, I keep my eyes on that edge, sure it must be some delusional prayer of a hallucination. But as I pick it up and tilt it in the light, there is definitely a border on one side of the picture.

A border!

Hurtling the remaining pieces onto the floor, I turn and turn them, trying to find the edges on all the pieces to put them together. It's not quick, but quicker than attempting to work them out blindly, and eventually, I have them all laid out 'right side up'. Now I've just to work out what goes with what.

It takes more time than I had hoped, but slowly and surely, the pictures begin to form, the magnets clicking them in place.

The sun.

Cards.

A river.

Piano.

A calendar.

And a coffin.

"Part one is complete," a voice says over the music, the sound echoing around the room before the music recommences.

Yes!

If I allow myself too much time to enjoy this moment, though, someone else could be opening their door and finishing their challenge before me. Sure, using the light to help find the pictures was quicker than working it out from the riddles, but was it quick enough?

And interestingly enough, it doesn't seem like The Sect is bothered about how you get the answers, so long as you get them. So, the rest should be easy, right?

"What is cut on a table but never eaten? A deck of cards."

"Correct. Five remaining."

"What has many keys but can't open a single lock? A piano."

"Correct. Four remaining."

Turning the cube, I look at the remaining riddles and the answers in front of me, attempting to work out what is what.

"What goes up but never comes down? The calendar."

"Incorrect."

"The days."

"Incorrect."

"Fucking great." The temptation to throw the thing against the wall again tickles at the back of my neck, my fingers already itching to do it, but who's already finished, and how long do I have left? Hang on a minute, how long do I have left!

"What goes up but never comes down? Your age."

"Correct. Three remaining."

Okay, sunshine, a coffin, and a river...

"What can run but never walks, has a mouth but never talks, has a head but never weeps and a bed but never sleeps?

That's water. It's got to be a river."

"Correct. Two remaining."

"A coffin can both break and fall so that doesn't work, but the person who uses it can neither see nor feel it. Okay, what breaks but never falls, what falls but never breaks? Daylight."

"Incorrect."

Fucking semantics.

"What breaks but never falls, what falls but never breaks? Day and night."

"Correct. One remaining."

"The person who makes it has no need for it, the person who buys it has no use for it, and the person who uses it can neither see nor feel it. What is it? A coffin."

"Correct. Challenge complete."

"Yes," I hiss, pumping my fist in the air, not giving the slightest fuck that someone is very obviously watching.

The door unlocks with a click, the music now silent as I step out and check the door opposite to see Jacob's timer still running. *Fuck.*

"You took your time," Wyatt calls from the other end of the building, drawing my gaze there and to the 'winners circle', where Stephanie is flicking through a magazine disinterestedly.

"Only ten minutes or so," I say, but checking the clock, I realise I've been in there a lot longer than I thought.

"Or so." He chuckles, holding his hand out. Our palms meet, and he pulls me in, slapping his hand against my shoulder before whispering, "They'll be fine."

We both know riddles and mind games are the staple

of The Sect, but neither thing are Oliver or Jasper's forte. Not that they're exactly Jacob's, either, but there's a good chance he'll make it out before one of them.

I should feel bad about it, but I don't.

Neither of us grab a drink as we take a seat, watching the clocks nervously and waiting for whoever comes out next.

Stephanie attempts to make conversation, congratulating us once we join her, but soon enough, she realises we aren't interested in anything she has to say and she goes quiet, continuing to flick through the glossy mag until security delivers her to Oliver's room.

"Is that good or bad?" I ask, watching Jacob's clock.

"Time will tell," Wyatt replies anxiously, sliding back in his seat before his knee begins to bounce to a tempo nobody else can hear.

ELEVEN

"How long do you think this is going to take?" Aimee asks as we load up the second film.

"As long as it takes," Penelope replies, rolling her eyes.

"Didn't sound like they were going anywhere nearby," Charlotte says, ignoring Penelope's tone. "So, I dunno. Like half an hour, forty-five minutes each way, plus however long this thing they're doing takes… at a guess."

"Tamsin was going out of her mind when Taylor disappeared for the entire afternoon. Do you remember?" I ask, thinking back to the two of us standing on the doorstep, hammering away with no answer.

"Oh, shit. Yeah. After we'd been with the Little Sisters," Penelope says, topping up the popcorn machine. Not that Aimee or I have made it very far through the last batch. "That was a whole afternoon. Maybe this will be the same, then? I don't think any of us were particularly invested in the guys enough to notice before that."

"Some of you weren't," Charlotte adds bitterly.

"Got something useful to add to the conversation?"

Penelope clips. "Like a timescale…"

She doesn't get it. She's not in this the same way we are, and that's definitely for the best, but still.

Charlotte had a thing with George before he left. What and how deep that was, I don't know, but it was real enough to her, and that's what's important. Aimee and Jasper were getting ready to do their wristbands tonight, before this interruption, so they're either in deep with each other, or they're playing it safe and banding together to get through this.

There's no question as to whether the guys are in this with me, we've declared that more than once, but what if Stephanie doesn't come back?

"No," Penelope replies, sliding her legs up on the sofa and curling them under herself. "I'm just saying."

"Do you think they'd let me out for a bathroom break?" Aimee asks, diverting the conversation and side-eying the door. All of us are acutely aware of the sizeable men on the other side of it.

"I should doubt it," I reply, accepting the drink she offers.

"I'll give it half an hour," she says with a sad smile, and the opening credits begin rolling. "Hopefully, they'll be back by then."

We settle in to the second film of the evening, none of us knowing how many of these we'll need to get through before the doors open and they return. And worse, who's going to be returning, because it's clear someone isn't.

We're on edge the entire time, and despite our concerns, Aimee gets escorted to the bathroom and back without any issue. But they're moving things on the other side of that door, and it feels like there's a stone in my stomach, or I'm about to be sick… maybe even both.

We're fifteen minutes into the third film when Aimee and I look nervously across the room at each other the moment we hear the door opening, and the bees that were swarming in my stomach take flight.

"Hola, bitches. We're back!" Stephanie singsongs as she strides in. "You guys totally missed out because that was so much fun."

My stomach turns.

If she's here, then Oliver is, too, and that means that any minute now, mine or Aimee's lives are about to be ripped to pieces again. The film falls to the wayside when Stephanie bangs the lights on, plucks a tub of popcorn from the side, and plops onto one of the sofas while we wait with bated breath for everyone else to come in.

Both mine and Aimee's gazes are locked on the doorway, barely paying attention to Charlotte, who makes her way to Stephanie. Oliver and Leo follow next, and Leo's sad gaze catch mine, and my heart lurches inside my chest.

What does that mean?

I want to be relieved he's here, that he's safe. I want to release the breath I'm holding, but I can't. Oliver's here, like we knew he would be, and Leo's here but disappointed. Does that mean it was Jacob, Wyatt… Nick?

Or was it Jasper? Are they all safe? Did they make it?

It's hard to let go of the hope that clings around my insides, steeling my heart and my spine for whatever comes next, but when Jacob and Wyatt follow, I know it's over. His arm is thrown over Jacob's shoulder while Jacob watches his feet, shuffling along, not even looking up at Leo or me.

Fuck. That's it.

I didn't realise I'd been half out of the seat until my arse lands back on the cushion, the wind completely knocked out of me as I begin to hyperventilate. Closing my eyes, I attempt to get it under control, just like Tamsin taught me on those weird nights when I had a panic attack.

Count.

1, 2, 3, 4, 5. Breathe in.

Count.

1, 2, 3, 4, 5. Breathe out.

Tears track down my face, and I'm sure the wailing echo around the room must be coming from me, until his cologne registers, hot hands are on my thighs, and eventually, I peek one eye open to find he's there. Nick.

Throwing myself at him, I almost topple us both to the floor, that relief I was hoping to feel finally making an appearance. Although it still tangles with fear and blind panic, and as the noise continues, I realise it's Aimee, not me.

"You absolute bastard," I manage to stutter out between sobs, most of the sound lost in his shirt. "Don't you ever fucking do that again."

"Sorry," he placates, his hand smoothing down the back of my head. "I was just making sure everyone was back and the security had left. I never thought."

No fucking shit.

Eventually, my heartrate returns to normal, the tears stop, and reality floods back in. "Why is Jacob so sad?" I ask, pulling back and wiping my face.

I thought it was because something had happened to Nick, but now he's physically here, right in front of me, where I can touch, taste, and smell him, it must be something else.

"It was down to Jasper and him," Nick admits quietly.

Jasper.

Aimee.

Here I am, completely relieved Nick walked through the door, my pure terror now her new reality.

Charlotte catches my gaze, waving me off.

Her and Penelope have got this. As sad as it is, I'm not the same part of their circle that I used to be. We used to sit around and laugh and joke, in small doses, because moving in with five other people took a hot minute to navigate, but a bond was formed. A friendship.

And I'm sure that even Stephanie's cold shoulder and aloof attitude are just a way to protect herself. She saw what happened to Charlotte when George left, and to me when Tamsin was taken. She doesn't want that pain.

I get it.

It sucks, but I get it.

And there are still two more to go.

Oliver and Stephanie are nowhere to be seen when I look up at the door banging back and Leo comes back in carrying two bottles of tequila.

"I'm sorry," he says, handing one to Penelope while Aimee's face is buried in her shoulder. He takes the other and leaves, and Wyatt, Jacob, Nick and I follow silently.

"I should really go and talk to her," I say, closing the

bedroom door behind us.

"Not now," Wyatt says as Leo cracks the lid. "You just won the lottery she lost. Give her a day or two to process.

"Yeah," I agree hesitantly.

Had the roles been reversed, I wouldn't necessarily want to see Jasper and her, either, but it would sure help to hear some comforting words from them. I'll find her soon. Tomorrow, maybe.

Leo takes a swig, handing the bottle to Wyatt, who does the same before passing it on, the four of them already sitting on the sofa, staring vacantly into nothing. It looks like they've been through it too.

"Bubble?" I ask, taking the offered bottle.

The bubble has become more permanent than I anticipated when Wyatt first suggested it. It was nothing more than a way to shut the world out and grieve, heal, but now it's so much more than that. It's a safe space, sure, but it's us, just us, against the world.

They nod, and the tequila burns on its way down, meaning I have zero control over the face I pull, or the shake of my head as they chuckle.

"I'll go get you something else," Jacob offers. "There's no need for you to wallow, too."

"No," I argue, resting my hand against his arm. "I'll get used to it."

When I hand it Leo, our fingers brush, and so it begins. We drink, some music gets put on, and eventually, all I can remember is the relief that they're all here, safe, and together.

Nobody talks about what would happen if one of them

hadn't made it, and nobody talks about the fact that Jasper isn't here.

We drink.

I dance.

Another bottle materialises.

And we drink some more.

We drink until everything is soft around the edges, and the world feels warm, my fingertips tingling.

Strong arms band around me, and Wyatt's chest is at my back as the two of us move to the music. "Are you okay?" he asks quietly.

"Uhm-hmm," I hum with a nod. "Grateful. You?"

"That's a good word for it," he agrees, his finger sliding under the edge of my shirt, setting fire to my skin.

It's been way too long since I felt the security of them all and the safety in their touch.

All the stress of worrying about if what Wyatt and I did was within the rules of our new group dynamic has worked its way under my skin. Leo said it was fine, nothing him and Jacob aren't doing, and nobody is complaining about that. And despite Nick's previously more than jealous outbursts, he's been quiet about the whole thing. Not pulling back like he did before, but quiet, observant, and when you wrap that up with the fact that Nick is finally starting to feel and look better, I know he's ready. We all are.

Worry and anticipation have been an interesting combination, and when you throw in terror, relief, and the freeing ability of alcohol, something is going to give.

Resting my head against his shoulder allows the two of us rock and move. My eyes close, savouring the peace of the moment as he runs sizzling patterns across my stomach, his breath fanning against my ear... until Leo joins us. His cologne wraps around me like a blanket, my body standing to attention as one hand glides up the column of my neck before cradling the back of my head reverently. My eyes open to meet his gaze just a step away from mine.

"I'll always bring them back to you, angel," he promises, his dark eyes holding a solemnity I wasn't expecting, stopping me short as he pulls in close, his lips hovering just inches from mine.

We haven't kissed yet, Leo and me.

Nick and I, yes. Wyatt and I, yes. Even Jacob and I have. But Leo has been an enigma for so long. And it's not like there haven't been opportunities, or moments I thought would be the ones, even before I realised he liked Jacob, and before I understood that we could have it all. It just hasn't happened yet.

Electricity zaps in the air around us, the room charged with more than just alcohol now. It's an unexpected combination of relief, fear, gratitude, and the understanding that no matter how much he says he'll bring them back, it's not a given. But here and now, we're together, and we should cherish that. Revel in it.

I tilt my head, and we meet part way, his lips soft but insistent as his tongue teases against the seam, waiting for me to open up to him as I melt into his touch. His kiss sends spirals of ecstasy rushing through me, and when he steps in closer, he presses me back against Wyatt, the three of us moving as one, lost to the tequila, the music, and the moment.

It feels like that time in the pool when he offered me a hand, revenge, and the promise that he'd always have my back and do his best to keep me safe—the words never said yet somehow understood. Sure, that's not always been the reality—the hole where my best friend used to be is still raw, after all—but he's held up his end of that deal in any way he could.

"You can't promise that," I eventually reply breathily as we pull back.

I know he'll try, but three is what they want—what they've demanded.

"We're working on it," Wyatt adds behind me, a promise too good to be true. "There are more moving parts than you know. Just trust us."

"I do," I admit.

After everything we've been through, how could I not?

"Good," Leo says, sliding his hands beneath my shirt, the two of them then working together to take it off. "Now, stop thinking so hard."

Wyatt's hips roll behind me, grinding my body against Leo's as his five o'clock shadow dances down the column of my neck. His fingers tease the lace of my bra before Leo unclasps it, then his lips are back against mine.

And then the rest of the world falls away, disappearing into nothingness. I wiggle my arms between them, pushing Wyatt's top up, and Leo helps remove it, catching Jacob's gaze over my shoulder. But the buttons on Leo's shirt prove way too difficult, so I give up and yank it over his head with a giggle instead.

"Smooth," Wyatt says, dumping it on the growing pile

of clothes beside us.

"Does watching them play with her get you hot?" Jacob asks Nick, his deep rumble a clear reminder that we're not alone and are currently on display for the two of them.

Not that we've not been on display before. Leo and Jacob were quite happily tucked up together watching when Nick and Wyatt set my body on fire the last time we were all together, but this feels different.

Nick sacrificed himself for us, and we've made promises since then. Promises we've not yet been able to cement as a group because of his broken bones and tumble into the dark place he's come through. But he doesn't like to share, and his jealous nature is a fine balance we're still working out.

"Yes," Nick admits on a rasp, the tone and appreciation tingling all the way down to my toes, but I dare not look, scared the spell will break, and I'll find this is all just a dream. "What about her playing with him?"

It's a weird conversation for them to have and to be the centre of, especially between brothers, but it doesn't feel anything like as awkward as it probably ought to.

God, if only Tamsin could see me now.

"Them… yes," Jacob replies.

Shuffling catches my attention, and I can't help but turn and look, just in time to catch the drop of Jacob's shirt, his broad shoulders, and toned abs a match for his brother, although the tattoos are different.

Sooner than I'm ready, he's at our side, dragging Leo's lips from where they hover in front of mine, and slamming them to his. Jacob holds Leo's chin possessively while the bottle of tequila hangs limply from his other hand.

I don't know if it's just being this close to someone else kissing, having never been this close before, or if it's the way Leo's testosterone fuelled dominance wanes just briefly, but the need that's been coiling in my stomach explodes. Their lips move, a moan tumbles from one or the other of them, and I catch the slide of a tongue snaking back as Jacob pulls away, and Leo swallows thickly.

"We're going to need more of this if you keep doing that," Jacob says, raising the bottle with a small shake of his head and a smile. "Now, this time, you're supposed to feed it to her."

Oh.

It was more than just a show of possession. The kiss was something else. A way to join us without crossing a line with Wyatt or me, despite the admiration they secretly share for each other.

Jacob takes a swig, the dark liquid sloshing in the bottle before he kisses Leo again, and I catch it this time. The second the tequila goes from Jacob's mouth to Leo's, and knowing it's coming my way next, has heat rushing through my veins. I know Wyatt notices how my nipples tighten, his rumble of appreciation causing goosebumps to break out, and a shiver to ripple through me.

Damn them all.

Jacob pulls back again, turning that amber gaze, and Leo, towards me. But it's a gaze I can't hold as Leo's lips come to mine once more, the sweet burn of the tequila rushing into my mouth, chased by his tongue, a surprise.

"Give it to Wyatt," Jacob whispers in my ear, waiting for Leo to pull back before we turn.

The two of us slide around each other until Wyatt's lips are pressed against mine, the tequila almost gone when I pass it to him before pulling back. All four of us turn to look at Nick with anticipation.

How far will he let this go?

"I swear to God, bro, if your tongue comes anywhere near my mouth, we're going to have a problem," Nick says, his dick clearly not getting the message as it strains against his zipper, despite the hand he holds up in warning.

Mischief twinkles in Wyatt's eyes when he takes a few testing steps towards him, swaying along to the music as he goes, reminding me of the first night we found ourselves thrown together. Or more accurately, *I* found myself thrown with them. Nick demanded me, and I went.

In retribution for that *demand*, my turn at 'truth or dare' found them doing a striptease for each other—something they both enjoyed way more than I intended as they got into the music and the moment—and just for a second, I think Wyatt's willing to risk it, until he turns, laughing, evidently just winding Nick up. Although there is a small part of me that wonders how far he'd have taken it.

"Here," Jacob says, taking another pull before dragging me up against him and passing the liquid from his mouth to mine. A surprised squeak falls from me, and then he pulls back and pushes me in his brother's direction.

"Go carefully. He doesn't always play well with others," he warns, like this is any kind of a surprise.

The burning liquid tangles its way around my tastebuds as I close the distance between us, carefully straddling Nick's lap before tipping his head back and letting it trickle from my mouth into his, licking along his lips as he swallows, then kisses me deeply.

Any sense of worrying about whether he's in pain or I'm hurting him disappears into the background when his arms envelop me, providing a sense of protection so deep, I don't have time to unpick it before he's pushing up onto his feet, apparently paying no mind to what everyone else is doing as he walks us to the bed, and they follow.

The sound of belt buckles and top buttons being opened drowns out whatever music is playing on the TV. It's even louder than the heartbeat that thunders in my ears when he lays back, shucking his shoes and T-shirt before pulling me back into the moment with him.

Most of the obvious bruising to his face healed a few weeks ago, but the shadows that cover his ribs are more stubborn, and a big part of the reason I've been hesitant to get too close physically. The last thing I want to do is cause him more pain.

Trailing my fingers around them makes goosebumps break out over his arms, and a shiver ripple over his body.

"Unfasten him. He's not made of glass," Leo says huskily, his teeth nipping at the lobe of my ear, and it's my turn to shiver as we all fall into place, with the three of them already gloriously naked.

With shaky hands, I unfasten the top button on Nick's jeans, catching Wyatt's gaze before he helps me pull them and his underwear down, and ultimately off. Nick and I shuffle awkwardly to manage it.

Then Jacob is throwing lube to Wyatt and Leo, and suddenly everyone apart from me is naked, their dicks hard and abs glistening, or the other way around. Nick unfastens my trousers, helping to slide them off, even as he categorises what's going on around us with vague interest, and the four of them turn into some well-oiled machine built for sex.

Wyatt is quiet as he joins us on the bed, shoving Nick's thighs wider, and pressing against my back even while I watch Nick for signs of the jealousy that creeps in now and again. Instead, he smiles, knitting his hands together, and resting them behind his head as he watches Wyatt nip and torture my already achingly tight nipples.

It's lucky the bed is as big as it is when Jacob climbs up beside me, and Wyatt's hip catches me off guard, pushing me forward to land on Nick's chest.

"Shit, sorry," I apologise, cringing when I think of the hurt I've just caused.

But as I look up into the eyes of the man that's given me more than I ever thought possible, there's nothing but lust and appreciation there, his gentle kiss catching me off guard, especially considering the tangle we're currently in.

Wyatt squirts some of the sticky stuff over my arse, and the cool liquid slides down over my pussy quicker than I expected, making me gasp at the contact.

"Show me," Nick rumbles, his desperation barely restrained.

Sitting back up, Wyatt's stubble grazes along my shoulders, his arm wrapping around my stomach as I lift slightly. Nick's cock bobs in front of me as Wyatt pours again, the viscous liquid covering us both while Nick watches, his attention rapt.

"He's been so good and waited so long," Leo says,

joining Jacob beside me, eyeing up Nick's impressive size over my shoulder. "Don't you think?"

It's strange to see Nick like this, patient and compliant. He's usually so bossy and commanding, like turning Wyatt down just moments ago, yet here he is, seeming to wait for Leo's okay, or mine.

Jacob's hand wraps around Leo's dick, and Leo jerks in response, his eyelids fluttering closed for a second before pulling Jacob's closer to him. Their thick cocks rub against each other, and I press my lips together, wishing I knew how exquisite that felt.

"Do you have any idea what pressing your lips together like that does to me?" Nick growls from beneath me, still not touching my body, still teetering on the edge of taking before he pulls me down, rearing up and slamming my lips against his. Wyatt's hands roam and squeeze along my back, his hips and arse sensually such a dichotomy to the frenzy of Nick's kiss.

My back arches, desperate for more than just the feel of Nick beneath and Wyatt behind me, both of them close enough to touch, yet far enough away to be nothing more than a tease, with Nick's cock pressing against my clit as he grinds against me.

"He can wait five more minutes," Wyatt decides quietly as he slides his dick through the lube before pushing in. My pussy clamps down around his massive intrusion.

A gasp and a moan tumble from me between kisses as I stretch around Wyatt thrusting slowly in and out as he grinds me against Nick's hard cock, the lube only making the friction more torturously glorious.

"Fuck," Nick says, grinding against me, holding my face in his hands as he rocks, licks, and sucks. "I want to taste you, to feel you come on my tongue. I want you to shiver and shake, then I'll fuck that tight pussy until you do it all again."

Wyatt's grip on my hips tightens as he fucks me harder, Nick's words clearly turning him on as much as they do me. He squeezes and releases my hips before pulling out and guiding me onto Nick, who flicks his hips upwards, catching me off guard as my body adapts to the change in angle and extra girth.

"Oh, fuck."

My head drops back, and my hair tickles against my sweat-slicked lower back before Leo pushes it away, turning my head to his and kissing me deeply, his measured strokes so different to everyone else's. Something this controlled and precise would usually come from Nick, and yet his frenzied touches set fire to my skin even as Wyatt soothes it.

"Can I?" Leo asks, pulling back and looking into my eyes, but I have no idea what he's asking, or even who he's asking as he turns to Wyatt over my shoulder. "Can I taste her on you?"

My pussy clenches, and Nick slows, his surprise clear as Leo looks to Jacob for something... acceptance, maybe? It's been the three of us and the two of them this whole time, and whilst Jacob showed me the ropes of how Leo's body works, I'm not sure this has ever been on the cards before.

Jacob licks his lips, and what taste he's imagining on his tongue, I have no idea, but Leo waits, his grip tight in my hair as Nick's hips roll, and Wyatt's hands massage, with his cock bobbing behind me, the moment feeling strangely poignant. The groan that falls from my lips is unintentional, but it seems to spur everyone on.

"If he's happy with it," Jacob finally relents, gesturing to Wyatt with his head, even as his fist glides up and down Leo's cock.

"Uh, fine," Wyatt replies, shocking more than just me as he peels himself from my back, placing a chaste kiss to my shoulder as he comes to my side, offering himself up.

The disbelief on both Jacob and Leo's face probably mirrors my own, until Nick rocks up, his added size hitting places I never knew existed, blasting stars behind my eyelids, reminding me exactly who I'm fucking with right now.

Someone mutters, someone whimpers, and Wyatt's fingers clamp around my nipple as I teeter along the edge of oblivion, as desperate to hang on to this feeling as I am to let it roll over me. Nick's fingers wrap around my throat, pushing me up to sitting, and dragging my gaze from where Leo wraps his lips around Wyatt's cock, the sight so sensual.

Wyatt takes my lips, kissing me hungrily, and I don't know or care whose fingers graze over my clit, but the next to nothing touch has my every nerve ending on high alert. Bracing one hand on Nick's forearm, and the other on Wyatt's chest, we ride the high that's like nothing else in this world, with me trapped between the two of them, once again, and the five of us connected in one way or another for the first time.

Leo's dirty words of encouragement have all but disappeared, and as those fingers rub my clit, I can't find it in me to care. The orgasm rushes over me like a hurricane, Nick and Wyatt both holding me steady as they draw every last second from my over sensitive skin, with Wyatt quickly following me over the edge.

Nick roars his release just seconds later, letting go of my neck to hold my hips, and pumping up into my pussy, even as I spasm around him. The crack of skin against skin echoes from behind me as I slump against Nick's chest, then slide off him to curl against his side.

"Well, that was different," Wyatt says between sated, panted breaths, dropping onto the pillow behind me.

An embarrassed blush creeps over my cheeks as I peek one eye open to find Jacob buried deep inside Leo's arse as he chases his own oblivion. Leo moans as he reaches back for Jacob's thigh. I've never done that, and even though my head knows it should hurt, it certainly doesn't look like it does.

"Don't even try and deny how much you enjoyed it. We all saw you lose it," Nick says to Wyatt from beside me, his heart still thundering beneath my ear. "His lips feel good, right?"

"Oh, yes," Wyatt replies, surprisingly accepting of the fact a guy just swallowed down his dick.

Jacob grips Leo's hips, pumping erratically until he comes on a moan, smacking his arse one last time before pulling out and tying off the condom, his chest bounding.

"He wasn't the only one who came at the drop of a hat though, was he?" Jacob asks, glowering at Leo. "You came all over the sheets, you can fucking change them," Jacob declares, standing on shaking legs before heading back for the tequila. "Some people have zero control over themselves."

Sated and surprised, we all move. Nick and Leo change the sheets as Wyatt turns on a shower for me and joins Jacob, grabbing a pair of shorts in the process. By the time I'm cleaned up, the bedding is changed, the bottle is traded for something without alcohol in it and some snacks, and there's a film on the TV. Finally, the five of us cosy up together like the stress of today never happened.

Except it did, and sooner or later it's going to catch up with us.

TWELVE

Nick

Stirring, whispering wakes me, and the daylight peeks in around the edge of the curtains, showing just how long we've slept in.

"Shh, you'll wake him up," Ivy whispers with a giggle.

"Too late," I grumble, stretching before wrapping my arm around her, pulling her back against my chest, and burying my nose in her hair. "You already did."

"Sorry, man. We were just talking about next week and the Christmas break. Do you guys have any plans?" Wyatt asks, his mop of hair tied up man-bun style.

That's a strange conversation for whatever goddamn time this is but whatever.

"We're heading home on Boxing Day or the day after. I can't remember," I grumble, attempting to wake my brain up enough to hold a conversation. "Sophie's doing some big thing at the house, I think. Fuck knows why. They'll all be in Italy for Christmas Day, so why on earth they're flying back here I have no idea."

"Who's Sophie?" Ivy asks, narrowing her eyes as she turns my way.

"Big sister," Jacob answers, the bedroom door closing behind him. "Bossy britches, organiser extraordinaire."

"And the glue that holds our dysfunctional family together," I finish, pulling Ivy back into my body.

"True," Jacob agrees. "Are you guys getting out of bed at some point, or are you just going to lie there and fester?"

"We'll get up," I reply, squeezing Ivy's boob. "Maybe we'll just stay here for a bit, though."

Ivy giggles as Jacob drops onto the end of the bed. "What are you guys doing?" he asks.

"For Christmas?" Ivy clarifies, turning to look at him.

Something wasn't quite right with him after everything last night. I'm not sure anyone else noticed, but he's off.

"Yes," he says, kicking his shoes off and jumping up, crossing his legs.

"It'll be a traditional family affair at mine," Wyatt says, watching him carefully. "I'll be heading home on Sunday, but I'll be back before New Year's Eve."

"Same, but I might be back a few days early if I can manage it," Ivy adds, and there's a sadness to her reply I wasn't expecting as she absentmindedly traces patterns on my arm. "It's not going to be the same without Tamsin, and my father and I kind of fell out before I came here. I'll be spending as little time there as I can manage."

She's made it clear they had some kind of disagreement, but I hadn't realised it was bothering her this much. Or maybe it's having to go home without her best friend that's the real problem. Either way, I pull her in closer, wrapping her in my warmth.

"Leo's going home on Christmas Eve until probably

Boxing Day, and we're here until Boxing Day at the earliest. So, whenever you need to come home someone will be here. I'm sure he'd skip out early for you if needed, too," Jacob says.

"As would we," I interject.

"That's not going to fly with this family thing, and you know it," Jacob argues, pining me with a look. "She asked us for one thing, one tiny little afternoon of our time, and she's damn well going to get it."

"Fine," I grumble by way of reply. "Where's Leo, anyway?" They're usually not too far from each other, and after last night, I want to know they're okay.

"I think he's in the gym. I went for a run."

"Are you guys good?" Wyatt asks, propping up on his elbows, clearly picking up on the same thing I am.

"We're fine," Jacob replies, brushing it off as he gets up. "I'm just going to jump in the shower."

And with that, he disappears, closing the door behind him.

"Maybe I should…" Wyatt says, gesturing to the bathroom door.

"Nah, leave him to it," I reply. There's no point poking the bear at the moment. "What have you guys got planned for today?"

"The tree I ordered should be arriving in a couple of hours, so my plan is to decorate this musty, old place. I just hope we bought enough lights," Ivy declares excitedly.

"Really?" I ask.

I've barely thought about Christmas. Well, aside from coordinating gifts for the family with Jacob, but that's much more his thing than mine, and I certainly hadn't considered decorating the house.

"Yep. It doesn't feel festive at all in here. So, whilst we were shopping the other day, I got a few extra bits and bobs. It seemed as good a moment as any."

"I bet the girls would love to give you a hand with that, too," Wyatt adds. "It might even help to brighten everyone up after what happened."

"That's what I was thinking," she says, yawning and trying to stretch whilst still wrapped up in my arms. "I've got a lecture in an hour," she says, checking the time. "And then it's time to get Christmas underway."

"Sounds perfect," Wyatt agrees with a small smile. "I've got lectures this afternoon, but we could pop out and get the ingredients for eggnog and Prosecco this morning, ready for when you're decorating the tree or whatever. It's tradition."

"Yeah, Leo could give us a hand with that," I add remembering he had something to tell us the other day before all the challenge chaos happened and we forgot about it.

"Sounds like a plan." She nods before attempting to extricate herself from our tangle of limbs and covers. "I'm going to jump in the shower quickly and get ready. The day is already running away with me."

"Is that an invitation?" I ask, watching her sexy arse climb over the bed before hopping off the end.

"Absolutely not. We don't have time for that," she argues with a wink.

"I can be quick," I counter with a smirk, not really sure

that's an argument I should be making.

"No, you can't," they both reply in unison, laughing before she disappears into the wardrobe to pick out her clothes.

It goes quiet, leaving Wyatt and me laid in bed together, and things start to feel a little awkward for the first time. Sitting up, I shove one of the cushions behind me, getting comfortable.

"So, I know Jacob's a little pissy about it right now, but are you okay after last night?"

Why the hell am I bringing this up?

"Yeah, I think so."

"You don't sound so sure." Smirking, I raise an eyebrow.

Sure, Jacob and I don't usually stick around to deal with the fallout from a menage night or an evening that goes further than we anticipated, but we're here, and I don't plan on going anywhere. I'm reasonably sure Jacob isn't either.

"Well, I've never thought about a guy like that, or I mean… you know, done things like that with a guy before," he admits, shuffling to sit up. "But he so badly wanted to taste her,…" he says, looking at me for understanding. "And you were busy fucking her, and you both seemed happy, so I figured if he wasn't going to be able to taste her himself, then, why not?"

"Sure." I shrug.

"And Jacob looked to be cool about it, interested even, if the way he teased Leo about it and then fucked him was anything to go by…" he ponders aloud.

"But?"

"But then a taste became a blowjob, and I've never

come so quickly in my life." He swallows, pulling the band from his hair before running his fingers through it and tying it back up. "Fuck, this is a weird conversation."

Kind of...

"Why?" I ask, doing my best to pretend it isn't. "I was right there," I say, pointing across the bed. "I think I remember you kissing Ivy while she rode my dick, so talking about it after the fact shouldn't be weird."

I've seen more of him, and him of me, than most normal guys would. Do I want to kiss him? No. Do I want him to suck my dick? No. Does it matter that he enjoyed it from someone else? No. It matters even less to me that the other person was a guy—one intimately linked to my twin brother.

"I've never done anything like this before," he admits quietly. "I've always been a one girl man, but you know how it is with her. I just want her to be happy, and *we* make her happy. All of us." He chews on his bottom lip, and I know he's not finished.

This is the first sign of vulnerability I've seen on him in a long time, and as much as it's Jacob people usually come to for advice, I'm here, and Jacob's really not in a place to help right now.

"Am I gay now?" he whispers, looking around nervously.

The amount of men that have let Jacob have his wicked little way with them and then demanded their wife, girlfriend, or significant other back for round two so they can assert their manhood again is ridiculous.

And that's just a straightforward trade off—nothing nearly as complicated as whatever this thing is we've found ourselves wrapped up in. I understand what he means about wanting to give Ivy what she wants and what she needs, but we're all important parts of this fucked up mess, and his needs are important, too.

His question doesn't hold the tatters of his masculinity in it. It holds a query. I'm still working out how to reply when Ivy appears from the walk-in wardrobe, smiling, and sending a finger wave our way before she steps into the bathroom and closes the door behind her.

"Do you still want to fuck Ivy?" I ask him.

"Yes." He nods.

"Cool," Well, not really. I'd much prefer for him and everyone else to fuck off and leave Ivy and me to it, but it is what it is. "Do you want to fuck Leo or Jacob, or be fucked *by* them?"

"I don't think so…"

"You're still not sounding sure here, my friend. And I guess, that's okay. We don't have the answers to all the relationship stuff we're still working out, so why would we have all the answers to this?"

"Good point," he concedes. "But your brother is quite intense while we're… you know…"

"Yeah… and you like that?"

Why did I ask that?

"Yeah."

"You enjoyed what you did last night?"

Stop asking these fucking questions.

"I did," he agrees.

Well, thank fuck for that.

"So, receiving is fine, and you might want to do that

again? Or you hated it and never want to do it again?" I ask, attempting to help him work out where his boundaries are right now, even if part of my brain is screaming to stop asking questions I don't really want the answers to.

Jacob and I may have done the sexual stuff before, but we've never stuck around for the relationship side of it. Though even I realise that when those two start to cross, shit can get tricky, and talking about it is important.

Wyatt takes a minute, pressing his palms together before cracking his fingers, his mind clearly a million miles away.

"Yeah, it was good," he admits, his brain processing things faster than I anticipated as he adjusts himself under the covers. "I'd do it again."

"Cool. So, I guess that means you know where your line is. You're good with what happened, and you're open to doing it again. There's nothing wrong with exploring something new, Wyatt."

"Yeah, I know that. I just always thought I was straight, you know? It never occurred to me that I might like something else. I mean, I've thought about what it might be like, but I never seriously considered it a thing…"

"And that's okay, too." I shrug. "I'm not trying to offer you a label or whatever. Straight, gay, bi, or other, it doesn't matter to me. You're an adult doing something that makes you happy, consensually, with other adults."

"It's that simple, is it?" he asks, not looking at me as he smooths down the covers.

"It is as far as I'm concerned. And as much as I can't speak for the others, I'm quietly confident nobody had any problems with you enjoying yourself last night. Equally, though. they would have been fine if you'd said no."

He nods, digesting the conversation.

"I mean, we're five people who swore blood oaths and promised each other the world," I add, attempting to break the tension that's creeping in. "The long and the short of it is that I care about the people in this circle, or this bubble, or whatever the hell we're going to call it, and I'm not interested in justifying that to anyone else with a label, okay?"

"You're always so blunt." He sighs, shaking his head with a small smile. "It's just confusing, that's all. We all came here with one goal in mind: to win. Now that's fallen to the wayside, and not just because I've fallen for someone, but because the lot of you stomped in and made yourselves known, too. I wasn't prepared for this."

"Who the hell was?" I ask, scoffing out a laugh.

He's not wrong, though. This has taken us all by surprise. Not just The Sect and the noose they're drawing ever tighter around our necks, but our relationship as a whole.

"Look, nobody expected this, and nobody really knows what we're doing, but we need to be open and honest with ourselves and each other, or this will crumble into nothing. I should know. I've still got the bruises from my attempt at sorting shit out on my own."

"I think we're going to need some help," he muses. "And that's maybe something we could get whilst we're out today," he adds, an idea formulating behind his eyes before he looks at the bathroom door wistfully. "Are you sure I shouldn't go talk to your brother?"

"Leave him. He probably just needs a minute. He'll be

fine by the time we're done today."

"Okay," he says, shuffling. "So, I didn't do anything wrong?"

"Definitely not. If Jacob wasn't happy with something, he's more than capable of saying so in the moment. He certainly wouldn't have waited until he'd got his before making it known. No, this isn't something you or anyone else did. He's probably just working out this new dynamic exactly the same way you are."

"Yeah?" he asks, hope laced through the singular word.

"Yeah. I get that was a big deal for you personally, but it changes things for all of us, you know?"

"I never thought about it like that."

I nod, getting it.

It doesn't change anything for me, and I won't be partaking in anything with the guys—that's not me or my thing—but I'm not going to look down on him because he might want to.

"Okay, well, I'll go grab Leo and then we can make tracks," he says, seeming to come to terms with it... for now.

"Sounds good," I agree.

The two of us climb out of the bed, with him sliding some jeans straight on and scurrying away just before Jacob reappears.

Well, I guess this is as good a time as any.

"So, what's got your pants so twisted up?" I ask while following him into the wardrobe and grabbing my clothes from the rail. Just because I told Wyatt to leave him alone be doesn't mean the same applies to me.

"Nothing. I'm good."

Of course you are. "I think you're forgetting it's me you're lying to, but even Wyatt noticed something's not right with you this morning."

"Honestly, I'm fine. It'll be fine." Jacob sighs, sliding his underpants on before taking a seat and tackling the socks.

"See, not fine yet. What gives? Are you not happy about Wyatt getting involved last night? Or was it because Leo was kissing Ivy? And you all say I'm the jealous one." I scoff out a laugh.

Jacob's been eying Wyatt up since we got here, and I know he was disappointed that he wasn't interested in the goods he was offering, so why the sad face now he's potentially got what he was looking for?

"What? No, that's all fine." He brushes me off. "Leo's been teasing me with him for weeks, and the way you guys work Ivy's body is hot."

Not a surprise.

"So, what's the problem?"

"Nothing, just drop it."

"Fine." I shrug my shoulders, turning and sliding my shirt on, knowing he'll spit it out when he's good and ready.

"He came so damn fast," he admits, stepping closer. "With Wyatt's cock in his mouth, covered in Ivy's come. Jesus, I'd barely even started when he came like a kid on his first time."

So, he's not upset because Wyatt and Leo were having a moment together. He's upset because it got the guy he likes so hot, he blew his load in seconds.

"Of course he did," I say dismissively. "The taste of the girl he's been chasing for months on the dick of the guy he knows you've got a thing for, whilst you're busy doing whatever the hell it is you were doing… I'm not surprised he came like a fucking freight train. It must have been like all his Christmases had come at once."

"So, they're better than me. Great." His head drops in defeat—something I've not seen on his face for a long time.

"Hey, don't be like that," I say, throwing a sock at him. *We really need to find those stress balls.* "Can't you see? Leo thinks they're good *because* of you. Without you, they might be fun, but with your touch, it's explosive."

"Literally."

"Exactly." I nod, fastening the last button on my shirt. "What did Leo say about it?"

"Nothing." He shrugs, stepping away to grab his clothes. "I went for a run to clear my head, but coming home to him shirtless, and you guys cuddled up in the bed, had all my insecurities rising fast."

And this is why we only do this shit with people we don't know and care about…usually. It gets complicated fast.

"There's no need for all that, bro. There's no retreat, and no surrender, remember?" I say, throwing our catchphrase at him. "We're taking the three of them all the way, and they're here for it. With us. With you. Can't you see that?"

"Yeah, I guess. It's just taking me a minute, that's all."

"You weren't ready for adding Wyatt into the mix after all, were you?" I ask quietly.

"Not quite," he admits. "The thought of it is hot as fuck,

and the reality is, too, to be fair. I don't know… I'm just in my head about it all."

"Yeah, I can see that," I say, pulling on my jeans. "You know that this is his first ever experience with a guy, and he thinks he's upset you. He's worried about your feelings, as well as the fact that he *also* came like a kid on his first time."

"Shit. I never thought about that."

"Use your fucking words," I say, tapping the side of his head.

"I can't believe you're the one having this conversation with me." He barks out an amused laugh. "Well, here we are, doing the one thing we said we never would: letting fucking people turn into caring about them."

"I'm pretty sure we cared about them before the fucking began, but whatever. So, Wyatt, Leo, and I are heading out. Ivy's got a lecture. Will you make sure she gets there okay, then hopefully you guys can get some time on that project? You'll get your turn with your new toy soon enough, I'm sure."

It's not that simple, and we both know it, but he needs the release that comes with me making light of all this. Hopefully, now he realises his reaction has consequences for other people too, he'll pull his head out of his arse.

"God, you're a dick." He laughs, finishing off getting dressed. "Thanks, bro."

"Any time," I reply before heading out. "And we need to find the stress balls. Every time I want to hit one of you, it's becoming a battle."

"I'll find them," he says, just as Ivy appears from the bathroom, the skirt she's wearing perfect for sitting in my lap, but less so for a draughty lecture hall.

"What did you lose?" she asks, stopping to slide the zipper up on her boots as she catches the tail end of our conversation.

"Stress balls."

"There are boxes of them in the office. I wasn't sure who or what they were for," she admits.

"For me not smashing their faces in every time one of them catches your eye," I admit.

Both Leo and Wyatt are far too appreciative of her outfit when they walk in at just the right moment.

Leo adjusts the towel over his shoulders, swallowing before turning to catch Jacob's eye as I slide my hand under her skirt, grabbing her arse, and pulling her up against me. With a surprised squeak she comes, willingly stepping in and bringing her lips to mine, any sense of hesitation long gone.

I'd love to sit back on the sofa and let her ride her way to victory again, but with us all in the room and on the clock, I guess that's going to have to wait for later.

"We're heading out," I say, leaving my hand exactly where it is as Leo disappears to get changed. "Do you need anything picking up?"

"I think we got it all the other day, but thank you," Ivy replies, stepping back and swishing her skirt down, her hand pressing against Wyatt's chest before she kisses him, too. *Fucker.* "Got a class," she says with a smile. "See you all in a bit."

"Jacob..."

"Yeah, yeah," he grumbles, grabbing his bag from the

side. "I'm coming. Catch you all later." He rushes to catch up with her while we wait for Leo, both lost to our phones until he finally graces us with his presence.

"I'll drive," Leo says, appearing from the walk-in, ready to go at long last.

"Over my dead body," I argue, following him out the door. "Neither Wyatt nor I are going to fit well in the back of that shoebox."

"I'd hardly call the Lexus a shoebox," Leo argues. "But we're not all compensating as hard as you are with the giant BMW."

"I think we are all well aware that I'm not compensating for anything in that department," I argue as we hit the ground floor before heading through to the garage.

"Or we could take both you argumentative pricks out of the equation, and I'll drive," Wyatt intervenes the moment we get to the garage. "Jacob took your car, and Leo's blocked in, so I guess we're taking the Alpha. Hop in, boys," he says gleefully.

Leo reaches the passenger door first, barging his way in while I climb in the back, rolling my eyes.

If he only knew what went on in here the last time I was in the back of this car.

"Are we okay to talk now?" Wyatt asks, just as I'm about to open my mouth.

"As far as I know," Leo replies as Wyatt backs out of the space.

"Good. We've got a couple of issues."

Seems like he's got his head back on straight, anyway.

"So, first up, they want three Devils. They're not going

to just let Jacob back out any more than they were going to let you do it," he says, catching my gaze in the mirror. "I've got a few thoughts, but I'm going to speak to my father about it when I'm home over Christmas. We'll be out from under the radar, and I'm hoping he'll have something useful to add, but I wanted to run it past you guys first. Is that okay?"

"Fine with me," I reply.

"Yeah, if you think it will help," Leo adds, no awkwardness in sight. It's almost as if he didn't have Wyatt's dick halfway down his throat last night.

"He came back to me about Timeless Inc," Wyatt continues. "They're the company that runs the Little Sister programme, and they're one of our companies, so it would be fair to say that it's being controlled by The Sect."

"Figured as much," I reply. They've controlled everything else so far. It would stand to reason they've got their hands in that, too.

"While we're talking about that," Leo says, pulling out onto the main road. "I don't think Ruby is who she says she is either. I think she's a plant from my father."

"How'd you figure that?" I ask, leaning forward.

"She has this close friend who told her to wear blue just after your thing happened—that's a code between my brothers and me, and one of our phrases just rolled off her tongue while we were out the other day. Oh, and the car that picked her up? That's definitely one of his."

"So, she's on our side, then?" Wyatt clarifies.

"My father isn't on anyone's side but his own, so it's hard to say, but she's involved here somehow."

"Yeah," I say, thinking out loud. "That camera you found was way too obvious to have been planted by The Sect."

"And?" Leo asks, turning in his seat.

"And I found her upstairs at the party. She was in our bathroom when I caught up with her, but she could have easily been in your room before that. But if she's sending messages from your brothers, is she with them rather than your father?"

"That would make sense," Wyatt agrees.

"It would, but he was too close. He arrived way too quickly up at the church that day for her not to be feeding back to him."

"But how would she have known?"

"If that camera is still active somehow, they'd have seen it on there."

"Except that it's unplugged in the office."

"Yeah, and where were you writing out your goodbye fucking notes before you left, huh?" he asks, the question hitting home harder than I think he intended it to. "Maybe it's got a backup battery or something."

"And your brothers? They wouldn't be working with your father on this?"

"No. If he trusted their information, he'd have just enrolled them at Pendleton."

"So, if that's the first issue, and the second, what else do we need to deal with?" I ask, dreading what else there could be.

"The fact that they want three winners paired up at the end. That's going to be a problem," Wyatt says.

"Yeah," Leo and I both agree.

"Any thoughts?" he asks, pulling into a car park.

And isn't that the biggest issue of all? The lack of information and answers.

We're fumbling around in the dark, and the days are rushing by quicker and quicker, the numbers dwindling faster than we're ready for.

THIRTEEN

Ivy

Light streams in through the glass panes that make up the entrance to the building, the warmth surprising considering the frigid temperatures held the other side of them. The winter sun is weak compared to its summer counterpart, and yet it holds more promise, it's hours fleeting. A gift.

Smiling, my gaze catches on a familiar head of dark hair, lost to his phone, sipping coffee, and paying no mind to the students that mill around him, or the puff of cold air as the doors open and close.

"Have you been sitting out here this whole time?" I ask, dropping onto the bench beside Jacob.

"Nah," he replies, looking up with a grin. "I took the opportunity to go and grab us a decent coffee." Pulling the takeout cup from its holder, he hands it to me.

"Oh, my God. You're an angel." After accepting the offered cup, I tuck my bag into the bench, and wrap my hands around it to take my first heavenly sip.

"Well, I think that title officially belongs to you at this point, but thanks." He huffs out a laugh, shaking his head. "And do you really think I'd leave you to walk back down there on your own?"

"I'm sure I'd be fine," I say, brushing it off. "It's the middle of the day."

It's not like I'd be walking through the woods on my own in the dark. No, I'd go down the middle of the driveway. Still a complete target to whichever idiot comes flying down there, but at least I'd be lit up.

"Sure. Still not happening," he argues. "Are you ready to go?"

"Absolutely." I nod. Jacob takes my bag as we head out of the glass doors and to the car that awaits us. "Do you think the three of them are okay?"

It's not been on my mind *all* day, and it's not that I don't think they're incapable of running a few errands together without it devolving into complete chaos. It's just that Nick and Leo aren't exactly known for seeing eye to eye, and then the whole thing between Wyatt and me that's not really been spoken about until now…

"Wyatt will keep them both in line, don't panic."

"And if Wyatt's on the receiving end?"

"Then, someone else will have to step in." He shrugs. "Honestly, they're big boys. They'll be fine."

"Fair enough. You seem to be in a better mood…"

"Coffee helps," he says, turning down the driveway. "With the perspective and all that."

"Yeah, and chocolate," I add.

"I'll try and remember that one." He smiles. "So, what's your plan for the afternoon?"

"Well, I'm hoping the Christmas trees I ordered have arrived so we can get them decorated."

"You could be on your own for that one, but I'm sure you'll have fun. Oh, actually, Charlotte and Aimee were around earlier on. Maybe they'll help?"

"Here's hoping."

He sounds much more confident than I do, but the short drive disappears quickly as we fall into easy conversation about the sociology project we've got to finish. The days before submission are running away faster than I'd anticipated, everything considered, and before I know it, we're home, walking into the huge tree perched in the entranceway. All the decorations I bought the other day are now removed from Leo's car and carefully piled up on the floor.

"I think I may have gone a little bit overboard with the baubles," I comment.

"Do you need me to call the guys and get another tree ordered?" Jacob asks. "I'm not sure where they'll put it with all the ego in that car, but that's for them to work out, I guess."

"I hate to admit it, but there's a smaller one in the den, and our room, plus the decorative ones to go in the dining room and kitchen."

"Oh. Then, that looks like the perfect amount of baubles," Charlotte says, peeking her head out of the den doorway. "I knew someone would have a clue about all this. The placement instructions were helpful, by the way."

"Oh, good. I wasn't sure if I'd be here when they arrived, so I figured better safe than sorry, you know?"

"Yep," she agrees.

"Well, this all looks way too delicate for my huge paws,

so I'm going to make a start on that work we discussed and leave you girls to it," Jacob says before ducking out and heading towards the stairs.

"Erm, how are we supposed to reach the top?" Charlotte asks, looking up at the tip of the eight-foot tree.

"Grab Ivy one of the dining chairs. Those long legs will finally come in useful for something." Jacob waves us off, his amused chuckle following him up the stairs.

"Charming," Charlotte comments when she steps out, looking over everything with interest.

"So, is anyone else here? Penelope or Aimee?"

"Pen's due back in like half an hour, but I'm not sure Aimee's quite in the festive spirit. You know… after everything with Jasper."

"Yeah, I get it," I admit, looking at everything. "Where do we start, then? With baubles?"

"Never decorated your own tree before?" Aimee suddenly asks from the doorway behind me, making me jump.

"Nope."

"What did you buy, and what theme are you going for?" she asks, crossing her arms beneath her chest.

"Uh, I just bought what I liked the look of," I reply, gesturing to the pile of stuff with a grimace.

With a sigh, she pushes off the doorframe and steps over to hopefully make sense of all this.

"Tell me you bought white lights," she says while shuffling the packs around.

"Yes. The long string is for in here, and the shorter ones are for the other trees. The lady in the shop said these were the ones to get." I nod, not above taking someone else's help.

"Well, I've already sorted out your centrepieces in the dining room and the kitchen island, so I might as well help you out with the rest," Aimee says.

"Yeah?" I sound way too hopeful, and I'd never admit it out loud, but I'm so out of my depth. But we needed something positive to really end the year with, and we need it more now than ever before…

"I've nothing better to do," she says, pushing her jumper sleeves up and starting to separate the boxes out. "These are for your room—I'm not venturing in there," she says, pointing at one pile. "These are for the den," she explains, pointing at another. "And everything else is for this beast of a tree."

"Right," Charlotte and I say in unison.

Charlotte moves things into the den, and I stash our bits by the stairs, ready to take up later, or ask the guys to take up later. Where the hell are they, actually? But I don't have any time to worry about them or what state they'll be in when they get back as Aimee sorts through the rest of the stuff.

"Lights first and then add the baubles, bows, strings, and whatever other decorations you want, depending on which tree you're decorating," Aimee explains.

"Perfect, thank you," I say, before heading into the dining room to grab a chair.

After pushing it up at the side of the tree, I check where we start while she pulls the massive roll of lights out and says, "Wherever you want."

I take the top, with Charlotte on one side, and Aimee on the other, and the three of us wrap the lights around and around and around. We're almost to the bottom, just adjusting them up and down the various branches to get an even spread, when the door opens behind us.

"Tell me you checked those first," Leo says before Nick and Wyatt come bustling through the doorway behind him.

"Uh…" Looking them over has me scrambling for words, but nobody seems to be limping, bleeding, or bruised.

"What if one of the bulbs is gone?" he asks looking from me to Charlotte and then Aimee.

"Erm… What?" I ask, scrabbling to follow the conversation as he hands his bag off to Wyatt before dropping to the floor and looking around.

"And where's your plug socket?" he asks from beneath the tree, barely giving anyone chance to answer one question before he tumbles into the next one.

"It's looking great," Wyatt says with a thumbs up.

"Very green," Nick comments, then the two of them sidle off into the kitchen.

"There's a plug socket on the left," Leo says, coming back out from under the tree.

"I know, and they're brand-new lights, so the bulbs should be fine," Aimee says once he finally comes up for breath.

"Perfect." Leo smiles, and there's a light in his eyes I've not seen before, when he kisses me, his lips soft, and the moment brief, and then he disappears into the kitchen with Wyatt and Nick.

"Girl, your love life is all kinds of complicated,"

Charlotte says, handing the last of the roll of lights to Aimee.

"You don't know the half of it," I reply quietly as she shimmies down the back of the tree, plugging the lights into the timer, and the timer into the socket.

"All done," she declares, climbing back out as the lights turn on.

"It's a bit of a tradition in my house"—Wyatt interrupts our excitement when he comes back through the doorway with two glasses in his hands—"that whoever is decorating the tree has to do it with a glass of something fizzy in their hand."

He gives the first flute to Charlotte with a smile, and the second one to Aimee with a nod, just as Nick arrives with two more. He gives one to me and places a quick kiss on my cheek. Leo hands one to Wyatt, and the six of us stand around the tree, watching its lights blinking gently.

"We've got plenty more of this, plus the ingredients for eggnog, and a boozy hot chocolate that's to die for… or so the recipe says," Wyatt continues.

"I know we're not all feeling very festive right now," Nick says, catching Aimee's gaze. "But I'm sure he'd want us to try our best. They all would."

Because while Jasper is the man Aimee's currently dealing with losing, we're also missing George, Emmerson, Taylor, and Tamsin. We've all lost someone close to us through this sick *game.* And someone you've grown close to isn't quite the same as your best friend of twelve years, but in this pressure cooker, it's not far off.

We toast to those who can't be here, and Leo connects his phone to the sound system. Then we make a start on the decorations, with Penelope joining us not long after as Wyatt heads to his class.

Stephanie and Oliver appear and disappear, and before I realise it, both downstairs trees are done, and the house finally feels like Christmas is coming, even if we don't feel fully festive ourselves yet… although the booze is certainly helping there.

"I'm going to leave you guys to sort the last tree out on your own," Aimee says when Wyatt reappears. His class finished in the time it took us to get downstairs done. "But thanks for this—I needed it."

"Anytime." I smile, squeezing her arm as the guys grab the boxes and a bottle of bubbly, then disappear up the stairs. "And I'm really sorry about Jasper; I know you were close."

"Thanks, chick."

"There's a bottle open in the kitchen for you!" Nick calls from the landing. "Don't let it go flat."

"As if that's going to happen," Penelope mumbles, heading straight there.

"I don't know when you guys are here or away or whatever, but I'm leaving tomorrow for the week," Charlotte says, stepping out from the den. "I'm assuming we're all back for New Year's Eve?"

"For sure," I agree, giving her a quick hug. "It's a date. Drive safe!"

"I will."

I leave them to their drinks, and disappear upstairs, hoping to get the last tree done before dinner, but there's not much time left. Luckily, when I get up here, the guys have it all in hand.

Once I drop onto the sofa, I get to enjoy the three of them joking around whilst putting tiny bows on the arms of the tree—something so many people are missing out on right now.

"I can honestly say this is a first," Jacob comments, coming out of the office and joining me. "Not that I'm complaining."

"Absolutely not," I agree with a nod, offering him my glass.

He takes a sip, then hands it back and grabs the bottle to top up both Leo and Wyatt's before handing them over with a smile.

When they're finally done with the fiddly bits, Jacob lifts me up to place the star on the top of the tree, with the guys making swift work of everything else. Considering this is the third tree of the day, it's hardly a surprise. They're a well-oiled machine at this point, and all too soon we're being called down for dinner, the festive cheer even in Stephanie's voice now, despite her earlier protestations.

Except, when we make it to the dining room, I realise it's not festive cheer in her tone but excitement over the large dress boxes laid out, and the black invitation in the middle of the table.

My stomach sinks like a lift hitting the ground floor.

Wasting no time, Leo heads straight there, picking up the card and reading the words enclosed as Penelope's panicked gaze catches mine.

"Angels and Devils, you are cordially invited to our New Year's Party. Come dressed to impress. This is your opportunity to prove you're The Sect material. Cars will arrive at nine p.m. sharp."

A lump lodges in the back of my throat as I imagine the group of us walking back into the lion's den. At least we're prepared a little better this time. We knew it wasn't over, but I guess I was hoping for something akin to a reprieve for the holiday season.

I should have known better.

"Ooh, open them, open them," Stephanie squeals excitedly as we take work our way around the table, finding the boxes with our names on them.

The gold calligraphy is embossed in the thick, black card of the boxes, and when I tentatively peel back the lid, white paper peeks out. Watching, lid in hand, the Devils' boxes hold fitted suits, each black, charcoal, or pinstripe, with waistcoats and pocket squares to match, while the Angels' boxes have gowns.

Not cocktail dresses for an evening of polite conversation over some canapes, having been dragged back out of our comfort zones. No, these are ballgowns. There isn't a thigh-high split or a plunging neckline in sight, just swathes and swathes of fabric.

Stephanie holds hers up against her chest, the modest neckline a long way from her usual style as black material with a red spider-web pattern worked through it cascades to the floor.

"That looks gorgeous," Charlotte comments as she pulls her silver dress out of its box, the sweet pea organza beneath giving it a pastel twist. The soft fabric hugs her across the sweetheart neckline, cascading to the floor in rivers.

Penelope's flint-coloured, straight neckline is heavily

brocaded, the jewels glinting in the light as she hauls it from the box. But as the skirt plunges to the floor, the jewels peter out, the crepe tulle a whole other centrepiece that moves as she does, swishing it around her feet with interest.

"Come on, girls. Don't just stand there," Stephanie says with a wink before gesturing to mine and Aimee's boxes.

With a thick swallow, I peel back the paper, only half seeing my own before Aimee pulls out a cool grey, off-the-shoulder dress that has ribbons of silver running from top to toe. It's beautiful.

But daring to take in my own dress is no easy feat.

Last time dresses arrived for us was during our very first week here.

We were full of excitement and nervous anticipation. We planned an entire day spent together prepping and laughing. It was the first time the six of us had sat down together and made an effort to get to know each other.

Now, Stephanie is cruel, Penelope is jilted, Tamsin is missing, and Aimee and Charlotte are mourning relationships that have barely had the opportunity to begin before they were over. These are not the dresses of that first week, but we are not the Angels of that first week either.

My fingers run over the jewels which line the creamy, grey-coloured, halter neck dress, and I lift the top to see them turn into three columns that drape from the bust line, the coffee-cream fabric beneath buttery soft. But there's even more to see as I pull it from the box. The columns taper out part way, being met and then replaced by black fabric at the base of the skirt. It intersects the coffee-cream mid-thigh at both the front and back, and when I turn it around, I see the jewels along the back of the dress look like they've been dipped in ink, acting as a stark contrast to the delicate silver of the front.

"Black for the Devils, Grey for the Angels, and you, my dear, seem to be caught somewhere in between," Stephanie comments astutely. "This is going to be fun."

"That's what she said about the last challenge," Leo comments under his breath, with nobody else catching it but me.

"I think we have different definitions of fun," Aimee says.

Beneath the dresses and suits, we find new masks—ones to match our updated attire. The hard plastic masks the Devils usually wear have been traded for black masquerade ones, although they still seem to hold their signature colours.

The attention to detail is worryingly good as I note the colours in my dress matched against different parts of theirs. The pocket square in Leo and Jacob's suits are silver, Wyatt's waistcoat is the delicate coffee-cream of my bodice, and Nick's charcoal shirt is offset with a blacker than black suit that matches the bottom of my dress.

Not that I'd expect any less.

"We could have a pamper afternoon," Charlotte suggests, turning the mask over in her hands. "Like we did for the first event here. Let's start the New Year right and get ready together. Unless, I guess, you want to get ready with your, erm… partners?" Her questioning gaze catches mine, clearly not sure what to say or call the guys.

"A girls' afternoon sounds perfect," I reply with a small smile, pushing down the dread that churns in my stomach.

The first time we received dresses and an invitation like this, we were dragged into The Sect and their silly games. What's going to happen this time? Probably nothing good.

The boxes are moved, and the dinner is served, the two guys who usually do the catering also doing the heavy lifting to make sure the delicate fabrics make their way to the right places in the house.

Interestingly, no comment is made about the pool house—the place most of us Angels are supposed to be sleeping at night. Well, all of us apart from Stephanie.

Unfortunately, the conversation is stilted, this invitation giving more than just me to pause for thought, but talk of Christmas plans and the opportunity for everyone to go home, even if just for a short while, eventually takes over, and by the time we get to desert, New Year's is almost forgotten.

Everyone is going home at some point, and the house will be empty, although just for one day. Hopefully someone will be here to water the trees. What will it be like when we all come back?

With the house empty, this is the perfect opportunity for The Sect to reset the playing field—to put us all back in our places. I'm not particularly looking forward to Christmas with my father, or New Year's celebrations without Tamsin. Now, I even have to consider what I'll be coming back here to.

Great.

FOURTEEN

Leo

The gates are rolling back before I even pull to a stop, the security guy waving me through with a nod. I pass my usual parking spot because a dark green Jaguar XF is parked in it, and it soon becomes clear why: my father is hosting a party.

On Christmas Eve.

Eventually, I find a free space, pull in, park up, and climb out. After throwing my coat on, I pull the heavy, wool collar up, attempting to keep out the worst of the winter chill as I drag my overnight bag from the back seat and head towards the entrance.

The door is ajar, the music loud and obnoxious as I push it open to find two drunk women loitering behind it. Neither of them recognise me when I stroll in while other contacts and colleagues welcome me as I go in search of my father, knowing exactly where he'll be.

Knocking twice, I wait for access to be granted before pushing his office door open.

"So nice of you to join us, boy," my father says when I enter, cigar smoke curling around him as he exhales.

"You're late."

"I had a few things to take care of, so I was late setting off." *By several hours because Jacob had to practically force me in the car to come.*

"Well, you're here now." His eyes narrow as his elbows come to the desk, his gaze not leaving mine. "Blaise, Josiah, you're with me. Everyone else, out."

"Can someone take this to my room, please," I add, holding out the bag and taking a seat once I shrug my jacket off, the heat in the house already stifling.

The three of us wait for the door to click shut, my father's second-in-command; Josiah, and one of only two men, until recently, that I'd die for; Blaise, both moving around behind me as my father holds my gaze —a power play I've seen him use more than once.

"It's a shame you missed the start of the party," Father says, opening his cigar box and offering them over. He waits until I've plucked one out and rolled it between my fingers before he smiles and nods. They're worth a fortune, hand-rolled on Cuban virgin's thighs, or some such bullshit. Part of a deal, I'm sure.

"Well, I'm here now."

He throws the matches on the desk while I cut the end, tutting before continuing. "I had a beautiful brunette all picked out for you. Just your type."

Like he has any idea what my type is. "I'm sure someone else will keep the girl company."

He knows all too well there's only one woman catching my eye right now, but throwing a girl at me in front of all the people here would have meant accepting her or risking offending him, and if you value your life, you don't refuse my father. Not privately, and certainly not publicly. Not even I am an exception to that rule.

"I think Van was keeping her warm, last time I noticed," Josiah comments over my left shoulder, standing beside the door.

"I hope she's not new." I scoff out a laugh, hoping for her sake, not his. The guy's a fucking monster. He takes the word '*rough*' to a whole new level.

"She is, or was, I suppose. Go save her," my father goads, watching with intent as I light the cigar. "Isn't rushing to rescue the damsel in distress your new thing?"

Nick

"Not quite," I brush off. "I'm sure she'll be fine." Not my circus, not my monkeys.

"You were invited to the New Year's event." It's a statement, not a question.

"We were."

"Good." He nods, pondering his next words carefully.

Will he be there? Will something happen? Is this another test or a challenge? Does he know something I don't?

Probably. Definitely.

"It's always an interesting event. New year, new revelations," he says cryptically, not that I'd have expected anything different from him, but a straight fucking answer would have been nice.

"Great, well. I'll see you there… or not, I suppose."

Awareness prickles at the back of my neck when Blaise's feet move behind my right shoulder—a warning of the disrespect somehow falling from my tongue.

One day soon, I'll be replacing him here, or moving on to something bigger—something better—and I'll be doing it alongside people I care about, not some woman I picked for her huge tits and ability to suck dick. It's crass, I know, to understand that about your own mother, but it's a truth he's thrown in my face more than once over the years.

"It's been a long drive. You must be tired," my father says dismissively, not picking up on or not caring about my flippant comment. "Perhaps an early night would be more beneficial than an evening of frivolity."

He may as well send me to bed with no supper, but I'm not five years old anymore.

"It would be rude to not say hello to everyone, wouldn't it?" I ask, standing. "Perhaps a drink will shake this tiredness right out of me."

"Indeed," he replies, standing, too. "Two more challenges. Just keep your head on straight now, okay?"

He turns away from me and walks to the drinks cabinet before I make my leave. Josiah winks as I open the door while Blaise's attention remains firmly on my father, even when the sound of the party pours through the open door.

"Yes, sir," I finally reply, then leave. Closing the door behind me, I head towards the kitchen in search of some kind of alcohol to numb the night away.

"He's not going to spend the whole night in there, is he? This is supposed to be a party," one of the associates slurs when he bumps into me.

"Why don't you go ask him?" I suggest, standing him up and wiping the spilt drink off my sleeve.

It would be signing his own death warrant, but if he's

stupid enough to do it, then he fucking deserves it.

"Yeah." He nods, heading back in that direction and walking straight past the office. *Idiot.* The office my father is currently holding court in with my, for all intent and purpose, brother… or one of them, at least. It smarts that he didn't even acknowledge me, but I get it. He's being tested too, no doubt.

Striding into the kitchen, I find a clean glass and grab a bottle from the top shelf, pouring two fingers of the dark rum and drinking them straight before topping it up and putting it back, the burn reminding me that I'm still alive, for now, even if I am back in hell.

I put the cigar out, and it doesn't take long to find Dex, his wide shoulders a dead giveaway as I strike up a conversation with some of the guys in the same room. After all, Dex and I have worked together for years, even if it is at a slight distance to everyone else. Dex, Blaise, and I have been a trio for as long as I can remember, and the heir to the throne can't be seen mingling with just anyone, you know?

Fuck, I can still remember the condescending tone my father used every time he got rid of an associate or two for getting too close, when he reassigned or removed them. There's no point wasting good talent, but those at the bottom are easily replaced. Not that the bottom of the food chain is somewhere I've ever been.

Rather than the usual dark corner we find out way to, Dex is making conversation in the main living room—my father's domain—tipping his drink to me in acknowledgement even if he doesn't come to greet me. Before long, my father arrives, taking centre stage as always.

Blaise and Josiah follow, but only one of them sits. Blaise heads straight to Dex before the two of them make a swift exit. I itch to follow them, knowing my father's here playing king of the castle, but it would also be noticed and obvious, so instead, I wait.

The music goes up, the drinks get refilled, and all too soon, the strippers appear.

Great. Just how we all want to ring in Christmas Day.

My gaze lingers on the doorway. God knows where they've gone and what my father has got them doing on Christmas Eve, of all nights, but I can't let it simmer or fester. He's made his point. They're his pawns to move. Aren't we all? So, for now, I smile and nod, joining in the conversation at hand until I can find myself somewhere else—anywhere else.

It only takes half an hour for me to find an opening, and I follow one of the guys out into the hallway in search of different liquor, the vodka being liberally passed around not doing it for him either… although one of the women clearly caught his eye. It looks like my father went all out and brought a bunch of new women in for the evening, as well as a few of his usual lovers, I notice, when a flash of dark brown hair catches my attention and a slender woman crosses my path.

The guy and I talk shop briefly as we refill the glasses before parting ways when he heads back to the blonde he had his eye on. I meander from room to room, surreptitiously seeking out Dex and Blaise but coming up short. Eventually, I give up, figuring I've spent enough time showing my face to fuck off out of the way.

Sticking my head around the den doorway—our usual corner of choice—I catch sight of the brunette in Van's lap. The one that was supposed to be for me.

She's not some top-tier pussy glammed up to the nines. She's barely more than a girl. The dress is too cheap and the heels too high, but her makeup is flawless, or it was until it was marked. Until she was marked. She's already sporting a selection of bruises along her arms and a split lip, and I don't know why I care, I shouldn't, but it grates.

"What do you think you're doing?" I shout, catching Van's gaze.

"It's a party, Leo. We're just having a bit of fun," he replies with a slur, the girl wobbling in his lap when he moves.

"Is that so?" My head tilts, my irritation obvious to anyone bothering to look, when someone turns the music down, evidently interested to see what's going to happen here. Taking another sip of my drink, I let it simmer before tearing my gaze from Van to address the terrified slip of a girl in his lap. "Come here."

"Woah," he interrupts, wobbling her even more when she attempts to get off his lap. "Your father said—"

"That she was for me," I clip out, cutting him off. "So, she'd better fucking come here, now."

The room goes silent, with all eyes on the altercation brewing between us. Sure, an order from my father is the law around here, but I'm the heir to that throne, and nobody fucks with me.

The girl's sad gaze turns frightened, my tone clearly not helping her confidence as she hovers over Van's lap, waiting for him to release her from his hold. Tension crackles in the air until I push off the doorframe and stand to my full height before he releases her with a sigh. She tucks a lock of hair behind her ear and walks my way, resignation pouring through every step.

"Sorry, Leo. We didn't realise you were still coming," Van apologises, unease thick in the air, despite him releasing the girl.

Taking two steps closer, I meet her part way, categorising the marks before gently touching the places he's hurt, but the way she flinches back from me the first few times has red descending, and no amount of swallowing down the rage or rum quashes it.

"Did he do this to you?" I ask her quietly—the room taking a collecting hissed intake of breath.

"Leo, Bro. You're father said—"

"I don't give a fuck, and I didn't ask you anything," I hiss, cutting him off.

Still, though, she stays silent, staring at the carpet to my right before she nods ever so slightly. The movement is tiny, likely missed by most people in the room, but it's all the confirmation I need.

"I don't care what my father said," I seethe, turning my attention to Van, who's now standing in front of the sofa, clearly ready to defend himself. "If a girl is for me, I expect her to be unmarked by someone else's hands when I get here."

"But—"

"*Don't* fucking interrupt me!" I yell, sick of being cut off, sick of being second guessed as I throw the glass at his feet. Van's stunned silence finally registers when I step closer and hit him square on the jaw, throwing his head back, knocking him out.

The entire room is silent while watching him fall back onto the sofa, not a whispered word being said.

"Don't touch someone else's present. It's just fucking rude."

"Your father did say it was open season if you couldn't be arsed to turn up on time," James says from the side, and my furious gaze flicks to his. "Not that open season excuses the marks, but just explaining the situation, sir."

The red haze dissipates slightly at the deference, not just because he's lower in the food chain than I am, but because there's history there. Fuck, it's a long time since anyone called me that, and the double entendre doesn't get missed as memories of his perfect subservience flash before my very eyes. No doubt that was intentional, but some of the tension coiled through my body finally releases.

"Get him some ice and a bottle of water for when he comes round. I don't want to see his face in this house tomorrow," I say, my gaze dragging from the dangerously light grey of James's eyes, all the way down to his perfect black brogues.

He's nothing like the clean-cut perfection of Jacob Barrett. James's hair is longer, curled around his ears, and his beard is trimmed short as he looks up at me through dark lashes. He looks good, his crisp white shirt and dark jeans ticking all the boxes I'm usually interested in, and yet somehow, it doesn't quite hit the mark it usually would.

"But—"

"I'll explain the situation to my father tomorrow," I say, already anticipating the questions, with James no doubt worrying about his reaction to one of his perfect men not being where he's supposed to be. "Put him on the gates. It'll be fine."

"Okay." He nods, getting up and unceremoniously throwing the rest of his drink in Van's face. "We'll sort it."

The rest of the people in the room move, and everything bursts back into action now Van is awake and breathing, spluttering alcohol all over the place. After grabbing her elbow, I guide the girl out and take her upstairs, away from everyone else.

My bedroom door slams closed loud enough to shake the frame before I stalk over to the bathroom and turn on the shower, more than ready to wash away the night.

"Here," I say, handing her the TV remote. "Grab a seat or make yourself comfortable on the bed. I'm getting in the shower."

Leaving no room for argument, I turn and walk out, her confusion clear as I grab some sweats and a shirt before closing the bathroom door, hoping and praying for just five minutes of clarity. I don't know what the hell I was expecting from tonight, but this wasn't it.

Quickly, I get washed up, dried, and dressed before heading back into my room. The young girl is draped over my bed, with soft music playing in the background, and the lights dimmed.

Here we fucking go.

Picking up the remote, I pull up a guide and find a half decent film as quickly as I can manage. Let's get the tone right before I attempt some kind of discussion with the damn girl.

"So, how old are you really?" I ask. The film's twenty minutes in, but it'll have to do.

"What do you mean? I'm nineteen," she says, attempting to be sexy, and failing.

Maybe it would have been sexy, until recently, or maybe she'd have looked as young as she does right now in the dimmed lighting of my bedroom, and I would have still sent her on her merry way.

"Fine, I'm seventeen," she admits on a sigh. "Me and two of my friends were offered a fun night and five hundred to come and party. It seemed like a no-brainer until they bailed on me last minute."

Genius. "So, you came alone?"

"Yes…" She cringes, realising, albeit belatedly, what a terrible idea that was.

Double genius. "And the bruises?" How on earth is she planning on explaining those when she turns up with Mummy and Daddy?

"I'd have ended up with those if I'd stayed at home, anyway," she admits sadly. "I'm a stupid temptation that shouldn't be there, or so my stepdad likes to tell me."

Fucking wonderful.

"He sounds like a great guy."

"Can't pick your family." She shrugs.

Don't I fucking know it.

"Did you at least get your money?" I ask on an exhale.

Please, dear God, don't let the girl have come here, get manhandled and bruised, and go home empty-handed and alone.

"Yeah," she admits sheepishly, tugging on the bottom edge of her skirt, her insecurities creeping in now we're alone and the drink is hopefully starting to wear off.

"How much have you had to drink?" I ask, conscious she seems sober enough, but if Van has given her something, I'd rather know now.

"I don't drink; that's how I ended up with this," she admits, pressing the back of her hand against her lip.

Yeah, that sounds about right, but at least she's chosen to be here, she's sober, and she's got what she was owed. It could be worse. Not that throwing a couple hundred her way and going back down there swinging would have been the end of the world, but I really don't need to be dealing with an overdose tonight.

"Final question, I promise. Do you have a curfew?"

It's not something I've ever been afforded, but then most people aren't doing the kinds of things we do in their formative years. Most seventeen-year-old boys are home by midnight and certainly not staying out on Christmas Eve.

"I'm already passed it," she admits, looking away.

With a roll of my eyes, I climb from the bed to grab one of my oversized shirts and a pair of shorts from the drawer before throwing them on the bed. "You might as well get changed if you're staying. There's no point being uncomfortable."

"You mean you don't want to…?" The sentence trails off, but it's obvious what she means.

Dimmed lighting, sexy music, her former perfect placement on the bed. She came here expecting sex, and hoping if she got ahead of it, I wouldn't be as much of a dick to her as Van has been.

"No."

Maybe Van would have rocked her world. Maybe he'd have fucked her and then passed her off to the next guy. Maybe she thought my show of protectiveness meant she'd get an easier ride of it with me. Well, this is going to be a lot easier than she thought.

"Are you gay or something? Fuck, you probably have a girlfriend," she splutters, her eyes widening in surprise like she didn't expect the words to come out of her mouth.

Can't even blame that on the drink.

"Something like that," I grumble. "Look, if you want to party, I'm sure there are plenty of guys willing and able to help you out with that downstairs," I say, gesturing to her split lip. "But if you've had enough, I'll drop you home in the morning."

I don't care if it's nothing she wouldn't have got at home anyway. It still pisses me off.

Her gaze flicks to the door and then back to my shirt before a small smile creeps over her face, and she grabs it and rushes to the bathroom.

Plucking my phone from my bag, I fly a quick message out on the group chat, letting everyone know I turned up safely before making myself comfortable. Eventually, the girl reappears, placing her dress and heels on the table, then joining me.

"I'm Poppy, by the way," she says. "Thank you for this."

"Consider it a life lesson: don't go partying with strangers, no matter how much they offer."

Knowing the guys my father deals with, she likely just sold her virginity for next-to-nothing to a complete stranger. Unknowingly or not, that's plain fucking stupid.

"You're at least as hot as they said you would be," she admits, not turning to face me.

Yeah, I bet they spun her an epic tale about how much I'm worth, and how many women want me. *Wouldn't it be great to beat all those other girls and be my gift?* Not knowing that I would never be the white knight she's looking for, and she'd be nothing more than a bed warmer for me, at best.

Or usually, anyway.

Now I'm putting my clothes on her and finding one of those stupid films that Ivy likes while she settles in under my sheets.

Merry Fucking Christmas.

***

Once I've waved the valet off, I park in my usual spot out front and make my way to the house with an accomplished smile now that Poppy is home safely. The house is abuzz with nervous anticipation as I close the front door behind me, hoping to escape back up to my room out of the way for an hour or so before the chaos begins.

"Been out already?" Josiah asks from a doorway, like he didn't see me leave with the girl an hour ago.

Well, I guess that's my escape foiled as he watches me intently, a mug of coffee in his hand.

"Yeah, I had a gift that needed returning." And a lesson

to hand out at the same time. "Whoever found Poppy and her friends needs to be looking higher up in the food chain." The shitty neighbourhood I dropped her off in was worth less than my car, and whilst my father loves a woman he can keep pliant with cheap gifts and promises he'll never fulfil, and when needed, drugs, I'm less interested.

"Noted." He nods. "Coffee?"

"Why not?"

There's no point slinking off to my room and hiding without Dex and Blaise, anyway, and neither one of them is anywhere to be seen yet, but I guess it is early in the day.

I follow Josiah into the room, and he pours me a coffee, adding milk before handing it over. The two of us sit on opposite sofas in comfortable silence while people move quietly around the house. Cooks, cleaners, servers setting up, and for what? It's nothing more than the opportunity to make sure everyone knows who's in charge.

"Merry Christmas," Josiah says, apparently remembering it's Christmas Day. "So, how are you finding Pendleton Prep?"

Talk about a loaded question.

"Merry Christmas." I smile, attempting to work out how to answer that one. "Classes are okay. Roommates are… a mixed bunch. It's proving to be an interesting endeavour."

"Hmm, I bet it is. Got yourself a girlfriend yet?"

"You want to know if I fucked that girl last night? Well, she left with a smile on her face, so I'll let you work that one out." I scoff out a laugh, not interested in playing that game.

He knows all too well what's been happening at Pendleton. He's the one with the spies around here after all.

He's the master of ceremonies.

"Nah, girlfriends are different. You've never had a proper relationship," he comments astutely. "Bed warmers, fuck buddies, they're what you've had. You'll know when there's someone special."

Oh, I know exactly what he's talking about, and I think he knows it. My father turning up to save our arses won't have gone unnoticed, and you don't do that for a casual fuck buddy.

"It's complicated. How have things been here?" I ask, changing the conversation. "Miss me yet?"

"Oh, yeah, like a hole in the head." He laughs, the sound deep and throaty, the kind of sound that warms you to your toes. Something familiar. "You know how it is, son. The record has got to keep turning."

"Yeah."

I'd put money on the fact that he's had daily, at least, reports about what's been going on, where I've been, what I've done, and who I've seen. The guy has so many spies, it's a wonder he can't see through the very walls… but then, they did try that with the camera, didn't they?

"It was interesting that you had Blaise with you last night," I comment, throwing it out there.

This isn't a conversation I'd ever have with my father, I'm barely more than a chess piece to him, but Josiah is different. He's the one who can connect, or more accurately, *will* connect with you if the timing is right and it suits.

Sure, my father is the kingpin, the one who coordinates the pieces and makes the decisions, but he wouldn't have a bloody clue if it wasn't for Josiah. He's the brain of the operation, and he's always understood that I'll be taking over. I don't have my father's maniacal ways. I'm cold and calculating in a completely different way—I've had to be— but I'm a beast worth keeping on side.

So, he feeds me titbits of information when I ask, when it's important, and I leave them to their own shit for the most part, just happy to do what I'm told and keep my nose out of it for as long as I can.

Not when it comes to my brothers, though.

"Really?" Josiah asks, cocking his head.

"I thought they were on an assignment."

"They were. They're back."

Duh.

And just because he's the one who's level-headed most of the time, it doesn't mean it's not like getting blood from a fucking stone when he doesn't want to talk.

"They're back, and he's shadowing you."

He nods. "I assume, one day, you're going to need them capable of being your second. With the wheels currently in motion, now seemed like an apt moment to share some insight with them, and Blaise happened to step up to the plate."

"And Dex?"

"Will receive further training in other areas if required."

Of course he will.

My father is a piece of shit most of the time, but even he isn't stupid enough to split the two of them up too far to risk them rebelling against him or getting hurt. I may be a pain in his arse most of the time, but if something happened to them, he'd see another side of me altogether, and I think he knows it. Everyone does.

"And nobody thought to discuss it with me?" I ask, sipping the coffee, the bitter taste clinging to the back of my throat. It's not as nice as the shit Jacob likes.

"No."

It's not my place.

It's none of my business.

My father runs things, just as he always has, and when and where he sends his associates is fuck all to do with me, heir or not, but these aren't just *anyone*, and he knows it. They both do.

"What If I was intending on bringing someone else in?"

I'm not. I won't.

Jacob may be my partner in this thing, more so than anyone else anyway, but I wouldn't drag him into this mess for anything. If we somehow make it through this whole thing in one piece, I'll be keeping him as clean as possible.

This is my mess, not his.

"There are protocols for that, as you know."

Yeah. Start at the bottom and work your way up. Nobody is going to take orders from someone who hasn't worked through the shit my father has sent their way—who hasn't earned it. It wouldn't work, not that I'd try.

"And you don't want the position?"

Josiah smiles, raising his eyebrows before placing his mug on the side table.

"Why on earth do you think I'd want to spend any more time than necessary doing this?"

"Necessary?"

If we're talking about financial necessity, he could have

stepped back a long time ago, but he's a core part of keeping my father on task. Keeping the booze and the women flowing is what keeps him happy and entertained. When he's bored he goes on rampages, and that also stands when he's hungry, angry, upset… basically anything that doesn't put a smile on his face. That's why no one likes going in there with bad news.

"You know what I mean," he says. "You'd all miss me too much, and the wife would be bored of me after a couple of hours." He scoffs out a laugh, no doubt imagining what a normal retirement might look like: boring as fuck.

"A couple of hours? No all-night loving going on at your place, then?"

"Just you wait, son. One day, you'll know all the buttons to press, and you won't have to try so hard and still fail." He winks. "Experience comes with age, and I'm aging like a fine wine."

"Great vintage, I'm sure." I smile, the mood lightening in the room, finally.

It's good to know the boys are safe, despite my father's threats. There aren't many people I'd go to war for—although the list is getting longer—but Dex and Blaise have always been at the top of that, and they'll always remain there.

"If you two are finished talking about your dicks, we'll have guests arriving in an hour. Office, now," my father clips out from behind me.

"Coffee?" Josiah asks, his smile lingering.

"No!" he shouts from halfway down the corridor, apparently not even waiting for us to join him.

"Maybe he'd prefer wine," I offer "Vintage wine."

There are always plenty of women around, usually in their early-twenties, dolled up and looking for a good time—the couple of *special* guests last night being the exception, I hope—but the women he ends the night with are often the same: Rita, Jessica, Louise.

A blonde, a brunette, and a redhead, not in that order, and they've got a good ten or more years on the ones he brings in for the boys. Most of the associates his age are married and not interested in playing with toys, or they're only looking for a quick fuck, so they don't care or probably never noticed, but I have.

Being sober in this house is a necessity, much like it seems to be with The Sect. You see lots of things other people miss in their drunken haze.

The redhead in question is closing Father's office door when we get there, wiping her mouth as she passes us, heading somewhere else to do something else. But as her gaze flashes briefly to mine, there's something familiar about it, something other than her being here, but I can't place it.

"Close the door behind you," my father snaps, probably having said the very same thing to Rita just a few minutes ago.

"I'd say Merry Christmas, but I think she just facilitated that," Josiah says with a chuckle, placing his mug on my father's desk and running his fingers through the thick of the salt and pepper of his hair before sitting, with me joining him.

The only words that come to my mind are sarcastic, not

likely to be helpful, and better kept to myself at this point, and after the night I've had, and the place I've been this morning, I finally remember to keep my damn mouth shut.

"There's something going on," Father starts. "People are moving, and I can't get any details about it. Things are changing, and I don't like it."

"Did nothing come back on those investigations?" Josiah asks.

"No."

"Give them time. This is going to need quiet conversations done delicately. We can't go in shouting, yelling, and hoping for answers."

"The Sect?" I ask, seeking clarification because none of this makes any sense.

My father nods, biting on the inside of his cheek briefly before releasing it.

"Things are happening behind the scenes, and I'm being locked out. So, I'm assuming that means it's to do with the new recruits, and that seems like information you might need."

"Appreciated." I nod. "We're down to the last five, so there are just two challenges to go. I guess it makes sense things are getting busier as we near the end." Especially with the curveball we've thrown them recently.

Silence permeates the air while he lights a cigar and the smoke curls out in a stream. "Is your head still in this?" he asks.

Straight down to business. As if I'd expect anything less.

"Yes."

"After everything at the church, I'm beginning to wonder."

He can't seriously be wondering that or we'd be having a completely different conversation, likely at the other end of his fists.

"I've got options for my partner at the end of this, and that's the only reason I was there: to keep them safe and well. Nothing more."

The seconds tick by as he weighs the truth of those words. Josiah cocks an eyebrow as he turns my way with interest.

It's not quite the whole truth, but they don't need to know that.

Nick means more to Ivy than I anticipated, but he was always going to be non-negotiable with Jacob. The biggest issue now comes with adding Wyatt into the mix. Now he's in, there's no way to extricate him, and I'm doing nothing more than hoping and praying they come up with something soon, because I have no idea how we're going to make it through this in one piece. I'm also confident my father isn't going to have any ideas or care about it. He's interested in making sure I get to the end of this thing, and nothing more.

"Fine," he eventually agrees, leaning back before grabbing something from his bottom drawer and throwing it on the desk. "Merry fucking Christmas. Don't say I never get you anything."

"I'm not a kid. I wasn't expecting a song and dance."

Sure, I've got something for him stashed upstairs, but I honestly wasn't thinking he'd bother.

"Yeah, well, just open it," he grumbles.

Sliding the black box open, I'm greeted with a set of keys, but not car keys.

"What are these for?"

"They're for an apartment in London, just in case you need somewhere to lay low. I got it ages ago, but it seemed like the right time to hand them over."

"Thanks." *I think.* "I've got something for you, too, but I'll grab it later."

I'm not sure if it's more concerning that he thinks I may need a way out, or because now's the moment he's choosing to offer it. Either way, he's clearly concerned, and that doesn't bode well.

"This is not an out if shit doesn't go your way," he warns.

No, because if he didn't hunt me down, The Sect would.

"Of course not."

"But you might need some space between terms that doesn't include the rabble here in your face all the time."

So, it's not only about The Sect after all. "You don't want me bringing my boyfriend home, is that what you're saying?" I ask, flicking the keyring around my finger in irritation.

"It looked like your dynamic was a little more complicated than that," he hedges.

Which means if he knows, Josiah knows, and that entire conversation about me having a girlfriend or not and what happened with the girl last night was nothing more than digging and filling the silence. A fun way for him to see what I was willing to divulge.

"Anyway, what do you think any of *those* people would

make of this," Josiah comments, his irritation bristling. He means Nick, Jacob, Ivy, and Wyatt. "Our money speaks, but our lifestyle isn't like theirs."

Understatement of the year.

"So, maybe you and yours might prefer a little privacy and a bigger bedroom." He shrugs. "Or bring your orgy home and see where the chips fall."

They've spent years telling me what I can and can't do. This is just another way for them to manipulate me.

"When are you going back?" my father asks, drawing my attention back to him and trying to draw a line under the argument brewing.

As soon as fucking possible.

"Either tonight or first thing in the morning. I've got an assignment to finish, and whilst the house is quiet seems like the perfect opportunity."

"You could have done it here."

"I'd have ended up out on a job, and you know it."

"Too true," Josiah agrees. "You know you'd be bored doing all that studying whilst everyone else is busy with the fun stuff. In fact, if you're free, I'm sure I can use your help with something later."

"On Christmas Day?"

"We got a new shipment of guns. They need testing. They're samples, but I thought you might appreciate a look," he explains.

Well, at least we're not knocking the fuck out of someone for fun this afternoon. Although that has been how we've spent other Christmas Days, because crime doesn't stop for the holidays.

"Sounds good."

"Guns after dinner, great," my father says. "Now, I need ten minutes with Josiah before we eat. The address that goes with those keys is inside the lid. Don't fucking lose it."

And with that, I'm dismissed.

"Merry Christmas," I say, standing. "Oh, and Van is on the gates today. He won't be making an appearance."

Father nods, waving me off as he puffs on his huge cigar. He's already moved on. Now just to make space away from the house so that Dex and Blaise can find me.

The hallway is busy when I close the door, with preparations well and truly underway. Once I've made it upstairs, I grab my coat, sliding the box and an envelope in my pocket before heading out into the gardens, where the cold air is biting. Luckily, it's quieter out here, and I head down the steps, no real destination in mind.

It doesn't take long for the familiar smell of cigar smoke to find me, and soon Dex falls in step with me before offering a pack of cigarettes out silently. Taking one out, he lights it for me, hands it over, and I let the poison fill my lungs.

"Thought you'd quit."

"Then, why offer?" I counter.

"It's only social. Totally fine."

It's been ages since I bothered. I'm not sure I'd even call it social at this point, but there's something oddly comforting about the burn in my lungs, the cold in my fingertips, and the crunch beneath our feet.

"Is it just us?" I ask.

"He's being watched right now."

Not a surprise.

"Are you guys doing okay?" I ask, rounding the corner as we push farther into the gardens, the house and its inhabitants almost a distant memory.

"Well, we're still here." He shrugs, blowing a plume of smoke out. "We got your message though. Thanks for that."

"How bad was it?" I ask, dreading the answer.

I knew calling my father would have consequences—ones he'd probably take out on them in order to take it out on me. After all, this would all be for nothing if I don't make it through, so I've got to be in good health.

We changed the bulbs to warn them, sending a coded gift, hoping and praying they were watching, and they'd see. Not that Josiah, my father, or anyone else would get the significance. And I got the returned message, the card for my new car just what I was looking for, but it didn't tell me whether they were okay, or if they received the warning and were prepared for whatever the fall out was.

We've been watching Nick heal, working shit out between us, and attempting to find some kind of normal, hoping that they weren't dealing with broken bones or worse. Yet here they are, both of them whole, in one piece, looking much better than Nick has been.

"We've dealt with worse," he comments.

That doesn't help much.

"I just can't work out where the girl fits into everything," I ponder.

He cocks his head.

"She was planted in with the Angels, and then there was a piss poor attempt at planting a camera in my room."

Although, if there's a backup battery and it's been in our office, it might have seen and heard more than I intended. "Oh, and then you picked her up. Well, I'm assuming it was you if Blaise is being watched right now. So, is she your plant or theirs?"

"It's not that simple."

"No?" I question, my steps slowing. "I have no doubt Josiah has people watching and listening. It wouldn't surprise me in the slightest to find out she's one of theirs. What threw me was one of our sayings tumbling out of her lips."

The silence is heavy, weighted, laden with all the words he isn't saying.

"Who is she to you?" I ask.

"No one."

"And to Blaise?"

"No one."

"Bullshit," I hiss, putting out the cigarette under my boot before we devolve into a fight in the middle of the gardens in the freezing fucking cold. "When did we start keeping secrets, huh? Telling each other lies?"

"When we got put in the kind of position we needed to," he counters, shoving his hands in his pockets, clearly itching for the very same thing I am.

Physical release.

Fuck. This is all my fault.

"I should never have gone."

There was no choice, we both know that, but these past few months have changed us both—changed us all. They've separated our trio in ways they'd never have managed to with me here, and I would never do anything to take away from the relationships I've formed, from the softness I've found, but the cost of that seriously fucking sucks.

"He'd have found another way, and you know it."

Yeah… "Can I trust her?" It's the only thing I really need to know. It doesn't matter who she's reporting to, or why, as long as I know if she's there to help or hinder.

Dex nods, swallowing when I turn to look him in the eye.

Never in my life have I questioned either one of them or their loyalty, but there's something about this distance that makes me uneasy. Or maybe it's just how close Ruby is getting to Ivy that worries me.

"There is more than just my life on the line. Can I trust her?"

"Did someone smack you upside the head this morning?" he asks, staring me down. "If not, maybe I ought to."

One second ticks over into two, both of us squaring up in the middle of the freezing cold gardens on Christmas morning. It's not something I'd hoped for, but I can't say it surprises me. She may have been sent by my father, but she's something to Dex, I can tell.

There's no way those words fell out of her mouth so lackadaisically without her being close, and there's even less chance he'd be this irritated over a stranger. The list of people he gives a shit about is even shorter than mine, though maybe that's not the case anymore.

"I'm glad you're still fucking in there." I grin, pulling him in and sliding my arm around his back as he whispers, "You can trust her."

Nodding, I pull back, glad we could have the conversation I'd hoped for, even if I didn't quite get all the answers I need. "So, where'd you two disappear to last night, anyway?" I ask, changing the subject.

"We got sent out on a last-minute job." He rolls his eyes, lighting a cigarillo before pocketing the packet. "I hear Van's on the gates today Something to do with your morning drive, I'm led to believe."

Yeah, living in a fish bowl is nothing new. "Fucking gossips."

He chuckles, the tension easing between us as we continue walking.

"I guess I don't need to fill you in on my life, then." I scoff out a laugh. *Why would bringing them here be an issue when the entire world knows what's going on with me already?* He raises an eyebrow, but we continue walking without any further explanation. "What's new with you guys, then?"

"Apart from the shit going on here, fuck all. Mum got a new boyfriend. That lasted until he looked at B the wrong way."

"Shocker."

Overprotective isn't even the word, and it never has been.

They involved my father to get rid of the piece of shit that left her for dead one night a long, long time ago, and since then they've always been over the top. It's just lucky they don't have a sister, I suppose. Although, the same could be said for me.

Overprotective men with access to lots of guns, drugs,

and ways to dispose of a body aren't exactly a girl's best friend… usually.

"Mum sent over some of those cookies you like. They're safe in our spot in the pantry."

"God bless that woman."

There haven't always been many highlights to living with a narcissistic fuck with more money than sense, and a dark side that's blacker than black, but the treats their mother bakes and sends our way is one of them.

"Of course she's blessed. She's got us," he declares.

And I know for certain he's talking about more than just himself and Blaise. I'm as much family as they are.

"Here," I say, fishing an envelope from my pocket. "It's not as good as those cookies, but she wouldn't appreciate my attempts at baking anyway."

"You know she's not going to cash a cheque," he dismisses, stashing it in the depths of his coat.

"I know. That's why I got her bonds instead." I wink.

"Well played."

"Are we good?" I ask as we turn, heading back towards the house.

We've never kept secrets before—never needed to— and there's a divide growing between us that's never been there before. It's more than just the physical distance my father has placed between us and the girl I know nothing about. Things are changing, and there's nothing I can do about it.

"Yeah, we're good." Dex nods. "Are these people important to you?"

"I honestly wasn't expecting it, but they are." More

than I am willing to admit.

"Only you could go on an assignment and catch feelings." He shakes his head, a bemused chuckle falling from him. "They'd better be worth all this hassle."

"They will be, and if they're not, I fucking am."

"Dick."

"Tosser."

"Come on. Blaise is inside, and if we're lucky, we might get five minutes with him before we've got to be social and remember our places in this world."

Great.

"Are you guys allowed to be seen with me today?" I ask, attempting to keep the sarcasm to a minimum, and failing.

I'm not saying the cold shoulder I got last night isn't understood, because it is, but it still fucking sucks.

"Can't see why not." He shrugs.

"How busy is this thing going to be?" I ask, already dreading it.

"It'll be the usual faces, I'm sure. Most people will be heading home to their families fairly swiftly, I would have thought."

Dinner has always been limited to those closest to us: Josiah and his wife, Dex and Blaise, and a couple of others. All the top-line associates will pop in over the afternoon. It's weird, but it's how it's always been.

"How long are you back for?" he asks, yanking the door open.

"Not long enough and way too long at all the same time."

"Helpful."

"I've got shit to do and problems to work out, and the quiet of that empty house is exactly what I need to do it."

He nods, knowing exactly how demanding life around here gets.

In a house full of chaos, sometimes you just need to be able to carve out a tiny amount of peace, and with my father throwing in a London apartment, maybe it's something I'll be able to get a little more often. Fuck knows, you don't get it here.

"Just don't forget, new year, new revelations," he says as we enter.

"Where have you two been?" Blaise asks, rounding a corner, and cutting off any questions I might have had. My father said pretty much those exact words to me earlier on, too. "Dinner's almost ready."

"Just for a smoke," Dex replies. "You all good?"

He nods, an entire conversation happening between them that I'm not privy to. It smarts, but the three of us make our way in together. The same way we have done for years, as a unit, and no matter what he does and the obstacles that are placed between us, we'll always come out together.

We may be slightly less so this year than previously, but they've got my back, and I've got theirs no matter what.

FIFTEEN

Ivy

The tree twinkles perfectly as I place my case beside it, and my mind wanders.

I have no doubt the decorators will be back in the next week, pulling down all the pristine work they've done and dressing the house full of its new year florals, because that's all this is: dressing. It's just another face, and just another mask. Picture perfect. Always.

I didn't see it before; didn't want to. It was just the thing that marked the changing of the season, and the movement of the year from one month to the next. The decorations changed, the throws and pillows got updated… it's like a regular mini makeover. But I know different now. It's more than that.

"Do you really have to go already, darling?" my mother asks, breaking me from my thoughts.

"I'm afraid so. We've got a New Year's event to prepare for, and I've got an assignment to finish before we're back to classes on Tuesday."

"You've only just got here," she complains. "I'd have never agreed to this if I'd realised just how much time this was going to take up."

Like she'd have had any say in it anyway. I certainly didn't.

"It's only the same as if I'd gone straight to university," I placate, knowing that was my original plan, taking her hand in mine. "I'm a grown woman now, with my whole adult life ahead of me. I'm not going to be coming home every week to check in on you."

"You'll always be my baby no matter how grown you get, and the door will always be open for you here," she says sentimentally.

It's been a prickly few days with my father, the tension high between us still despite the months I've been away. Now that I've seen the crack in the façade, I can't unsee it, and it's making me question everything, even the damn decorations.

"Why don't you leave the car here and I'll drive you down?" my father offers, coming out of his home office and closing the door behind him. "It would be a good opportunity to get a look at this campus I'm paying for, anyway."

"I'll need the car to get to class," I lie, conscious there's always someone coming or going around the same time but needing the space nonetheless.

"I thought everything was within walking distance?" my mother asks.

"The house I'm staying in is farther away than I expected." *Understatement of the year.* "So, no can do, sorry."

"That's a shame, baby girl. I'd have liked to spend a bit of time with you," Dad says. "I've barely seen you since you came home."

Hiding out in my bedroom hasn't been easy. Normally, I'd have been at Tamsin's, but that's not an option anymore. She's not there, and I'm not sure how I'd even explain it to her parents. But maybe The Sect have already taken care of it. They have everything else.

"Well, have a great New Year," my mother says, intervening in the awkward conversation. "And we'll see you soon."

She wraps her arms around me, a comforting embrace I'd forgotten felt this good, albeit brief. Placing a quick kiss on my father's cheek, I grab my case and head for the car, dropping a message in the chat to let everyone know I'm on my way home.

Home.

When did it become that?

When did this stop feeling like home? Was it when that glass hit the wall behind me, and the mask my father had been wearing crumbled into nothing, or when the men at Pendleton Prep became my lifeline?

After turning up the music, I wave at my parents before backing out of the driveway, sadness wrapping around me. The last time I left here was with trepidation but with my best friend in the passenger seat—a ray of sunshine I miss so badly.

By the time I make it back to the house, I'm exhausted by the whole thing and ready to sleep for a week, but I have a feeling that's not how it's going to go when I see all bar one of the cars already parked in the garage as I pull in.

Taking a minute, I close my eyes, exhaling long and

deep, the sense of relief intermingled with fear intoxicating.

"Do you need a hand, sugar?" Nick asks, tapping the window beside me, making me jump.

I've been back for less than two minutes, and I'm already close to having a heart attack.

"Stalker," I mouth, opening my eyes, and unlocking the doors with a sigh. "It's one bag. I'm sure I can get it up the stairs without assistance."

"Well, you could, but now you don't have to." He grins.

"Did you hit your head whilst you were ice skating?" I ask as he pulls my bag from the back seat and throws it over his shoulder before wrapping his arm around me, pulling me into his warmth and safety.

"You'll be pleased to know that I'm perfectly fine, and I missed you, too."

"That's not what I—"

He cuts me off by tipping my chin up to meet his soft gaze. I did miss him, strange as it is to say. I missed them all.

The hint of a smile creeps over my face as his affection seeps into all the crevices of my soul—the ones I'd been revisiting on my way back.

"I think the girls wanted to do some pre-party pamper warm-up tonight, but you're more than welcome to skip out on that if you'd like. I know Wyatt's not back until tomorrow, but I'll give it a go at running one of those baths you like if you need it," Nick offers, picking up whatever the hell is going on with me in just the few minutes I've been back.

"I honestly don't know what I need," I admit, stepping

farther in and wrapping my arms around his waist, resting my head against his shoulder, and breathing him in.

This. This is what I need.

"What the hell did you put in this bag?" he whispers after a few minutes, his arm wrapped comfortingly around my back. "Rocks?"

"Worse," I admit. "Shoes."

"You don't have enough pairs here?" he asks, peeling back to catch my gaze.

"Not the right ones for that dress," I admit. "I'll show you when we get upstairs. They're worth the weight."

"Sure." He shrugs. "But before we go up, are you okay? Has it been an emotional few days?" he asks seriously.

"Yeah, something like that. It's just hard coming back here alone, that's all."

He nods before pressing his lips against mine, gently at first, then becoming more insistent when I open up for him, melting into his touch. *Home.*

"That's not insignificant, sugar," he says, pulling back before taking my hand and leading the way to the boot room and entranceway.

He's not wrong, and the acknowledgement soothes some fractured part of me I couldn't name as he whisks me upstairs and away from the rest of the world.

"Hey, angel, nice to see you back," Leo says, looking up from his laptop.

"Oh, and it's nice to finally see a smile on *his* face," Jacob comments with a grin as he gestures to his brother.

"Ignore him," Nick says, placing my bag by the door. "So, tell me what you want: tea, wine, tequila? Your wish is my command."

"I think it's probably a bit too early for tequila." I chuckle, joining Leo and Jacob on the sofa. "How about we have a chill afternoon and then I prep with the girls later on?"

"Actually, are you up for a review on that project?" Jacob asks. "I had a bit of a re-write on those notes you made, and I've adjusted a few other things, too. It would be nice to get it finalised if we could."

"Sure. Let's do it," I agree, then follow him into the office.

Ten minutes turns into half an hour, and half an hour turns into an hour, with Nick coming in to let us know the girls will be making a start shortly if I still want to go before we even realise how long it's been. Luckily, we're just putting the finishing touches to it and are pretty much set to call it a day. *Perfect timing.*

"Take your phone and let us know if you need saving," Leo jokes when we reappear. "No doubt lover boy will be down for his face mask in half an hour."

"There's nothing wrong with looking after your skin," Jacob counters way too quickly for it to be unintentional or as defensive as it sounds.

"And here I thought all that stuff in the bathroom cabinets was Ivy's," Leo ponders, teasing in his tone, and mischief in his eyes. "Maybe I'm wrong and really it's yours."

"There are two clearly defined different sets," I say, intervening. "Not that it matters. And I'm sure you'd all be welcome to join us if you'd like a pamper."

"Or we could all go to the gym and fight it out…" Leo offers.

"I think I'll settle with watching some more of that silly triad thing we had on the other day," Nick says, dismissing both comments. "And of course, we'll be available for rescue, should it be required."

"Such a gentleman." I smile, then head into the wardrobe to grab some pyjamas and get changed.

If we're going to be sitting around doing nails and pampering, I'm going to be comfortable, too.

The guys wish me good luck and reiterate the offer as I hold up my phone and disappear out of the door as unobtrusively as I can manage before making my way to Aimee and Penelope's room. Aimee's been texting, letting me know where they're at.

It's not that I haven't missed the guys over the last few days. I've missed them like crazy, and, as comforting as it would be to curl up with the three of them and watch a film, it still feels like there's a part missing: Wyatt. Plus, I really need to spend some time with the girls.

After losing Tamsin and moving in here with the guys, it's like there's been a void open up between us. We're supposed to be the Angels, and we're supposed to be a team. Not in the same way the five of us are, but I miss my best friend, and these girls get it in a different kind of a way. They don't want to exact revenge on the people who caused me pain, and despite being in the middle of this, they're not fighting in and against it. They're just attempting to make their way from the start to the end.

"So nice of you to join us," Charlotte comments when

she opens the door, stepping back to let me into their private place. "I wasn't sure if you'd be spending the night with your harem ahead of tomorrow night."

"It's just a party," Penelope says, peeling the cucumber from one eye and looking our way as we close the door. "You're such a conspiracy theorist, Charlotte."

"I'm not sure it's possible for it to be just a party with The Sect," I say with a smile, sitting on the edge of her bed.

"Yeah, well, you know what I mean. Everything has to have an ulterior motive. Can't it just be a party to celebrate the New Year, and that's it?" She shuffles her feet, laying her head back, and replacing the cucumber slices. "Not everything is nefarious."

"Sure it can," Charlotte replies with a shrug. "But there's no way these people have gone to all the trouble of making sure we're all here and have suitable attire just for a *party*."

"I guess we'll find out soon enough," Aimee says cutting between their bickering, and not for the first time if the roll of her eyes is anything to go by. "There's a bunch of make your own face masks on the side. Pick one out, and I'll show you how to do it," she adds, gesturing to the row of tubs on what used to be her work desk.

I guess it still is… kind of.

Tamsin would have loved this.

Any kind of pamper event was totally her thing, but girls' nights were her speciality, and these would have been exactly her kind of product. She'd have known the perfect combination for every skin type and tone, for every problem area and type you can imagine and, once again, I'm struck with the similarities and differences between coming here for the first time back in September.

We did this once before, after all.

Although, that did have a whole bunch of professionals, an entire house to space them out in, and a lot more Prosecco…

"Nice choice," Aimee says, looking at the one I'm apparently holding. "Are you okay?"

"Sorry, it's been a long day. Is Stephanie joining us too?" I ask, changing the subject.

"No, she's spending the evening with Oliver," Charlotte replies. "Hence, we thought maybe you'd be spending the night with your guys, too."

"Ahh."

"To be fair to her, Oliver only got back this afternoon, so I get wanting to do something together," Aimee says.

"Yeah. *Do something together,*" Penelope repeats, her inuendo and jealousy not missed by any of us.

Aimee finishes mixing my mask before shooing me into the bathroom with a bottle of cleanser. Taking the moment, I cleanse my skin with the new, soft cloths left on the side for this very purpose. The bathroom, much like the room itself, is a mirror of the one Nick and Wyatt used to be in—the one we first formed our bubble in after I found out about Tamsin being *removed from the competition.*

"Did you find everything you need?" Aimee asks, peeking her head around the doorway.

These girls have been nothing but good to me since I turned up here full of trepidation about sharing a home with other women, and that was yet another fear Tamsin had eased. Not that it was warranted.

"Yeah, sorry." I pat my face dry and take in the vacant look in my eyes before following Aimee back into the middle of a conversation about their time at home.

"Now, you're supposed to be still and not crack it by talking," she says, waiting for me to sit before smoothing the silky concoction on my skin. "But you can see how well that's gone for the rest of us. Feel free to put your feet up, though. Oh, and I love that you dressed comfortable too. It's perfect."

Looking around, I notice they're also in pyjamas, so at least I got the theme of the evening right. Then my phone vibrates on the table.

"Do you need to get that?" Charlotte asks.

"No, it's fine." I know it's likely the guys already harassing me about needing rescuing. "Did you have a good Christmas break?"

"My little brother is still as much of a pain in the arse as he was when I left, but it was okay. One of these days, he'll wake up in the real world, and I'll get an apology for all his shit. Until then, I just have to smile and accept the old lady soap he bought me. You?"

"It was okay. Just me and my parents for a few days."

"Well, it was chaos with us," Penelope says. "Jasmin and her wife brought their two feral children and their dog to stay. There is food, or hair, or food *and* hair on just about everything I took with me. But I did remember the pashmina I wanted for tomorrow evening, so that's good."

"I hope that didn't end up with food on it," Aimee comments with a smile, Penelope's horrified look going her way before she rushes over to her bag, pulling the safely protected and clean item out.

"That was just mean," Charlotte says, dropping the cucumber slices into a bin and heading into the bathroom. We hear the water running shortly after.

"There are warm towels on the rail," Penelope calls, with some half-garbled reply of acknowledgement coming back our way when my phone vibrates again, twice.

"Nobody is going to be offended if you check it," Aimee says quietly, picking hers up. "It's totally fine."

"I'm good. It's just the group chat, probably."

"Group chat?" she asks with the raise of her eyebrows. "Oh, because you're all like a group-group." She winks.

"Something like that." I smile.

It's strange. I spent all that time trying to work out who to give my wristband to, wondering who I needed the most, and I never actually had to make the decision after all. Leo linked us all together, and then after everything with Nick and The Sect, and them cutting them all off, it just kind of became the five of us against the world. No wristbands required.

"Yeah, what *did* happen there? I feel like we've been on the outside looking in, just along for the ride," Charlotte says, coming back in, fresh faced, as Aimee swaps places, going to wash her mask off, too.

"It's complicated."

"Relationships always are," she says. "And then there was the thing with Nick, the doctor, and all broken bones. What was that all about?"

"That's also complicated, and not my story to tell. He

did something stupid but what he thought was right at the time, and it didn't go to plan."

My phone vibrates on the table again.

"Is he okay now?" Penelope asks.

"He is, and I guess, in some ways, it brought us all together," I admit, thinking of the promises we swapped in the days following. *To love, to care for, and to protect, until death.*

"So dramatic," she says, pulling out the nail files.

"But none of you have bands now," Aimee says, coming back in. My own face mask is more than dry and cracked, ready for washing off. "So, you're in the same boat as us."

"Yep."

"Even if you do have the four of them keeping your bed warm."

"Well, three tonight. Wyatt's not back until tomorrow," I clarify.

"I thought Jacob was gay, anyway?" Charlotte asks as I make my way to the bathroom.

"He is," I reply.

"So, how does that work? Wait, scrub that question. I don't want to know. Just be aware that you're totally living the dream. Those boys are hot."

Knowing everything I know about The Sect, it's safe to say they're mistaken.

My best friend is likely never coming back, probably dead and buried in an unmarked grave. And at least one of the men my heart is tied to isn't going to make it through to the end of this *thing*, either. Ignorance really would be bliss.

My phone's vibrating again when I walk back in the

room, all eyes going to it with amusement.

"Maybe I should just check it…"

"Maybe I should," Penelope says, taking a step towards the desk.

"You don't know the PIN." I wink, snatching it up and turning the stupid vibrate function off.

Hot Stuff: You bored yet?

Leo: Shut up, you idiot

Hot Stuff: The rescue party is at the ready.

Leo: Seriously, leave her alone!

Wyatt: Huh?

Hot Stuff: Ivy has been kidnapped by the girls and is being forced into face masks and sexy pyjamas.

With a smile, I reply, hoping this will be the end of it.

Me: I'd hardly call them sexy, and I'm choosing to be here, Wyatt. Don't panic, all is well!

Talk about scaring the guy half to death.

I've not even put it back on the desk before a reply is flashing up.

Hot Stuff: Just remember, I'm ready whenever you need me.

I really should change Nick's name in my phone.

Leo: We'll keep him busy. Enjoy!

Wyatt: Good to know some things don't change. See you all tomorrow, and don't have too much fun without me. ;-P

"It should be good now," I say, putting it back on the desk. "Just the cavalry offering to rush in and save me."

"Yes, nail varnish fumes can be toxic, don't know you?" Aimee says seriously.

"And all those heavy clays could cause a rash," Charlotte adds, trying and failing to keep in her grin. "They miss you, then, huh?"

"Something like that." I smile. "There's plenty of time for us to catch up, and I never get to see you guys anymore. If I'm being honest with myself, it's nice to have the excuse to do something girly."

It's not that I've been shying away from it or from them—not consciously, anyway—but I suppose after Tamsin *disappeared*, I have pulled away from them, as well as anything that reminds me of the friend that's supposed to be here and isn't.

"We're literally downstairs. You know you can come any time. What do you think to this colour?" Penelope asks, pulling out a bottle and changing the subject just as it's touching on something deeper. And thank the Lord for it.

"It's nice, but maybe a bit too red. What about this one?" Aimee offers, getting out another bottle. "I think it's closer to the colour of that underskirt."

"Oh, how gorgeous are the dresses this time?" Charlotte asks, flicking through the colours laid out. "And a petticoat turned up in my room at some point. It was hung up with my dress. It may be worth checking yours, too."

Great. More coming and going in our *private* spaces, unannounced.

It should come as a surprise, but it doesn't.

Penelope picks a colour, and I make a start, smoothing it down her perfectly manicured nail.

"I'm just glad to find everyone and everything where I left it," I admit. "I had visions of coming back here to find all of our stuff back in the pool house or something."

"Yeah, that would have been awkward," Aimee says, cringing.

"Luckily, the only change is the new dress additions," Charlotte says with a smile. "I'm looking forward to tomorrow night. It's going to be fun, I can tell."

"It's going to be something," I reply with a chuckle, but I'm not sure 'fun' is the word I'd use.

"Well, the last party we got dressed up for went well, so that's a good start," Penelope muses. "If you don't count the mud I got on my skirt when we traipsed through the gardens."

"For Tamsin's mirroring ceremony." I scoff out a laugh. "Yeah, that one worked out well for everyone, didn't it?"

"Shit. I didn't mean…" she says, the sentence trailing off once she realises there's no good way to end it.

"I know you didn't. It's fine. It's just on my mind a lot right now, that's all."

"I get that," Aimee says, her smile small as she looks at me over her shoulder. "But this is girls' night. Angels only. It's a safe space. There's been way too much negativity this year, and I, for one, am choosing to leave it at the door, and not take it into the new year. Good things from here on out."

"Now, that's a thought I can get behind," Charlotte agrees, with Penelope and me nodding along.

There's no way I can leave Tamsin behind, not even in

spirit, but I get the sentiment, and the idea of manifesting positivity. Hopefully, The Sect do, too.

SIXTEEN

Nick

The text message said he would be here by now.

The windows light up either side of the door as a car passes. Quickly, I yank on the handle, hoping it's just Wyatt's car on its way around the building, and not The Sect pulling up early. Looking up the driveway, though, I see nothing but darkness. No headlights yet. Great.

"Talk about cutting it fine," I grumble when Wyatt finally slides through from the boot room. "Your suit's hung up in the wardrobe. I've steamed the shirt for you."

"You're a star, thank you," he replies rushing up the stairs while I close the door and follow.

"What happened? You were supposed to be here hours ago."

"I know, I know, but apparently a single male on a main road isn't high priority for recovery assistance, especially when they've already been out to you once."

"At least they managed to sort it."

"Engine valve replacement and a puncture repair on the way back. It could have been worse, but still…"

He pushes the bedroom door open, taking off his shirt before we're even through.

"Shower's already running," Jacob comments.

"Great. You can give me a hand," Wyatt says, heading straight there.

"*Ookay*," he says.

Everything seemed to be good with them before Wyatt left for Christmas, whatever awkwardness had been eating away at Jacob over and done with, but calling him in alone seems out of character. After all, Wyatt's the one coming to terms with his new inclinations, not Jacob.

"Do you think this is one of those 'three's a crowd' kind of moments?" Leo asks, watching as Jacob disappears without another word.

"No idea." I shrug. "But we really don't have time for any of that. They said nine p.m. sharp."

"That's still fifteen minutes away. We've got loads of time," Ivy says, swishing into the room and stealing all the breath from my lungs.

Holy fuck.

The jewel covered top hugs her perfect tits, pushing and lifting them together before wrapping around her neck. The light brown fabric is taken over by ink black at the bottom, and it only gets more amazing when she turns and we see the back is open, the silver jewels surrounded by black along her lower back.

"Close your mouth," Leo whispers, nudging my shoulder with his as he passes me, heading straight for her. He wouldn't have known if we were wearing our usual masks. Instead, these bloody masquerade things show everything. "You look amazing," he tells her.

"Thank you," she replies, adjusting one of the soft curls at her shoulder before pushing it back to join the rest of her thick hair, black sparkles peeking out as she moves.

I'm sure he only does it to irritate me, but he takes her hand, twirling her around with a smile before attempting to dance with her. He's useless, but she looks like an angel, and in more than just name as the black twirls around her feet.

The bathroom door opens and closes to my side, the walk-in wardrobe following suit, with Wyatt and Jacob whispering while moving from one to the other as he rushes to get ready, the minutes steadily ticking by.

"Can someone give me a hand with—Holy Mary, mother of… Look. At. You," Jacob says, pulling up short when he looks up with a shirtsleeve in hand. "And I think you've knocked him mute, too," he says, looking at me before placing his cufflink in my hand. "Would you mind?"

Managing to drag my gaze from Ivy is a Herculean task, but I quickly fasten his cuff, then make my way to her, with Leo relinquishing space to adjust Jacob's tie or something.

"You look… breathtaking," I whisper, reaching up to cradle her head in my hands, desperate for a touch, a taste. *If only we were dressed up for a nicer reason.*

"And the shoes?" she asks, lifting her skirt slightly.

Sure, she showed us them the other day, going into great detail to explain why they're better than all the other pairs she's got lined up. Not that anyone wanted or needed the explanation, but it seemed like she needed to give it.

"Perfect," I agree without looking.

She could have work boots or slippers on, and I wouldn't give a flying fuck. She's always gorgeous as far as I'm concerned, but the extra effort she's put in for tonight makes her look even more beautiful, if that were even possible.

She giggles, looking up at me with the smallest smile, and I want to bottle it, that look: heat, innocence, care, all wrapped up with a huge amount of hope.

Tilting her head with my hands, I bring my lips to hers. Ivy meets me part way, and I kiss her gently, reverently, hoping to not walk out of here with a semi, or ruin her makeup just minutes before we have to leave.

Her tongue tangles with mine, her luscious tits pressing against my chest, and hell if I don't want to rip the damn thing from her body and worship her properly, but I can't.

"I've got something for you," Wyatt says, clearly finished dressing and turning up with the best timing in the world. "Oh." The walk-in wardrobe door closes behind him, and we pull back, the same lust glittering in her eyes as in mine.

"That colour does suit you though." Jacob sniggers.

"Huh?" I ask, turning and looking his way.

"The lipstick…"

"It's lip stain, and it's dry," Ivy says, stepping back. "You're good."

"Uh, sorry about that. I didn't mean to interrupt, but I got you something while I was back home, and I was hoping you might wear it tonight," Wyatt says, holding a rectangular-shaped box out to Ivy.

"You guys need to be quick. We've got less than five minutes," Jacob warns, hovering near the doorway.

Narrowing my eyes at Jacob, I step away and pull my camera up to check I'm not actually wearing Ivy's lipstick before we leave.

Quickly, Ivy and Wyatt close the distance, with Ivy's eyes going wide as she takes in the necklace.

"It's black obsidian, to absorb negative energy," he tells her, taking it from the box. "And to protect you."

She moves her hair so he can fasten the heart shaped pendant surrounded by a row of diamonds that continue throughout the chain.

"It's perfect," she says, touching the stone before looking up into his eyes.

There's a small, silver drop at the back that disappears under her hair as he places it all back, carefully teasing a strand or two.

"Just like you," he replies, kissing her.

The air in the room is charged with anticipation, and a lust so thick you could practically cut it with a knife. I know we've been apart for a few days, but the tension wrapped around us is palpable. I think we all know there's likely to be more than there should be to this evening and are wanting to be sure everything is said that needs to be.

Wyatt pulls her forward and she leans in, the two of them coming together so perfectly, it's almost cheesy. I could almost feel left out if she hadn't been exactly the same with me just minutes ago.

"Sorry to cut this short," Leo says, "but we're going to be late."

They pull back, an embarred blush creeping over Ivy's cheeks before the five of us make our way out, but not before Leo also steps forward to kiss her, too.

"Jesus Christ," tumbles from Jacob's lips as he rolls his eyes. "You go in the bathroom with one hot, naked guy, and this happens."

"Jealous, bro?" I ask with the quirk of an eyebrow, making my way to the door, with Wyatt following behind.

Leo and Jacob escort Ivy down the stairs. The rest of the house is already waiting by the front door when we get there, nervous excitement filling the room as the girls show off their outfits. Oliver joins us at the bottom of the stairs.

"Thank fuck you're here. If I have to hear about the perfect eyeliner for one more minute, I might go crazy," he says.

Because, clearly, he's been pretty sane up until this point.

"You could totally get away with a little bit," Jacob says. "Just to outline those eyes." He winks before walking away with more sway in his hips than usual.

Such a diva when he wants to be.

"Seriously?" Oliver asks, deadpan.

Someone knocks on the door, and the room falls silent before Oliver steps forward and pulls it open to reveal three cars waiting—the driver already on his way back to open the door.

Well, it's a good job we weren't any later.

The frigid air cascades in. Oliver and Stephanie step forward first, the girls next, and then Jacob guides Ivy down the stairs while I wait for Leo to lock up safely.

The driver closes the car door before saying, "Angels in the next car, please."

It pulls forward, with four seats spaced out to take all the damn skirts about to be shoved in it. As much as I want to throw Ivy in our car and go with the girls, if only to give her the best chance if something were to happen, I also know we have no say here. So, Jacob helps them all in, winking before closing the door and stepping back, then ours is pulling up just seconds later.

We pile in, following the other cars around the fountain and down the driveway. Their car waits at the end, and we all drive away together.

"Well, at least we can see their car," Leo says quietly.

"True," I agree.

Wyatt and Leo make conversation about his car issues this afternoon, the two of them making plans for remaps and whatever else while my mind wanders. *What are we heading into here?*

"Don't worry, we've got this," Wyatt says, catching my attention when, eventually, we pull through high, black security gates, watching more cars coming out than going in before we head down the country lane until the building finally comes into view.

It makes The Manor look insignificant in comparison as we pull up.

When he gets out of the car, our details are passed over by the driver before he returns to open the doors and let us out. The girls are already fluffing their skirts out when we make our way over. Then Leo pulls Jacob back before kissing him deeply.

Because, of course, he waits until now, when we have an audience. There's more than one woman fanning herself, despite the freezing temperature out here. The gentleman at the bottom of the stone stairs eventually manages to get everyone's attention, though, and gathers us together, ready to explain the next steps.

"If you could get into order, please. Pairs first, then Angels, and finally, Devils," he says, while someone else ticks off another couple and ushers them up the stairs and into the imposing building quickly. "There are drinks in the entrance. Please help yourself."

Turning, we follow him up the stone stairs, the entrance a full flight up, with two huge, stone pillars either side of double height glass doors. After selecting glasses we aren't likely to drink from, we follow him farther through the open entrance without time to look at any of the things inside the glass cabinets we pass.

It would have been nice to have the opportunity to take in exactly where we are. After all, someone has gone to a lot of trouble to get us here. The least we can do is appreciate it. Instead, two heavy double doors are peeled back to showcase a grand ballroom full of people—people who turn and look at us as when the man steps to the side and declares, "Ladies and gentlemen! It is my great honour to introduce the Angels and Devils of Pendleton Prep."

Oliver and Stephanie step forward first, his cocky attitude and her irritating smug smile taking centre stage before the other girls follow, with the four of us close behind.

We're the centre of attention, a spectacle, and we have no idea where to go.

"So nice of you to join us," someone says, coming over, his suit pristine. The woman on his arm wears a deep red dress that hugs her every curve; their masks matching. The voice is familiar, but I can't place it. Maybe he's one of the ones who's been to the house. It's hard to say.

"Thank you for the invitation," Wyatt replies, stepping forward and shaking the guy's hand.

If it irritates Oliver—the man who took centre stage just seconds ago—he doesn't show it, instead faking it brilliantly as he also steps in to shake his hand.

It wasn't so much of an invitation as a demand, but it breaks the ice all the same.

"This place is magnificent," Stephanie says, looking around.

"Thank you. The team do a fantastic job of decorating," the lady gushes. "And just wait until you try the food. It's always perfect."

I'm sure it is. Everything here is done with such precision. How could it not be?

"Ladies and gentlemen, if you could make your way through to the dining room!" is called from somewhere beyond the throng of people, and as we follow everyone else through, it's clear that we arrived later than the rest of the guests.

Groups chatter together, finding their tables on the seating chart before disappearing into the expansive room. It could be a wedding banquet or a summer charity event for the lusciousness of the set-up—something Jacob and I are all too familiar with after years of being dragged out and shown off at our mother's philanthropic events.

While others catch up and network, we're all placed on a table together somewhere central, where we can be seen.

There's comfort in the familiarity of the people around us, and the fact that both Ivy and Jacob are close to hand, but what is the point of bringing us here and showing us this opulence without any obvious cause?

We're not all going to make it through, they've made that clear time and time again, so why are we here?

The food is fantastic. The fish is flaky, the steak tender, and the mini desserts are the perfect ending, even as my anxiety eats at me throughout the entire thing.

"Take a breath," Jacob whispers, leaning in. "Your knee is going to bounce the table off in a minute."

If he noticed, then who else did?

I look around, but everyone else is chatting away, our table one of the quietest as we talk about our Christmas breaks. Not that most of us haven't already caught up. But then someone asks about a project, and we end up discussing schoolwork and preparing to head back to class.

"New Year will be ringing in within the hour. If you would all care to make your way to the ballroom, the music and dancing will begin imminently," someone declares over the conversations.

And like some modern version of *Pride and Prejudice*, the men stand, helping their partners up, and making their way back into the other room. It's a swathe of designer suits and hand-made gowns in just about every colour and design you can picture.

"It's just dinner and dancing," Jacob placates quietly as we move through the room. "Nothing to get stressed about."

"That's all well and good," Leo says, leaning in. "But I have no idea how to do this kind of dancing."

"Just follow me," Jacob says with a wink. "I'll lead. You'll be fine."

"Great, the only two guys dancing together," he grumbles while waiting to let a couple through the doorway.

"Actually, I think there are a few others," I comment, looking around. Maybe our group dynamic isn't as much of a first here as I thought it was.

Music is already playing when we enter the room. Aimee takes Ivy's hand and twirls her along before the two of them join the dance floor and the couples already dancing there.

Stephanie asks Oliver, who declines, preferring to head to the bar, leaving her to shrug it off, but even I can see she's hurt. So, making my way to her, I offer her the opportunity if she'd still like it. Sliding her gloved hand into mine, she looks around for Oliver before accepting with a small smile.

Her skirt swirls around us when I pull her into hold for a waltz, much like Ivy's as we pass her and Aimee, their smiles resplendent. But after a couple of songs, I can't see Jacob and Leo anymore.

"Are you ready for a break?" Stephanie asks.

I'm not sure if she can tell I'm distracted or if she's really had enough for the moment. Maybe she wants to go and find Oliver. I don't know, but it's appreciated all the same.

"Would you help me locate the ladies' room in here?" she asks quietly.

"Of course." I guide her to the side of the dance floor before breaking hold and guiding her away.

More than one couple is watching the two of us with

interest, conversations occurring that I can't hear. They may not even be talking about Stephanie and me, or the Angels and Devils, but it certainly feels like we're a big part of the entertainment for the evening.

Struggling to find anything on this side of the room, we head to the bar, asking for directions before finding our way there. Unfortunately, I don't find Leo or Jacob on our travels, and when Stephanie disappears into the bathroom, I take the moment to look around.

Oliver was going to get a drink, and now he's nowhere to be seen. Wyatt was on the dance floor with Penelope, but I can't see them now either, and Jacob and Leo have moved, too. When Stephanie comes out, we can do another sweep. They've got to be around here somewhere.

"This way please, sir," one of the security team says, stepping in front of me. A flicker of apprehension courses through me, the masquerade mask showing more than the usual ones as I take in the scar on his chin, conscious that anything could be important here.

"I'm just waiting for someone. She'll be out momentarily," I stall.

Suddenly, it doesn't seem accidental that I can't find any of the Devils, and if Stephanie comes out to find I'm not here, is she going to make the connection that there's something more going on? Or am I just another Devil she can't count on?

The security guy doesn't say anything straight away, instead, waiting as two others appear from the throngs of people surrounding us and place themselves either side of me. *Fuck.*

"I'm afraid we're going to have to insist."

"But—"

"It's just you, sir. I'm sure your partner will be just fine until you return."

If we return.

They don't leave any room for negotiation as they step in closer, so rather than make a scene in the middle of the event, I go with them, moving along the outside of the room and out of the double doors, where we head deeper into the building through a rabbit warren of corridors. Eventually, one of them pushes open a door before stepping to the side to allow me access.

The office is more spacious than I anticipated, the contemporary decor a contrast to the old wood panelling and deep red carpet. Three sofas create a U-shape at one side, but nobody sits there. Instead, the heavy-set chairs hold the missing Devils, and that anxiety twists in my stomach.

"It took us a minute to find you there," our host says, dragging my attention to him and the dark blue of his mask. He gestures to the cigar box and glass decanter on the table, like we're going to sit here and chat about the weather and the stock market for the next hour, but I shake my head, knowing that's not going to be the case.

It's also an event, which means we're under different rules to the rest of the guests tonight, and now more than ever do we need to be on guard. Unfortunately, looking around doesn't ease any of the concern swirling around my stomach. Everyone is silent in their seats, various shades of uncertainty reflecting back at me.

Great. At least we're all together, I suppose.

"No, thank you. May I?" I ask, gesturing to the seat beside Leo.

"Of course." The host takes a sip of his drink and perches on the edge of the desk, ignoring everyone else, his interest following my every move. "Are you enjoying the evening?" he asks conversationally.

Perhaps they've all been sitting here discussing how perfect the steak was tonight, but the tension that ripples from Leo belies that assumption.

"Yes, the orchestra is beautiful," I reply matching his tone as I sit. "And the catering was fantastic."

"I'll be sure to pass that on." He nods, turning to address the entire room. "Now, I'm sure you're keen to find out what on earth this is all about and get back to your Angels. So, I'll make it brief. We've got another challenge for you."

I stiffen, the tension ramping up in the room as each second ticks by.

"It's a new year," he continues. "Which means before you set your resolutions, it must be time for some new revelations. Actually, do you make resolutions?" he asks, cocking his head in interest. Silently, we all shake our heads, while Leo's fingers tap away on the chair arm in my periphery. "You should. It's always good to have a goal or achievement in mind. Anyway, this evening you'll be undertaking a little soul searching. Solo, of course."

"Not with my Angel?" Oliver interrupts, leaning forward. "Because I could call her in before, and she's around here somewhere."

Yeah, I left her in the ladies' bathroom.

"These are the kind of revelations that should be kept to

yourself, I imagine. If you choose to disclose them at a later time, that's totally down to you, but at this point, it's Devils only," he explains, pushing off the desk.

Well, at least that means he doesn't have an advantage this time.

"Shall we?" he asks, not waiting for any further questions before going straight to a side door. I guess with his wife or significant other around here somewhere, he's keen to get this over and done with, and it sounds like I've given them enough of a wait as it is.

We follow him through into another smaller corridor that has five doors opposite.

"Your names are on the doors." *As always.* "If you're ready…" He gestures to the doors from left to right. "And don't forget, discretion is key here."

Jacob and I catch each other's eye as we line up. The security guard at each door pulls them back, allowing us to step through before the doors close behind us ominously.

Let the challenge commence.

SEVENTEEN

Ivy

"**W**here the hell is your boyfriend?" Stephanie snaps as she joins us at the side of the dance floor, with more than one look of surprise being sent our way. "He was supposed to wait for me, but when I came out of the ladies' room, he was nowhere to be seen."

"How long were you in there?" Penelope asks with a snigger.

"Not helpful."

"I'm sure they're around here somewhere. A guy came to collect Wyatt for something earlier on. Maybe they're together."

"Collect… what do you mean?" I ask, the hair on the back of my neck standing to attention.

I knew something was amiss tonight. I just knew it.

"He said he was needed elsewhere but would be back shortly. No big deal." Penelope shrugs.

"Yeah, they said that when Jasper didn't come back," Aimee says quietly, huddling in.

"And when we left Tamsin and Taylor," I add, aware

this shit just got very real.

"Great. They've gone into a challenge, and I've been left here with you lot," Stephanie says, folding her arms across her chest in irritation.

"I'm sure if you were needed, someone would come and find you," Charlotte says with a roll of her eyes. "It's not like we're far away, is it?"

"Not the point," Stephanie clips out.

"Can I interest you in a dance?" a man asks, interrupting the hushed conversation as he holds his hand out expectantly for mine.

"Won't your wife mind?" I ask, scrambling for some kind of delay, or distraction, or... something.

He turns, gesturing to a twirling woman in dark green with a soft smile. "She looks pretty happy to me," he says conspiratorially, stepping closer. "You ladies looks like your evening needed spicing up a little, that's all."

"Her evenings are already pretty spicy," Charlotte comments, mischief twinkling in her eyes.

"If you'd rather not, that's totally fine," he says, moving to stand beside me instead of opposite, making the expectation significantly less.

There's something about the voice I recognise. The jawline. The lips. I'm sure it would be obvious if it weren't for these damn masks. Everyone feels like someone you think you know while also being a complete stranger at the same time.

I'm not going to be able to help anyone standing here and overthinking everything. The Sect has already proven how easily they can move people without anyone noticing, even in the midst of a full event.

"No, that would be lovely," I say, offering my hand out.

He smiles warmly, his straight white teeth glinting in the light as he takes my hand and guides me onto the dance floor before pulling me in close.

"So, how are you finding this evening?" he asks.

"Oh, uh, it's lovely," I reply, not sure what the correct response should be. *It's great, but there's clearly something untoward going on that we're being dragged along for.* "You?"

"It's always interesting seeing the beautiful women they bring in. Not that my wife isn't stunning, but you're always such a combination. The Angels, I mean."

"Have you seen many groups?"

It's hard to gauge his age. There are no wrinkles around his eyes, no greys in his hair, and the perfect amount of dark five o'clock shadow. He could be anything in a fifteen-to-twenty-year range. Not helpful for narrowing down who he is either, unfortunately.

"One or two," he admits. But despite his words, there doesn't seem to be any inuendo in them. "What are your dreams, little Angel?"

To make it out of here in one piece.

"I want to open my own therapy suite offering services to the stars," I admit, not seeing any reason to hedge or lie. What would be the point? The men involved in The Sect seem to know everything without any words needing to be spoken anyway.

"Well, you're in the right place. I can think of at least a dozen people who need exactly that just off the top of my head," he says with a smile. "The land of the rich and famous certainly has plenty of people who could use an unbiased ear, that's for sure."

Once again, I get this strange sense of knowing that I've heard versions of those words, that tone, somewhere before if only I could place it.

"That was my thinking," I admit. "How many people's careers have stalled, destabilised, or ended completely because they've enjoyed, and then relied upon unhealthy coping mechanisms. Drink. Drugs. Sex. Other people who don't have their best interests at heart… too many."

"What an interesting observation."

The music changes, and we swap, adjusting our hold as we move effortlessly across the floor. I'll have to thank my mother for the ballroom lessens that were part of my life for as long as I can remember. At least they're coming in useful now.

"What do you do?"

"A little bit of this and a little bit of that," he replies evasively.

"Come now. I've shared my dreams with you. Surely I've earned a little quid pro quo," I argue. After all, I don't even know this man's name.

"Ah, well… my dreams, I can share with you. I'd love to see my wife achieve another one of her dreams and open a school or build some housing in a third-world country."

"Wow, that's a big dream."

"The sky's the limit, little Angel, but I think that's our time up," he says looking over my shoulder. "Enjoy the rest of your evening, and good luck."

His wife cuts in, and I thank him before ducking out and making my way back to the girls. Charlotte is on the dance floor herself now, but the guys… they're still nowhere to be seen.

EIGHTEEN

Nick

The small office is basic at best, consisting of a desk and a chair sitting against one wall, and a bookcase lining the other, but it's the white envelope on the desk that draws my attention.

After pulling out the seat, I sit and read.

"In the pack you'll find four statements. Three are true, and one is a lie. Work out which is the lie, then hand it to security before moving on to the next location."

Great, more hide and fucking seek.

"The clock is already ticking, and the road ahead is winding. Use the clues to make your moves and see what you could be learning."

Because, of course, we're on the clock.

Opening the envelope, I slide out four pieces of card, interested to see what they've picked out.

"Let's start with something easy and reveal something recent. Which of the following is untrue? The girl you love loves somebody else. The home you have isn't yours to keep. Lies and deceit keep you in a powerful seat. The work you do now will help you in the future somehow."

What the fuck?

Well, the house is clearly true because we're at Pendleton Prep. So, moving that one to the side, I line up the others.

Sure, Ivy has feelings for Wyatt, Leo, and to some extent, Jacob, but is it love? Is any of it love? How would I even know?

Lies and deceit are the solutions of The Sect, not us, and what we're studying is definitely to pave the way for our futures. So, which is the lie? That she loves someone else, or that lies equate power.

A door opens and closes, the sound echoing in the silence as someone moves on to the next section already. Panicking, I grab the lies and deceit slip, open the door, and hand it to the security guy, who looks it over and hands it back with a shake of his head.

Fuck.

Throwing that one down on the table, I make a grab for the first slip: the girl you love loves somebody else. At least that would be good news, I suppose.

Wyatt's door opens at the same time as mine, both of us handing over slips, but I miss his clue because my security guard whispers my next instruction. "The clue you seek isn't hard to find. Just hand this card to the man making drinks of any kind."

Because, obviously, one set of truths would be too simple, right?

"Drinks of any kind," I mumble, taking back the card and shoving it in my pocket.

So, not one of the servers wandering around with their shiny trays full of drinks that I dare not touch because of the damn two drink rule, but a bartender would do…

Silently, Wyatt falls in step with me as we make our way to the end of the corridor and through the wooden door, both of us totally fucking lost.

"You okay?" I ask, not knowing if his things were the same as mine.

What if he's just found out that Ivy doesn't love any of us, too? Or maybe his was something else, and he's just had a dose of some truth that's left him reeling.

He nods. "I'm going outside, apparently."

"Cool. Bar."

We walk together, meandering our way from corridor to corridor, through turn after turn, with a dead end or two before we make it back to the entrance. Was the discretion supposed to be aimed at each other and the secrets we shouldn't share, or at the rest of the people and the Angels who are here?

"Good luck, man. No doubt we need to be anything but the last ones," I say as he turns to step away.

"Same to you," he replies with a small smile and a wink, shoving back whatever thoughts have been plaguing him while we walked together. "We've got this."

Well, I'm glad someone thinks so.

Heading for the double doors we walked through just a few hours ago, I heave them open, stepping back into the busy room as inconspicuously as I can before sliding along the edge of the room and making my way to the quiet bar area.

Most of the guests are dancing, talking, networking, and making the most of their evening together while I loiter at the bar awkwardly, attempting to get the bartender's attention without being obvious.

What feels like a lifetime goes by before he comes towards me. Pulling out the card, I hand it over to him before he gets chance to ask me what I'd like to drink. *Anything at this point.* He reads it over before sliding it under the bar and handing me a key.

"In a bedroom that's blue, you'll find the next clue."

"Thank you," I say, turning and making my way back towards the doors, but not before I attempt to peek through the people loitering around, selfishly hoping to see Ivy, even though I know it isn't a good idea.

She will have questions I can't answer, and it would take time I can't spare, but the disappointment sinking into the pit of my stomach is real as I turn and walk away, heading for the staircase and a bedroom that's blue.

The sound from the party echoes up the staircase and through the floor as I try door after door, with none of them being the match to the key in my hand. Turning, I try the next one, again and again, on and on, until I must be almost out of rooms. Either that or the bartender lied and gave me the key for somewhere else. Wasn't there something said about lies and deceit?

Just as I'm about ready to give up, finally, the lock turns, the door opening up to reveal an old Victorian bedroom, with a rich, royal blue bedspread laid out on the end of a four-poster bed. The wall lights lit, and there's a fire stoked opposite.

I guess that means I've found the right place.

"It's about fucking time," I grumble, checking the

corridor for signs of anyone else around here before locking the door behind me and heading straight to the white envelope on the bed.

"In your past are secrets you keep, but which one of these was indiscrete?" Pulling out the other statements, I lay them out on the bedding. "A playdate that finished earlier than intended, a time that had been so radically amended."

Think. Think. Think.

That's got to be the time I told my friend's mother I had to be home for an event, only I didn't. Tyrese was just so boring, I couldn't take it any longer. I think I was all of eleven or something, but I knew well enough how to get out of something I didn't want to do. Luckily for me, Andrew was home and happy to lie on my behalf. Not that he let me forget it, but isn't that what brothers are for? Saving your arse.

"Away from a test you did sneak, and into drum lessons you did peek."

There's definitely more than one test Jacob took on my behalf, and vice-versa, and I'm reasonably sure that I attended his drum lessons at one point or another. I'm sure he made his way through a couple of levels on a brand-new game one time… but how would anyone else know that?

"The days went flying with your father beside you, the trip of which your mother never knew."

Again, there's more than one trip my father and me went on without my mother's knowledge. And it wasn't favouritism. He did the same with Jacob and Sophie, just not usually to the shooting range. That was our thing. Shooting never interested my mother or siblings much, so when we got the opportunity, we took it. What nobody else knew wouldn't hurt them… or us.

"The one you called Angel you've already met, in a garden of green with a climbing wall set."

She pushes up from the ground with a glare, the watery sadness from earlier long gone as she gives the climbing equipment one last, longing look, completely ignoring my outstretched hands.

"Fine."

She drops the hem of her dress, the white edge catching in the blood, a red smear staining what was once shiny and clean.

"It's this way," I say, gesturing with my head back past the sandpit.

She grabs her sandals as we pass, sliding her feet back in them with a wince before falling into step silently. It's not too far back to the house, and there's a short cut just farther ahead, but somewhere down the line, a bush scrapes against her leg, and she starts to limp, pushing me away when I offer her my arm.

Well, if she wants to be like that, we can take the long way back, and it's got nothing to do with the hedges that are overgrown on each side of the shortcut. Nothing at all.

So, I skip the short cut, taking her back the way we came in and enjoying the silence whilst it lasts. The limp turns into a stumble, and I catch her tiny body in my arms, only this time she doesn't try to shake me off, accepting the help with a grumbled, "Thanks."

"Can we go back there?" she asks. "After."

I nod with a shrug of my shoulders, but once everyone

else finds out where we've been, it won't be the same. They'll all want to come, and I won't be able to watch her unguarded or enjoy her excitement in the same way. It'll be tainted, like the delicate yellow flowers on the bottom of her dress.

She leans in to me as we make it around the last corner, and I wonder for just one second if she knows it won't be the same too, the sound of our families laughing and enjoying themselves breaking through the quiet we've been settled in this whole time.

"Oh, no. Nick, what happened?" a blonde lady asks, coming over to see us.

I have no idea who she is, but she clearly knows me well enough to pick me out from my twin brother.

"She fell," I reply, still not sure of the name of the girl now huddled into my side.

The lady places her drink on a table before dropping to the ground, her skirt puffing out around her before she asks, "Can I?" holding the edge of my new friend's dress.

"What's up, Posey?" one of the men asks from behind me, making me jump as I turn to glare at him. Doesn't he realise I'm holding her up? She's already fallen once.

"I fell off a climbing frame, Daddy," she finally says, her watery gaze coming back to me briefly before going behind me to his. "I got lost in the gardens, and then we were playing, and now this has happened."

"Best get you cleaned up, then, huh?" he asks, narrowing his eyes in my direction like he knows that's not the whole story. Well, it's not like I pushed her off the damn thing. *"Fran, do you have a first aid kit around here*

somewhere?" he calls, scooping her into his arms and striding away without so much as a thank you.

My mother fusses, finally jumping up from her chair, with her friend tagging along as they continue their conversation in Italian, oblivious to the attention of half the people here.

"I'm sorry her father never thought to say it but thank you for bringing her back and trying to help," the lady says from in front of me, breaking me from watching the trail of tiny red drips along the pristine patio.

"Is that her name? Posey?" I ask.

"No, but her father always wanted to call her Rose. His little Rosey-Posey. The nickname kind of stuck."

"Oh." That's weird.

"Her name is Ivy." She smiles. "And it looks like your mother and aunt have got it all under control now. Why don't you go and find the other children?"

"She's not my aunt."

"Family is about more than blood, Nick. I'm sure one day you'll understand that. Some of the other children are in the games room if you'd like to join them. I can send her through once she's cleaned up."

I nod with a smile, heading through the kitchen and into our den—the place I should have known everyone would be, not looking around the gardens for me.

"There you are," my cousin Isabella says with a grin. "You took your time."

Nobody else pays any attention as I come in, joining her in the huddle of bean bags and reading books.

"Got lost. Got found. Helped some girl who fell over," I reply succinctly with a shrug.

"Jacob said you went to the bathroom." Of course, he did. I roll my eyes. "And that's why no-one came looking for me."

"Sorry, sunshine." She pats my leg in consolation before picking her book back up. "That's family for you."

"Throwing your hat in that ring?" I ask with a smirk.

"With the two of you? Absolutely not. We might be family, but there's no way I can deal with your kind of crazy."

"Fair," I agree. "Where's Sophie?"

Isabella gestures with her head to the games console over the other side of the room, and the dark-haired Italian boy pressed up against my sister whilst he shows her how to use the controls.

"Andrew already gave him an earful about it. Just leave them to it," she says, practically picking the thoughts from my brain.

"Whatever," I grumble, finally spying Jacob. "If a little girl with a plaster on her knee comes in, watch out for her, yeah?"

"Sure."

She goes back to her book, and I grab the nearest hand-sized bean bag before throwing it at the back of my brother's head. His returning grin tells me he's been waiting for it, and the barrage of plastic balls that get pelted my way tell me he was prepared, too.

The two of us fall into competition, play-fighting or whatever, but more than once I'm distracted by a noise from the doorway that he takes advantage of. She never turns up, though...never finds us.

It's strange how disappointment turns sour in your stomach, and how a fleeting encounter can bring out such big emotions. As my body adjusts to no longer having her weight on my arm or her heat at my side, my mind struggles to catch up, and more than once I'm caught out looking for something, or someone, that never appears.

Fuck, it was Ivy.

NINETEEN

Ivy

"**H**ow long do you think this is going to take?" Stephanie asks, stepping in conspiratorially. "Do you think they'll be back before the New Year countdown?"

"No idea."

"Probably," Penelope says with a nod.

"Maybe," Aimee hedges with a grimace.

"I'm just going to say it. No," Charlotte says with the shake of her head. "No, nope, absolutely not, no."

"Helpful. Did the guy say what Wyatt was needed for, or how long he'd be?" I ask, the thought starting to twirl around my mind as we step away from the dance floor, and from the noise and the people.

Historically, when they've disappeared, they haven't exactly been quick to return, but I guess it's hard to say how much of that involves travelling, and how much is actually whatever it is that they're doing in these challenges. But that's not what this is, is it?

What if I'm wrong and they've been dragged into a challenge whilst we're here at an event, celebrating the start of a new year together. Or not, as I guess the case might be.

"No, he didn't say anything much at all," Charlotte says. "Just that he was needed. He was kind of scary though, so I wasn't going to argue with him, and it didn't look like Wyatt wanted to, either."

I know Stephanie had suggested they'd been pulled into a challenge earlier on, but I wasn't really taking it seriously. Maybe I should have been. Nick has disappeared, and I thought Leo and Jacob were dancing, but come to think of it, I haven't seen them either.

"I love your gloves," a lady comments as she passes us by, and a gap opens in the throng of people as we make our way farther away from the dance floor. Where to and why, I'm not really sure, but doing something feels better than just standing there waiting for whatever inevitable thing is to come our way.

"Is that Leo?" Charlotte asks, pointing across the room before dropping her hand and turning so I can look over her shoulder without drawing as much attention.

Hope dances across my skin as I peek over, attempting to see what she saw. If Leo's here, then they're not in a challenge, and it's just a miscommunication. Then it will all be okay. But hope sinks like a stone the longer the seconds pass and I can't find him… until I realise who she means.

"It's hard to make out the tattoos at this distance, but he looks too tall. Too narrow in the shoulders," I say waiting impatiently for him to turn. "Yeah, that's not him," I admit, disappointment laced through each word. "Leo's mask has silver through it, not purple."

"Ah, sorry chick," she says.

"Well, that might not be Leo," Penelope says, narrowing her eyes before gesturing to the bar. "But that's got to be Oliver."

"Of course, *you'd* be the one to pick him out," Stephanie grumbles despite the excitement on her face as we all move towards the bar. I guess I'm not the only one hoping for good news or an explanation. Anything really at this point.

His gaze flicks over his shoulder as if he can feel us coming towards him, and he catches Stephanie's gaze before shaking his head and turning back to the bartender.

"Did he just...?" Stephanie says, surprise colouring her features. "He did not just shoo me away." She huffs, stomping her way over to him while the four of us hover nearby.

That way, we're close enough to step in if we're needed, but far enough away to be observers rather than participants in whatever is about to unfold. Oliver and Stephanie have proven more than once how volatile their relationship can become, and we're supposed to be representing the Devils and the Angels. Nobody wants to get tangled up in that.

The bar area is surprisingly quiet, with just a couple of small groups loitering around talking, and whilst the music is quieter back here, the room is no less impressive. The thick carpet is spongey beneath my heels, the chandeliers sparkling overhead as we wait for our friend, hoping she returns with some kind of answers.

"Nice to see you, ladies," Oliver says, coming up to join us with a wink "But I've got to run."

Stephanie's fingers are interlaced with his as the two of them cross the room, quickly making their way to the doors, but security stop them before they can make their escape. An argument ensues, and as much as I'd like to turn away, I can't do anything other than watch and find out what happens.

I don't know if I want them to be let out together and

know that wherever the guys are, there is something going on, or for them to be turned around, and for us to get the answers I dread but want more than anything. What I'm not expecting is the way Oliver kisses Stephanie, and then walks through the door without her, leaving her to come back to us with defeat laced through each step.

"That didn't look to go well," Charlotte comments.

"No," Aimee agrees, stepping to the side and adjusting her skirt to make space for Stephanie to join us.

"Well, that was just rude," Stephanie says, rotating her wrists and stretching out her shoulders.

"Go on. What happened?" Penelope asks with more interest than I dare to conjure up.

"They're in a challenge. Some new year, new revelations thing, and he had to get something from the bar, but the security won't let me through with him."

"But I thought the Angels were allowed to help?"

Not that it does me or mine any good now that we aren't linked anymore, but it might make a difference for her. Although, if Oliver gets through this, that means one of mine doesn't.

Fuck.

My stomach turns, and I'm reasonably sure that entire dinner is going to come back up as she continues to rattle on about how unfair it is that he doesn't get the benefit of his mirrored partner by his side. Like she would be any kind of advantage to him.

Maybe I'm being disingenuous because it would put the men I care about at a disadvantage, but we won't find out now.

"Can we sit down somewhere? Just for a minute."

The closest seating is likely in the entrance hall, but

after security has already sent Stephanie away, I can't imagine them letting the rest of us through. So, I make my way back to the dining room, not sure if I'm going alone or if everyone else is following me as I head for the beacon of light.

Quietly, servers move around the room, collecting plates and removing linens, the music nothing more than background noise in here now, and as I pull out the closest chair and sink into it, it's like I can finally breathe. Daring to suck air into my lungs without worrying about falling to my knees or throwing up.

They're in a challenge. There's nothing I can do.

Appearances must be kept, so this weakness must be reined in.

But what if one of them doesn't come back?

"Are you okay?" Penelope asks as she pulls a chair out beside me, adjusting her top before sitting.

"I just need a minute."

"Totally get it." She nods while I concentrate on the tablecloth in front of me, attempting to block out all the thoughts running riot around my brain. "When you're ready, we'll go back in, find a glass of champagne, and have another dance. This dress is too gorgeous to waste."

Yeah, that's exactly what I was thinking… or not.

The coffee-cream fabric in my bodice may be the only link to Wyatt that's left. The silver of the jewels on my dress the same as Leo and Jacob's pocket squares and masks. The black my only tie to Nick.

What if the only parts of them I get to keep are what's on my body right now? The key in my purse, the knife on my thigh, and the jewels around my neck.

Panic threatens, and I press my lips together, desperately

pushing back the fear and the tears. Resting my elbows on the table, I hold my head in my hands, letting the feeling simmer inside me before counting to five.

That's it. That's all I get.

Five seconds to drown in the emotional trauma that threatens to pull me under, because my fear, my tears, they're not going to help them, and they're not going to help me.

Now's the time to suck it up, put that mask back in place, and push through. Wyatt once told me that everything we're doing is being observed and monitored, so I have no choice but to assume this isn't only a test for them, it's a test for us, too.

And as much as I don't want Stephanie to disappear, I also need every one of those men to come home tonight.

"Do you ladies need a drink? Some water or a tea, or something?" one of the servers asks from behind me, reminding me that we're not alone in here.

There's always someone listening. Someone watching.

I just want it to be over.

"No, thank you. We're heading back in now, anyway," I reply, turning around and sucking in one last fortifying breath.

It's time to get that game face back on.

TWENTY

Nick

All this time, I've been led, guided. My own fucking sex life isn't even my own.

Sure, we've always known The Sect picked everyone. So, sure, there's always been an amount of manipulation. But to know how long that's been going on, or that they've looked for women of my age from my childhood, or hers, or theirs… that's messed up.

My phone rings in my pocket, jolting me out of my thoughts as an unknown number flashes up. *What the fuck?*

"Hello?"

"In your past are secrets you keep, but which one of these was indiscrete?"

Fuck.

Looking over the options laid out before me, I grab the only one that makes sense, reading it aloud. "A playdate that finished earlier than intended, a time that had been so radically amended."

Holding my breath, I wait for an answer, hoping this is the end of it.

"The next clue you'll find outside in the cold, hidden

somewhere near a stallion of old."

The line goes dead in my hand. My marching orders have been received and, clearly, they have nothing helpful to say or add. Shocker. Shoving the cards back in the envelope, I leave it on the bed, saying goodbye to the heat of the fire before pressing on.

After letting myself out, I lock it behind me, and head back through the corridor and down to the entrance before following the direction Wyatt went earlier on, making my way to the back of the museum and hopefully out of the building.

Though it's easier said than done, and knowing that not only is the clock ticking down, but all the other guys are wandering around this place just as confused as I am doesn't help. Mix that in with the fact that the girls are probably wondering where the hell we are and what on earth is going on doesn't help to keep my head or my thoughts straight as I push through another door only to find myself in a kitchen.

Fucking hell.

"Does anyone know how to get out of here?" I ask frustratedly, a couple of people turning to look my way in confusion. "To get to the gardens or a back entrance, or something?" Anything.

"There's a fire escape over there," one of the chefs answers, pointing past everyone. "But I'm not sure if it's linked to the security systems."

Yeah, the last thing I need is the entire building being evacuated while I attempt to make my way from one clue to the next.

"Thanks," I reply with a sigh.

Heading back out, I hustle my steps farther along the corridor. If there's a fire escape at that end, there must be one at the other end, so hopefully, access for the rest of the world must be somewhere in between. Randomly, I pick a door, pulling it back onto a drawing room, another holds a library, and just as I'm about ready to give up and go back to the entrance, I find it: two glass doors hidden between a pair of ancient looking curtains.

They should probably be drawn to keep the cold night air out, but they're partially open, and when I try the handle, it opens.

"Yes," I hiss out, barley containing my excitement as I step out into the cold.

Pulling my phone out, I turn on the torch—not that it helps much—but following the path along the back of the building eventually brings me to a junction; a sign finally giving me a clue as to where the stables are.

Hope grows as I draw my jacket closed, doing my best to keep out the freezing winter air that swirls around this monolith of a building, the tension coiling around my muscles setting solid as each minute passes.

We've done enough of these now for me to know that worrying about Jacob, about the others, does nothing for me or them, but I can't help myself, and my thoughts spiral downwards.

Wyatt was coming outside earlier… Did he go to the stables, too? Did he find answers with a horse? Or was he sent somewhere else, and now he's tucked up safely in the heat of the house?

Has everyone gone from pillar to post, working their

way from clue to clue, through a myriad of rooms, with what feels like nothing but more questions at the end of every turn.

And what if theirs were closer, easier? What if they're all done and I'm the last one? Out here, wandering around in the cold, not knowing that my time is already up.

Light spills from a building as I round the corner—a literal beacon bolstering the hope that was so quickly dwindling. After pulling back the stable door and letting myself in, it's clear to see I'm alone. I go from stall to stall and find each mare is clean and brushed, their hay bales already half empty as they turn to look at me before going back to their food. Just another interloper not there to interest them.

After all, it's too cold and too dark for anyone to be seriously considering taking them out safely.

But stall after stall holds a mare, not a stallion, until the last two.

A chestnut, and a heavy-set dark grey that looks familiar, as is the name and the age when I look at the details pinned to the stall door.

"Well, well, old friend. What are you doing here?" I muse, asking the horse as much as anyone else when I open the stall door and let myself in.

His neck is silky soft beneath my fingers, and he bristles, just for a moment, shaking his mane before letting me continue stroking down his neck, and he turns to look at me. If there's any recognition there, I'm not sure I see it, but it's definitely the horse I picked out a million years ago on a trip with my sister.

She was less than impressed that I came away with something as well as the mare she wanted. Even more so when I'd turn up in the stables to help with the mucking out and brushing and cleaning. But someone once told me that sisters are a gift, and that I should look after her…or words to that effect. We were only about eight, after all.

Now I know that little girl is closer than I thought; that memory and this horse saved far, far away until right now. It's not coincidental, I'm sure, and as I stroke his velvety nose, I ponder, "Now, where the hell is this envelope?"

There's nothing obvious, nothing pinned to the walls or the door, and as I carefully make my way around the stall, there's nothing hidden in his tack or blankets. So, where the hell is it?

"He said with a stallion of old. You're old and mine. Here when I didn't expect you to be…"

Giving up, I let myself out, shining the torch around the other stallion's stall before quickly doing the same with the mares'. There's nothing on the desk, nothing tucked in the medicine cabinet, and short of sifting through the hay on the floor, I'm coming up empty.

Except… hay. That's got to be it.

Thank God for helping Sophie out with the horses.

I pull over the ladder and look up, finally seeing the two catches, and slotting the top rungs in place before climbing up into the hay loft, cursing the mess I'm going to make of my suit. Shining the torch around does nothing more than light up the bales in front of me, forcing me to check over and around each one until I eventually find the black envelope right at the very end.

"Four statements you've found, family secrets abound. For your next clue, work out which one isn't true."

Balancing my phone on the hay, I drop to the floor, way past giving a fuck about the trousers as I pull the cards from the envelope, the wind whistling ominously outside.

"The Angel selected wasn't the Devil's first love."

Nobody has said shit about love yet, but I certainly haven't felt this way about anyone before. But then, this is about family, so it could be about Jacob or Dad? I'd have known if Jacob had his heart broken. That's the kind of shit you can't hide from a twin, and certainly not one that's as close as we are. But then, there's never been the same kind of bond between our parents as I feel with the guys now.

It wouldn't surprise me to find out that Francesca Barrett had spent half her life chasing the ghost of my father's first love, so that's probably true.

"A murder has happened, done completely in cold blood."

My mother might be a spiteful bitch when she wants to be, and she's more than shown those colours recently, but murder? That's got to be too far. There's no way anyone in my family is capable of that—clay pigeons aside.

"Your destiny was written when you were a child."

Now that I remember everything about that meeting with Ivy, that's probably another one that's true. They've been manipulating us our entire lives. But why?

"The mafia is linked through more than just blood."

There's no way we're linked to the mafia. It doesn't even exist. Sure, Sophie's fiancé is Italian, but that assumption is stereotypical as fuck, and certainly not something I think he'd see the funny side of, even if family is more than important to him.

So, which one is the lie? The mafia or the murder?

My phone rings again, making my stomach sink because I know who this is now. I know they want an answer, but this can't be right.

My family are good people, for the most part. Sure, they're a little eccentric sometimes, a little off the wall, but this? No way.

Swiping to answer, I put it on speakerphone so I can still see the damn cards, my stomach coiling tighter and tighter while I wait for the words to come.

"Four statements you've found, family secrets about. Which one is untrue?"

Fuck. Fuck. Fuck.

What happens if I pick the wrong one? Am I out? Is it over? Is this a life-or-death decision I didn't realise I was making?

He repeats the statement again, the voice cold and dead as I close my eyes, reaching out for whichever one feels right. "The mafia is linked through more than just blood."

"La Famiglia is real and nearer than you feel."

No.

Heat crawls over my body, sweat slicking at the back of my neck as I swallow, waiting for the final words to be said or a bullet to end this.

"Four statements you've found, family secrets about. Which one is untrue?"

Holy mother of…

The relief that pours through my body is unwarranted

because this isn't over, and the words continuing to be spoken don't stop me from checking over my shoulder, swinging the torch blindly around the loft, looking for anything or anyone untoward before reaching out for the other card and reading aloud.

"A murder has happened, done completely in cold blood."

"The murder is true, someone close to you. A retribution given for deeds unforgiven."

What?

Deeds unforgiven.

Retribution.

Who on earth is capable of doing that?

But without any time to consider who or why, he says, once again, "Four statements you've found, family secrets about. Which one is untrue?"

Two left.

Fifty-fifty chance.

So much time has already been wasted. I can't afford to choose wrong here, but they both feel like truths.

I met Ivy as a child—they've already revealed that to me tonight, of all moments. But my father definitely never treated my mother like I'd treat Ivy. Like we all do. And they've already said that lies and deceit are part of their ways. They admitted as much in the first set of clues tonight. So, what if it's a misdirection? A lie.

"Your destiny was written when you were a child."

Silence echoes down the line as the wind howls, nothing louder than my heartbeat in my ears, my fingers tingling with anticipation while I wait.

"More answers you're due, with this final clue. Your concluding room is almost ready, and this is the time for you to be steady. The drawing room will hold more answers, it's full of information for you to decanter."

Unsurprisingly, the line cuts out, my brain running circles around everything I've just learned, and all the details they haven't given me.

Great. Back in the house.

Dusting the worst of the hay off, I climb down the ladder and put it away before making my way back into the winter air and towards the house—autopilot mode fully engaged as my mind hurtles around all that information.

This isn't quite the night of dinner, dancing, and entertainment I was anticipating, but then weren't we warned that time with The Sect wouldn't be. If only we'd known.

I'm practically praying when I flash the torch towards the glass doors. There's no way I'm making it through if I have to find my way around the entire building to the entrance. The wrong answers and misdirection have taken up more than enough time as it is. The rollercoaster this evening has become something more than I ever imagined it could be as I push the handle, hoping it opens, which it does.

Sliding back in, I close it, rubbing feeling back into my fingers before reorientating myself and going back in search of the drawing room. I'm sure I found that earlier on. Trying the first couple of doors brings nothing, but I'm sure it was somewhere near here, and the third one finally has someone in. Someone clad in black, sitting and waiting beside a roaring fire.

Swallowing thickly, I close the door, stepping into the dimly lit room as he gestures to the seat opposite him. Part of me wants to stand, to brace myself for whatever else is to come. Part of me wants to warm myself by the fire and finally be able to feel my toes again. The biggest part of me, however, wants to turn and run.

To step away from this entire endeavour and take them with me.

To know that my brother is safe.

Ivy is safe.

Wyatt will be safe.

Hell, I even want to know that Leo is safe, and that's fucking saying something after all the shit we've been through.

Sure, he was the one who pushed me out of line, that tried to sabotage me from the beginning. He was the one The Sect used to make an example out of my brother back on that very first night. The man who took no prisoners. Who gave no quarter.

But he's more than that now. We all are.

Leo protected my brother the same way I would have done, even if the motivation was different. Wyatt is the man who garnered information to protect Ivy, and found a way to tie her to me. Jacob is a literal part of my body, of my soul, and Ivy is the glue that binds us together.

And these revelations, these truths, they're needling their way in. They're creating confusion, chaos, fear. They're another way for The Sect to push us where they want us, and they'll get it. They always do.

So, nervously, I don't walk away, and I don't stand by the fire. I sit opposite the man who holds the answers, and I wait.

"Two choices are in front of you, one cold and bleak, one guided through."

More choices. More statements.

It's not over yet.

"For if you choose to leave The Sect, your family would, no doubt, be vexed. So, be careful with your choices now, and pick the one to make them proud."

Because all this is about family, isn't it?

My present. My past. My family secrets.

These are individual. Tailored. Delivered with precision. As always.

"Behind door one, more answers come, but a life in debt isn't yours to set."

A lifetime in debt to The Sect. What kind of a life would that be?

A glorious one, potentially. More power than we ever considered was possible as the youngest twin brothers in the Barrett empire. The spoils of war go to the eldest. At least, so far, they have. This is our chance, our opportunity to do more, to be more, but at what cost?

"Door two holds freedom, yes, that's true, but a life that's free isn't easy to keep."

Freedom, but we wouldn't be free for long.

That first night we were told there were only two ways to leave The Sect: through death or excommunication. Neither sound like power to me, and neither sound like safety.

I'm already in this—we all are. If I walk away now,

then what was the point in any of it? In all the work we've done? In the people we've lost?

"Door one."

He nods. "The answers you seek are yours to keep. They can be found where you held the first round."

"Thank you."

I'm up and moving before my brain has even registered it happening, going on autopilot out of the room and back to the entrance, working my way back to the offices, and praying I'm not too late.

If ever there was a moment to have a barrel of stress balls to hand, this is it, and just as I step through the doorway and into the last corridor, a door ahead of me clicks closed.

I'm not the only one here.

I head straight to the one I was in earlier on, and the security guy opens it, then closes it behind me.

A laptop is now set up on the desk, with a couple— the lady in a charcoal dress, and the man matching sit opposite—silently waiting for me to sit, I assume. While dropping into the swivel chair, a strange sense of confusion wraps its way around me. *What else can be on here?*

"Press play on the video when you're ready," the man says.

With trepidation, I press play, the black screen fading away as my father comes into view, sitting quietly at the desk in his home office. I can almost smell the leather top of the desk, feel the ancient wood panelling under my fingers before I'd sit with him. Not that I can do that now.

A lump forms in my throat as he coughs, training his gaze on the camera, and smiling as it focuses. Those were few and far between in those final weeks, and something I've not seen for far too long.

"Congratulations, son," he says excitedly, and even though I know it's a video—one that was recorded some time ago if his reasonable state of health is anything to go by—I can't help the tears that prick at the back of my eyes.

He knew we were coming, and he knew we'd do well.

"I knew you'd be able to put everything together and keep yourself on task. My smart, handsome boy." Pride beams through the screen at me, and it's something I saw so little of in his life that it takes my breath away. "There are a few things you've learnt tonight that need an explanation, so let me begin."

Crossing my ankles, I straighten up, moving the screen so it's at a better angle. I only get one viewing, no doubt, and I can't imagine there will be other opportunities to hear his voice or see his face and gain the wisdom of the man I miss so dearly. The one who sent us here.

"I'm sick. Very sick by the time you watch this, no doubt."

No, you're already gone.

"So, the first thing you're probably wondering is, why you boys? Why not Andrew? Why not Sophie? Well, it's straightforward really. Andrew will be taking his place at Barrett Enterprises, and he's going to need your sister's help. I am in the very fortunate position to straddle the worlds between The Sect and La Famiglia."

The mafia.

"But Andrew won't be able to do both. He's too stubborn—too black and white about everything—so he's going to take up his legacy with Barrett Enterprises, and Sophie is going to support him with the transition to famiglia life. That means it falls to you, my youngest boys, to step into the spotlight with The Sect."

The mafia is definitely real, then, and the man my sister is engaged to is, most likely, involved, and she probably knows so, too. Fantastic.

"There have been several changes happening recently, and a girl… well, a young woman now, has been added to your Angels. I'm not sure if you'll remember Ivy or not, but you met at a few events when you were younger, and I know how this is going to look, like it's been a fabrication, your entire life manipulated and engineered. I just want to be clear that that's not the case."

Of course it isn't.

"Any relationship, forged or otherwise, during your time at Pendleton Prep is entirely your own. You weren't pushed together as children in preparation for this moment. It's entirely coincidental, okay? The world doesn't revolve around you." *Said only in the way a parent can say it.*

He coughs again, this one catching in his throat, and I lean forward, ready to help him if only he were something more than a picture on a screen. But he isn't, and he stops.

"Sadly, parents don't get updates on the initiates, but if you're watching this, then you're doing great, and you're almost there. Keep going, son. I'm prouder of you than you'll ever understand."

The lump in my throat is getting harder to swallow by the second, and I blink repeatedly, willing the tears back when the screen goes black, conscious that I'm not alone.

"Your challenge is complete, but more answers you seek. Three questions we're claiming before you return to your evening," the lady says, her ice-grey eyes ethereal against the deep red and black of her mask.

Three questions.

Just three.

So, what should they be?

Fuck, even I'm rhyming now.

My father answered some of the things that were plaguing me. Ivy is her own person, and so am I. We are linked to the mafia. He did know we were coming here. So, that just leaves one thing to ask.

"The murder. Who was involved, and why?"

"Someone attempted to kidnap Sophie Barrett a long time ago. With the help of her new famiglia ties, she was able to gain retribution."

"Sophie…"

Sophie killed someone.

My quiet, gentle, older sister.

The one who bosses everyone around.

That managed to coordinate dinner for a room full of people in our family home because this was the first year my father wouldn't be with us.

The one who bought me a stupid fluffy jumper with teddy bear ears on it, amongst other things.

Of all the people I thought they might have said, Sophie wasn't it.

"Two questions you've asked, one more will last," he says.

Shit.

I didn't think when the words tumbled out of my mouth, and I never expected that would count as two, but these aren't the kind of people to argue with.

What else is there to ask? What else is important right now?

"If I make it thorough, or don't, will my Angel and my family be protected?"

"An Angel is linked to a Devil. Their fate will mirror your own." I think I already knew that, but we're not linked—not anymore. "Family will always be protected. They're an extension of yourself as part of The Sect," the man answers coolly, like I've just wasted a huge opportunity.

And very quickly, I wonder if I have.

Three questions. Any questions.

This could have been the moment to find a way to get Jacob into the Angels, or to get them to accept four instead of three as their final number, or how the five of us will get to the end when they're looking for three pairs.

If only I'd been thinking about the future, about what comes next, but I wasn't. I was thinking about all the things I've learnt tonight, about what would happen to the woman I care about, and to my family if I was the last one.

"Make your way to the door opposite ready to return to your evening," the woman says with a soft smile.

Numbly, I nod before standing and letting myself out, with the security guy following me closely for the four steps across the corridor. He then opens the door, waiting for me to step through, and then locking it behind me. When I look around, I suddenly realise why.

Leo's head drops into his hands, and my stomach sinks

when Wyatt stands, taking two steps towards me, but I know it's really over when Oliver lets out a cheer, and all of my blood turns to ice in my veins.

Where the hell is Jacob?

Darkness wraps itself around my vision, the room tilting before almost disappearing as I step forward, my stomach twisting as all my strength disappears in a breath and I collapse, with Wyatt catching me before I hit the desk or the floor.

"Gentlemen, if you'd like to follow me. Let's return to our evening, shall we?" our host asks, not that I'd even seen he was here.

All I heard was Oliver, and then I knew that was it.

My life was over.

My brother is gone.

How long have they been sitting here waiting to find out which one of us was going to come through that door? And what do they have in mind to get the other one back? Because I'm sure as hell not going anywhere without my brother.

"Where's Jacob?" I ask, the words coming out whispered and hoarse before I manage to get my feet beneath me, pushing back the pain that lances through my lungs, and forcing myself forward. "I'm not going anywhere until you tell me where my brother is."

I can't. I won't.

This fucking game has opened my eyes to so many things I didn't need or want to know about myself, about my family, about the men who stand beside me. I had no expectations laid out before we arrived here, but no expectation could ever live up to *this*.

"Nick..." Wyatt starts, his tone placating, but I hold my hand up, waiting for an explanation from the only person who can give me one.

I'm not leaving here alone. I refuse to. And I expected more from Leo. More than sitting there with his head in his hands, defeated. More than this reluctant acceptance as I turn to face the man who holds the information I seek.

"Jacob Barrett has been removed from the competition."

The words slash through me with painstaking accuracy, and with that one sentence, it feels like my entire world crumbles to ash between my fingers.

He's gone. It's over.

But it's not over for us. not yet. We're still here, with more challenges to come.

"Ten of you kneel here, three will stand at the end. I'm interested to see who makes the cut."

So, we're going to lose someone else. Not today, not now. Eventually, they're going to come for another one of us, and we'll have to run through their hamster wheels and see who's going to come out on the other side, but nobody will be the same.

We're different already.

If I think back to the group of us that started... that first mixer night.

I was pissed off about not being able to drink, but in the end, that worked out in my favour, but we were all fresh-faced and hopeful. We're not now. Now, we're brow-beaten, and no video from my father saying how proud he is of us will change the fact that I'm going ahead alone.

Wyatt lets go of me as I push off the desk, heading straight for the man in a black mask with red slashed through it as I look around the room. There is no security in sight.

Jacob's been removed. Fine. But I'll find him.

"Mr Barrett, I'll remind you that *you* are still part of this initiation," he states, like he can read the thoughts straight out of my mind. Or maybe he can just read the anger in my footsteps and the hatred pouring from my face. "And we have rules in place for events. You will not like the outcome if crossing The Sect."

Because it worked out well for me last time.

My steps falter, his words hitting home. Getting myself killed is not going to help Jacob. No, but finding him will.

The man steps past me before going to the door, opening it, and marching straight out.

Wyatt's hand comes down on my shoulder as I turn and glare at him. I'm three seconds away from tearing this place to shreds and going in search of Jacob myself, but as much as it angers me, our master of puppets is right. I'm still in this initiation. The three of us are.

We could hang back, process this shit, and go find him ourselves, but they're not going to tell us where he is, and the chances of us finding him in this bloody maze of a building, if he's even still here, are slim to none. We're also under scrutiny here, now more than ever.

So, with a resigned sigh, I follow him—we all do—and we're returned silently to the ballroom, with our host soon disappearing. I grab the first drink I can find and down it, daring a glance at Leo.

Resigned acceptance. Defeat. I guess I reek of it, too.

"There's a two drink rule," Leo hisses in my ear when I reach for another. "Don't give them an excuse to get rid of you, too."

His callous words hit me like a train, but they do the job they were intended to, and I drop the glass, turning to seek out Ivy, but I can't see her either.

"We need to find the girls," I clip out, because Jacob isn't the only one here they can hurt us with.

Silently, Leo heads to one side of the room with his head down and his jaw clenched, but a fight in each step as he moves. Wyatt goes straight through with nothing more than a nod, going to the last place we saw her: on the dance floor. Meanwhile, I make my way right, going to the ladies' room, and the very place I left Stephanie, but there's no sign of them there either.

Not even after five minutes.

And not even after I ask some random woman to check for five women loitering in there, as a dread I'm not ready to admit exists swirls inside me like a tornado.

Finally, I head back to Wyatt, daring to hope that one of them has better news, but deep down in my soul, I know they don't.

"Any luck?" Wyatt asks, looking over my shoulder as if they're somehow hidden behind me, ballgowns and all.

"They're not over there," Leo says despondency radiating from him.

He doesn't ask if we've found them, and they both know I've come up empty, too.

A numbness I've never experienced before crawls over my body, wrapping around every organ, bone, and muscle

I have.

"They're gone."

To be continued...

Thank you for reading Their Hell. I hope you enjoyed it.
Get ready for more in ***Our Heaven***
Can't wait for more? Keep in touch with me here:
https://authorhlpacker.com/keep-in-touch/

ACKNOWLEDGEMENTS

Go on, it's okay, you can admit it. You were just waiting to get through the book so that you could read what on earth our "heroes" had to say… I know, I know, they're cool. I get it.

Leo – What the fuck, man? I'm out.

Nick – Yeah, what he said. *Slams door*

Wyatt – Well, I'm not sure any of us ever expected the two of them to agree on something, but here we are… Hey, thanks for popping in. I get it, they sort of got the raw end of the deal this time, but it will all work out just right, don't worry. I've got them, we've got her, we're good. Cheers!

Ivy – These guys are useless. Thanks for being here. Thanks for coming along this journey with us. Thanks for trusting the process. I swear to God if this author fucks the next book up, we're going to have problems.

Well, that was fun…

So, for me, the author, I have to start by thanking my husband.

I know, I know, I say this every time, but honestly, he is the best.

He's the one listening to me ramble on about the ridiculous thing that I can't work out, the plot that I've managed to tie myself in knots with, and the characters that come up with the most ridiculous stuff ever. Thanks for sticking with my crazy, you're awesome!

A huge thank you, as always, has to go to the team;

Donna, Angela, Karen, Christina. Thank you for your feedback, your notes, your encouragement, and all the other things you do. You're the best!

And, of course, a massive thank you has to go to anyone who has picked this book up and read it. Boogers, readers, reviewers, you're all making this little dream come trust. Thank you for taking the chance on this book and the insane characters that live inside it. Hopefully there will be more answers coming your way soon.

About the Author

HL Packer is quite frankly, a busy bee.

When she's not running around after her free-spirited three children, and husband. You can find her tending to the dogs, bearded dragons, and snakes that also reside with them.

When she finished her office job for maternity leave, her husband purchased a Kindle E-Reader to give her something to do, and oh what a journey that has been. From reading to reviewing, then blogging and creating Romance Readers Book Box UK. And now, her own words being put out into the world.

When she is not coordinating her worlds, you can find her soaking in a bubbly bath or enjoying a glass of wine, often still with a book in her hand.

Newsletter: https://bit.ly/3rdYAny

Also by H.L. Packer

Fated Series

Home

Within Reach

Within Hope

The Shadow

Amore

La Familglia

The Ties that Bind

The Bonds That Break

Broken Lies

Fractured Truth

Pendleton Prep

The Sect

Her Devil

His Angel

Their Hell